Advanced Dungeons & Dragons®

Player's Handbook   **Rules Supplement**

The
Complete
Ranger's
Handbook

by Rick Swan

Distributed to the book trade in the United States by Random House, Inc. and in Canada by Random House of Canada Ltd. Distributed in the United Kingdom by TSR Ltd. Distributed to the toy and hobby trade by regional distributors.

ADVANCED DUNGEONS & DRAGONS, AD&D, WORLD OF GREYHAWK, DRAGONLANCE, FORGOTTEN REALMS, DUNGEON MASTER, and MONSTROUS COMPENDIUM are registered trademarks owned by TSR, Inc.

The TSR logo is a trademark owned by TSR, Inc.

©1993 TSR, Inc. All Rights Reserved. Printed in the U.S.A. Fourth printing, October 1996

TSR, Inc.
201 Sheridan Springs
Lake Geneva,
WI 53147
U.S.A.

TSR Ltd.
120 Church End,
Cherry Hinton
Cambridge CB1 3LB
United Kingdom

Table of Contents

Table of Contents

CREDITS
Design: Rick Swan
Editing: Elizabeth Danforth
Black and White Art: Terry Dykstra
Color Art: Julie Bell, Clyde Caldwell,
Fred Fields, Keith Parkinson
Icon Art: Tony Diterlizzi
Typography: Nancy J. Kerkstra

Special thanks to Bear Peters

Introduction

The ranger is one of the most popular character classes in the AD&D® game. A woodsman and tracker, as well as a dangerous fighter, he combines good combat skills with a few extra abilities that give him many options and decisions during play. He boasts the courage and strength of a warrior and the stealth and self-reliance of a thief. He combines the druid's affinity for the outdoors with the devotion and magical aptitude of a priest. He's a hunter, a tracker, and a survivalist. By temperament and by choice, he's a loner, often preferring the company of animals to people. Without question, he's one with nature, sworn to protect the inhabitants of the wilderness and preserve the integrity of the land.

The ranger's origins can be traced to the time when isolated human settlements were first founded in areas of unclaimed wilderness, or in areas occupied only by savage humanoid tribes. Those who were at first hunters, trappers, and guides were turned by the necessities of survival into canny wilderness warriors; and ultimately into the principle protectors of the scattered settlements of humans and demihumans, which had to fend off countless humanoid raids.

Few in number, but effective far beyond the power of local militias or the occasional military patrol of a ruling lord, the rangers have kept a protective watch on the forward frontier of human expansion. There are seldom more than one or two to be found in any place, but somehow, as a group, they manage to cover huge areas of the frontier. Where the tide of expansion has been turned back, they are the last to fight a desperate rear guard action against encroaching hordes of evil humanoids.

In more civilized areas, it is common for kings and wealthy nobles to annex large tracts of forests for personal use. Some are maintained as private game preserves, others are harvested for the valuable timber. As a king's wilderness holdings grow, so does the need to protect them. But suitable candidates are hard to come by. Often, from among local woodsmen and hunters, able-bodied and trustworthy retainers are recruited as forest justices or wardens. Skilled in the management of land, wilderness survival, and natural lore, the forest justices are charged with guarding the king's holdings, preserving his game from poachers and his subjects from outlaws and brigands.

In other places, the local authorities have either lost control or become tyrannical. Perhaps the local order has broken down and the land is overrun by bandits or robbers. Perhaps a bad ruler has taken over and driven the peasantry beyond all possible tolerance. At such time a hero may arise, striding out of the wilderness, setting right the wrongs, returning a just overlord to power, and then disappearing back into wild and unknown lands. Such is the stuff of legends. Such is the legacy of the ranger.

Overview

The ADVANCED DUNGEONS & DRAGONS® 2nd Edition *Player's Handbook* and *DUNGEON MASTER® Guide* contain all the basic information you need to create and play ranger characters. But for players wanting to go a bit deeper, *The Complete Ranger's Handbook* provides a wealth of detail that expands on that basic information, adding more options and rules to make your rangers come alive like never before.

For instance, we'll examine the ranger's talents for tracking, animal empathy, and nature lore, suggesting methods for using these abilities in ways you might not have considered. If you've wondered what a ranger does with his followers or exactly how he acquires them, you'll find the answers here. If you're tired of playing ordinary rangers, there's more than a dozen new character kits for your perusal, including the Giant Killer, the Pathfinder, and the Stalker. There are also plenty of new spells, proficiencies, and equipment to expand your ranger's horizons. Use what you like and ignore what you don't.

Though much of this material will be of interest to the Dungeon Master, particularly the clarification of old concepts and the introduction of new rules, *The Complete Ranger's Handbook* is a supplement to the *Player's Handbook*. Every word is intended for the players. Note, however, that all of material is optional, and none may be incorporated into a campaign without the express permission of the DM. These caveats aside, feel free to turn the page and enjoy.

How to Use This Handbook

If you're a casual player, or have only a passing interest in the ranger character, begin by looking over the table of contents and noting any topics that catch your eye. Read the most appealing sections, skim over the rest, and consult with your DM about any new ideas you'd like to try. Later, you can read the entire book at your leisure, or keep it on the shelf as a reference, along with the previous handbooks in this series (including *The Complete Fighter's Handbook, The Complete Priest's Handbook, The Complete Wizard's Handbook, The Complete Thief's Handbook, The Complete Psionics Handbook,* and *The Complete Bard's Handbook*).

Players who take their rangers seriously are advised to read the entire book. You'll discover a host of new ideas and character options, expanded tables, and tips for fine-tuning your role-playing techniques. As mentioned, all of the rules in this book must be cleared with the DM before you can use them in a game.

Players of all persuasions should take a look at the new ranger character sheets located in the back of the book. The sheets have been custom-designed to record virtually every detail about a ranger character, and also feature a number of helpful notes to minimize the amount of time spent referring to the rulebooks. And speaking of the rulebooks, we've also compiled all of the key rules from the *DUNGEON MASTER Guide* and *Player's Handbook* relevant to rangers; you'll find most of them in the first three chapters. We've also made every effort to elaborate on the most interesting concepts from the *DMG* and *PH*.

Before We Get Started...

...here are a few more points to keep in mind:

First Edition Rules

The ranger has undergone several changes since the publication of the 1st Edition AD&D® rules. For that reason, those using the 1st Edition rules may find the ranger character described in these pages all but unrecognizable. Our suggestions: (1) take the plunge into the 2nd Edition rules, and become familiar with the 2nd Edition *DUNGEON MASTER Guide* and *Player's Handbook* before considering the ideas in this handbook, or (2) ignore the chapter references in this book, as they all refer to the 2nd Edition rulebooks. Find the relevant material by consulting the indexes or contents pages of the original books, then carefully adapt the handbook rules of your choice to the style of your campaign. For reference, a summary of the 1st Edition ranger rules can be found in the Appendix of this book on page 122.

Proficiencies

The ideas in this book lean heavily on the concepts of weapon and nonweapon proficiencies introduced in Chapter 5 of the 2nd Edition *Player's Handbook*. If you haven't been using proficiencies in your campaign, we suggest you review the rules before proceeding with this book. (And if you're not using the proficiency rules, you ought to reconsider—they're not that hard, and they make the game a lot more fun!).

A Note About Pronouns

For convenience and clarity, masculine pronouns are used throughout this book. This in no way implies favoritism towards the male gender; in fact, males and females are equally represented in the ranger population. In all cases, read *he* as *he or she,* and *his* as *his and her.*

Let's begin our examination of the ranger with a look at the numbers—the statistics, adjustments, and level progressions that define the ranger class. This is the raw data common to all rangers, regardless of their backgrounds or personalities.

This chapter compiles the basic information in the *Player's Handbook* regarding the ranger class, as well as the relevant material from the warrior section. In addition, some concepts, such as armor adjustments and level improvements, are clarified and expanded. A new concept, *primary terrain*, is also introduced.

In later chapters, we'll be discussing the ranger's special abilities in more detail, along with role-playing tips and options for refining his personality. But for now, we'll concentrate on the fundamentals, beginning with the most basic consideration of all—the ranger's class requirements.

Ranger Requirements

It's tough being a ranger. The requirements are high, among the most demanding of any character class.

Table 1: Class Qualifications

Ability Requirements
Strength	13
Dexterity	13
Constitution	14
Wisdom	14

Prime Requisites
Strength
Dexterity
Wisdom

Races Allowed
Human
Elf
Half-elf

Alignments Allowed
Lawful good
Neutral good
Chaotic good

As any player knows who's tried to roll up a ranger using the standard method (Method I, that is, described in Chapter 1 of the *Player's Handbook*), the dice seldom cooperate. In fact, it's just about impossible to generate the high die-rolls required for a ranger by this method. Method II isn't much better, and though Methods III and IV improve the chances somewhat, the odds are hardly favorable. Only by using Methods V and VI do you have a fighting chance of rolling up a ranger from scratch.

Not all Dungeon Masters allow these alternative methods, effectively restricting the number of rangers in their campaigns to a tiny minority. Players wanting ranger characters may find such restrictions frustrating, but remember that good DMs usually have their reasons for imposing these limitations. Perhaps rangers aren't prevalent in the campaign world, or he may feel that rangers will introduce problems of balance; rangers are, after all, a most formidable character class.

However, if your DM is agreeable to having rangers in his campaign, Table 2 is a quick way to generate ranger ability scores. Roll 1d12 and use the statistics indicated.

Table 2: Pregenerated Ability Scores

D12 Roll	Str	Dex	Con	Int	Wis	Cha
1	15	14	17	14	15	10
2	15	15	18	13	14	6
3	14	16	15	14	17	12
4	15	14	15	14	16	9
5	15	15	14	13	15	13
6	16	13	15	13	14	8
7	18*	13	14	15	14	7
8	13	15	15	13	16	10
9	16	13	14	14	17	14
10	13	14	15	16	15	14
11	14	17	14	13	14	15
12	16	13	16	13	14	13

*Make a percentile roll with d100 to find the ranger's exceptional Strength Score.

Level Advancement

As rangers earn experience, they advance in level at a different rate than normal fighters. They acquire 1d10 hit points for each level up to 9th, and thereafter gain 3 hit points per level. The rates of advancement and hit point acquisition, along with the ranger's THAC0 scores (the number rolled on 1d20 to hit armor class 0), are listed in Table 3.

Two adjustments to these figures also apply:

- Rangers with Strength, Dexterity, and Wisdom scores of 16 or more receive a 10% bonus to their awarded experienced points. A ranger must have 16 or more in all three of these abilities to qualify for this bonus.

- Rangers with exceptionally high Constitution scores are entitled to a special hit point adjustment. A score of 17 give the ranger a +3 bonus per hit die, while a score of 18 results in a +4 bonus.

Table 3: Experience Levels

Level	XP Needed	Hit Dice (d10)	THAC0
1	0	1	20
2	2,250	2	19
3	4,500	3	18
4	9,000	4	17
5	18,000	5	16
6	36,000	6	15
7	75,000	7	14
8	150,000	8	13
9	300,000	9	12
10	600,000	9+3	11
11	900,000	9+6	10
12	1,200,000	9+9	9
13	1,500,000	9+12	8
14	1,800,000	9+15	7
15	2,100,000	9+18	6
16	2,400,000	9+21	5
17	2,700,000	9+24	4
18	3,000,000	9+27	3
19	3,300,000	9+30	2
20	3,600,000	9+33	1

Table 4 summarizes the proficiency slot allowances and saving throws applicable to the ranger as he advances in level. Note that, like a fighter, if a ranger uses a weapon with which he isn't proficient, he incurs a –2 penalty.

Table 4: Level Improvements

	Prof.		Saving Throws				
Level	W	N/W	PPDM	RSW	PP	BW	S
1	4	3	14	16	15	17	17
2	4	3	14	16	15	17	17
3	5	4	13	15	14	16	16
4	5	4	13	15	14	16	16
5	5	4	11	13	12	13	14
6	6	5	11	13	12	13	14
7	6	5	10	12	11	12	13
8	6	5	10	12	11	12	13
9	7	6	8	10	9	9	11
10	7	6	8	10	9	9	11
11	7	6	7	9	8	8	10
12	8	7	7	9	8	8	10
13	8	7	5	7	6	5	8
14	8	7	5	7	6	5	8
15	9	8	4	6	5	4	7
16	9	8	4	6	5	4	7
17	9	8	3	5	4	4	6
18	10	9	3	5	4	4	6
19	10	9	3	5	4	4	6
20	10	9	3	5	4	4	6

Proficiency Abbreviations
 W = Weapon proficiency slots
 N/W = Nonweapon proficiency slots

Saving Throw Abbreviations
 PPDM = Paralyzation, Poison, or Death Magic
 RSW = Rod, Staff, or Wand
 PP = Petrification or Polymorph
 BW = Breath Weapon
 S = Spell

Spell Use

When a ranger reaches 8th level, he can learn priest spells of the animal and plant spheres. He acquires and employs spells the same way as a priest. Chapter 6 lists the spells available to a ranger. Chapter 9 explains the special relationships between rangers and priests.

Table 5 shows the number of spells a ranger may have memorized at each level. The "Casting Level" indicates the level at which spells are cast. For instance, the 1st level *invisibility to animals* spell cast by a 12th-level ranger has duration of 1 turn + 5 rounds (the spell lasts for 1 turn + 1 round/level, and the 12th-level ranger casts the spell at 5th level). The 2nd level *warp wood* spell cast by a 16th-level ranger has a range of 90 yards (the range is 10 yards/level, and the 16th-level ranger casts the spell at 9th level).

Regardless of his actual character level, a ranger's spells are never cast beyond 9th level.

The following restrictions also apply:
 • Unlike priests, rangers don't get bonus spells for high Wisdom scores.
 • Rangers may only use magical items specifically allowed to the warrior group. In no case may a ranger use clerical scrolls.

Table 5: Spell Progression

Ranger Level	Casting Level	Priest Spell Levels		
		1	2	3
1-7	-	-	-	-
8	1	1	-	-
9	2	2	-	-
10	3	2	1	-
11	4	2	2	-
12	5	2	2	1
13	6	3	2	1
14	7	3	2	2
15	8	3	3	2
16+	9	3	3	3

Armor and Weapons

Like all warriors, the ranger is allowed to wear any type of armor. However, lighter armor provides him with special benefits, while heavier armor imposes a few restrictions.

A ranger may use two weapons simultaneously without the standard penalties (which are –2 for his main weapon, –4 for the second weapon) when wearing studded or lighter armor (armor with an Armor Class of 7 or more). The following restrictions also apply:
 • The ranger must be able to wield his main weapon with one hand.
 • The second weapon must be smaller in size and must weigh less than the main weapon.

• The ranger can't use a shield when using two weapons.

The ranger's choice of armor also determines whether he can hide in shadows and move silently. Armor with an AC of 6 or less—scale mail armor or heavier—is too inflexible and too noisy to enable him to take advantage of these special abilities.

Table 6 summarizes the AC, costs, and weight of the armor available to the ranger. The table also notes whether the armor allows the ranger to fight with two weapons without penalty, and to use his abilities to hide in shadows and move silently.

Table 6: The Ranger's Armor

Armor	AC	Cost (gp)	Weight (lb.)	T-W	HS/MS
Leather	8	5	15	Yes	Yes
Padded	8	4	10	Yes	Yes
Studded Leather	7	20	25	Yes	Yes
Ring Mail	7	100	30	Yes	Yes
Hide	6	15	30	No	–
Brigandine	6	120	35	No	–
Scale Mail	6	120	40	No	–
Chain Mail	5	75	40	No	–
Splint Mail	4	80	40	No	–
Banded	4	200	35	No	–
Bronze Plate	4	400	45	No	–
Plate Mail	3	600	50	No	–
Field Plate	2	2,000	60	No	–
Full Plate	1	4,000+	70	No	–

Abbreviations

T-W = Two-weapon fighting penalty. ("Yes" means the standard penalties for two-weapon fighting are ignored while wearing this armor.)

HS/MS = Hide in shadows/move silently. ("Yes" means these abilities can be used while wearing this armor. A "–" means these abilities can be used if the DM uses the Optional Armor Adjustments; see Table 13.)

Rangers can use any weapons listed in Chapter 6 of the *Player's Handbook*. As they rise in level, they're able to make more than one attack per round, as shown in Table 7.

Table 7: Ranger Attacks Per Round

Level	Attacks/Round
1-6	1/round
7-12	3/2 rounds
13-20	2/round

As explained in Chapter 9 of the *Player's Handbook*, a character fighting with two weapons is allowed to make an extra attack each combat round with his second weapon. This is added to any multiple attack routine the ranger receives at higher level. For instance, a 13th-level ranger normally makes two attacks per round (see Table 7). However, when fighting with two weapons, he's allowed *three* attacks per round, two with the primary weapon and one with the secondary weapon.

Thief Abilities

A master of stalking and tracking, the ranger shares the thief's talents for hiding in shadows and moving silently when he is in a natural outdoor setting. As a ranger's level increases, so do his abilities, as shown in Table 8.

Table 8: Base Thief Abilities

Level	Hide in Shadows	Move Silently
1	10%	15%
2	15%	21%
3	20%	27%
4	25%	33%
5	31%	40%
6	37%	47%
7	43%	55%
8	49%	62%
9	56%	70%
10	63%	78%
11	70%	86%
12	77%	94%
13	85%	99%
14	93%	99%
15+	99%	99%

The base percentages in Table 8 are modified by the ranger's race, Dexterity score, and armor. Tables 9-11 list these adjustments. Table 12 shows adjustments for the character kits described in Chapter 4. These adjustments reflect the predispo-

sitions of various character types for hiding in shadows and moving silently.

When attempting to hide in shadows, the ranger armor is assumed to cover his armor. Except for leather armor and elven chain mail, which can be concealed by normal clothing, a cloak or equivalent is needed to cover armor.

If a ranger attempts to move silently or hide in shadows in an indoor or underground setting, his cumulative chance of success is halved. Further considerations and restrictions of a ranger's thief abilities are discussed in Chapter 2.

Regardless of modifiers, the ranger's chance to hide in shadows or move silently can never be more than 99% or less than zero.

Table 9: Racial Adjustments

Race	Hide in Shadows	Move Silently
Human	–	–
Elf	+10%	+5%
Half-elf	+5%	–

Table 10: Dexterity Adjustments

Dexterity	Hide in Shadows	Move Silently
13-16	–	–
17	+5%	+5%
18	+10%	+10%
19	+15%	+15%

Table 11: Armor Adjustments

Armor	Hide in Shadows	Move Silently
None*	+5%	+10%
Leather	–	–
Padded	–20%	–20%
Studded Leather	–20%	–20%
Ring Mail	–30%	–40%

*This includes magical apparel such as cloaks and bracers, but not large or bulky garments.

Table 12: Kit Adjustments

Kit	Hide in Shadows	Move Silently
Beastmaster	+5%	–
Explorer	–	–
Falconer	–	–
Feralan	+10%	+10%
Forest Runner	+5%	+5%
Giant Killer	–	–
Greenwood Ranger	–	–5%
Guardian	–	–
Justifier	+5%	+5%
Mountain Man	–5%	–5%
Pathfinder	–	–
Sea Ranger	N/A	N/A
Seeker	–	–
Stalker	+10%	+10%
Warden	–	–

Optional Rule: Normally, thief abilities are denied to rangers wearing armor heavier than studded leather. However, the DM may decide to override this rule in his campaign, allowing rangers to wear any armor they like and still be able to hide in shadows and move silently. (Also, certain character kits described in Chapter 4 allow rangers to hide in shadows and move silently when wearing armor of AC 6 or less). Table 13 lists adjustments for optional armor.

Table 13: Optional Armor Adjustments

Armor	Hide in Shadows	Move Silently
Hide	–20%	–30%
Brigandine	–30%	–40%
Scale Mail	–50%	–60%
Chain Mail	–30%	–40%
Elven Chain	–10%	–10%
Splint Mail	–30%	–40%
Banded	–50%	–60%
Bronze Plate	–75%	–80%
Plate Mail	–75%	–80%
Field Plate	–95%	–95%
Full Plate	–95%	–95%

Primary Terrain

Though rangers work well in all types of outdoor settings, most of them have one particular environment with which they are exceptionally familiar and feel especially comfortable. This environment, called the *primary terrain*, may be similar to the area where the ranger grew up, received his training, or currently calls home. A ranger operates best in his primary terrain, thanks to his intimate knowledge of this type of setting.

A ranger's primary terrain has no particular function in and of itself. Rather, it's used to generate special benefits and other variables described elsewhere in this book. For instance, certain character kits in Chapter 4 grant bonuses to rangers when they occupy their primary terrain. A ranger's primary terrain also helps determine his species enemy (Chapter 2) and followers (Chapter 3).

Types of Primary Terrain

The concept of primary terrain presumes that similar survival techniques, modes of transportation, flora and fauna, and physical features prevail in similar environments, regardless of where in the world they're located. Therefore, primary terrain doesn't refer to a particular area, such as the High Moor of the FORGOTTEN REALMS® setting, but to a general category of terrain, such as swamp or mountains. Conceivably, any combination of geographical features and climate could serve as a primary terrain, but for convenience, we'll confine the possibilities to nine general types:

Aquatic. This terrain type includes all areas consisting primarily of water, such as lakes, oceans, and rivers. At the DM's discretion, this category may also include islands and coastal regions.

Arctic. This includes any region covered with ice and snow where temperatures rarely rises above zero degrees. The North Pole is good example of arctic terrain.

Desert. This includes any barren, flat areas covered with sand or hard-packed earth. Desert climates are extremely dry and hot, with daytime temperatures commonly in excess of 100 degrees, followed by much colder nights. Vegetation is usually sparse, with special adaptations. Much of a desert may be unsettled or unexplored.

Forest. This category comprises any woodland areas in temperate climates. At the DM's option, subarctic and subtropical climates may also be included. Forests abound with a variety of animal species, and vegetation flourishes. Not surprisingly, Forest is the primary terrain of choice for the majority of rangers.

Hill. These are highlands, often wild and rough, which may or may not be forested. They usually form an intermediate zone between lowlands, such as Plains or Desert, and the highest lands, which are Mountain terrain.

Jungle. These are tropical lands (including rain forests) overgrown with dense vegetation and trees, and teeming with animal life. Such regions are often hot, humid, and hostile to civilization.

Mountain. This category includes terrain consisting of high rocky peaks, typically 4,000 feet or more above sea level, with sparse vegetation, severe slopes, and jagged cliffs. Subtropical to subarctic climates are typical, though a wide range of temperatures is possible.

Plains. These are flat areas with stretches of low rolling land, including pastures, meadows, fields, and farmlands. Grazing animals are common here. Such regions are usually covered with

grasses or scrub vegetation and are usually temperate in climate.

Swamp. This includes bogs, marshes, and other low elevation areas with standing water or waterlogged soil. Many species of reptiles, birds, and insects live in these regions. Vegetation grows in abundance. The climate may be oppressively hot and humid or cold and misty.

An ambitious DM may wish to define these primary terrain categories more precisely. Instead of a general Aquatic primary terrain category, he may include both Freshwater Aquatic and Saltwater Aquatic, or distinguish them further by designating Temperate Freshwater Aquatic, Tropical Freshwater Aquatic, and so on. In such cases, the DM will need to adjust the primary terrain references elsewhere in this book; for instance, creating his own Freshwater Aquatic Species Enemy Table like the tables in Chapter 2.

For most campaigns, however, the nine categories listed above should suffice. Though obvious differences exist, say, between saltwater and freshwater settings, a ranger's associated skills—the ability to swim, an understanding of aquatic ecology, a familiarity with water-breathing creatures—are applicable to both. Hence, a ranger whose primary terrain is Aquatic is presumably comfortable in a variety of watery environments.

Choosing a Primary Terrain

The player chooses his ranger's primary terrain as part of the character creation procedure, subject to the DM's approval. Each ranger has only one primary terrain. Because the primary terrain reflects many years, perhaps a lifetime, of exposure to a particular environment, the primary terrain never changes. In exceptional campaign circumstances, however, the DM may allow a ranger to discard an old primary terrain and choose a new one; for instance, if a ranger whose primary terrain is Forest spends a few decades exploring the Great Glacier, his primary terrain may become Arctic. But as a rule, the primary terrain remains constant throughout a ranger's career.

In most cases, the choice of the primary terrain will be obvious, as it usually derives from the ranger's background. It will be similar to the area where the ranger was raised, or the region where

he's spent most of his life. The primary terrain of a ranger who grew up in the barren wastelands of the WORLD OF GREYHAWK® Sea of Dust would probably be Desert. A ranger trained to oversee a private hunting reserve in the Wendle Wood of the DRAGONLANCE® setting would probably have Forest as his primary terrain.

A ranger's primary terrain can be randomly rolled on Table 14. The results are subject to the approval of the DM.

Once the ranger has a primary terrain, it can be used as a basis for developing the character's personal history. If the primary terrain is Arctic, for example, consider how the ranger might have become familiar with such an extreme environment. Was he hired by a king to oversee a seal refuge? Abandoned in the Great Glacier as a youth when his explorer parents were killed by a polar bear? Accepted as an apprentice by a famous white dragon hunter? Let your imagination soar!

Table 14: Random Primary Terrain

D100 Roll	Primary Terrain
01-04	Aquatic
05-06	Arctic
07-10	Desert
11-50	Forest
51-65	Hill
66-75	Jungle
76-85	Mountain
86-95	Plain
96-00	Swamp

Optional Rule: Primary Terrain Specialization

As an option, a ranger may be allowed to specialize in his primary terrain. This confers a +2 bonus when tracking in that terrain, a +2 bonus when training animals from that terrain, general a +2 bonus on any proficiency check associated with that terrain, and an additional –2 penalty to anyone trying to track the ranger through his primary terrain. On the other hand, the terrain-specialized ranger has a –2 penalty in all terrains except the one in which he is specialized. This specialization in terrain does not cost any proficiency slots. The ranger cannot specialize in more than one type of terrain.

Regardless of whether they're wardens of private game reserves, arctic explorers, or freelance monster hunters, all rangers share a set of special abilities that distinguish them from other character classes. Just as wizards have an innate aptitude for casting spells and thieves have a natural talent for picking pockets, rangers have the inborn ability to track other creatures, hide in shadows and move silently in outdoor settings, react to specific enemies, empathize with animals, understand the complexities of nature, survive in extreme conditions, build strongholds, and acquire followers. Quite a list—but that's what makes the ranger such an exceptional character.

We'll spend this chapter examining each of the ranger's abilities in detail, looking at their applications and special rules. The ranger's ability to attract followers—a topic complex enough to merit special attention—will be saved for the next chapter.

Tracking

Thanks to his keen senses and thorough understanding of animal behavior, the ranger is an expert tracker. He reads an impression in the mud or a bend in a twig like words on a printed page. He can determine the identity of his quarry and how fast it was traveling by the depth of a footprint. He can tell the size of a slug from the trail of slime it left behind. He can track an orc in the darkest forest, a rabbit though the thickest jungle, an escaped convict across the most desolate mountain range.

A ranger's tracking skills apply to characters as well as creatures, and to underground and interior settings as well as all types of outdoor environments. His tracking skills are inherent; that is, he receives the Tracking nonweapon proficiency automatically at the outset of his career, expending no proficiency slots.

Pre-Conditions

A ranger can't just track anything, any time he likes. In order to track a particular quarry, the following conditions must be met:

1. The quarry must be capable of leaving a physical trail. Elements of a trail may include footprints, bent twigs, waste matter, or any other physical signs that a ranger can follow. Certain categories of creatures—including swimming and flying creatures, small insects, and ghosts and other non-corporeal creatures—seldom leave physical evidence of their passage. In most cases, such creatures can't be tracked. However, since tracking involves all the senses, not just sight, it's possible that the aroma of burning metal might linger after the passage of a particular spectre, or a ghost might reveal itself by its eerie voice, heard faintly in the distance. Still, only the most skilled rangers are capable of following trails devoid of physical evidence, and the DM should allow such tracking in only the rarest of circumstances.

2. The ranger must be able to find the trail. If the trail is outdoors, the ranger must actually see the creature (he spots a fox darting into the brush), notice obvious signs of his quarry (such as footprints or droppings), or hear reliable reports of the quarry's whereabouts ("Looking for that old silver dragon? She likes to drink from the pond by the twin palm trees."). If the trail is indoors, the ranger himself must have seen the quarry within the last 30 minutes, and begin tracking from the location where the quarry was last seen. As always, the DM is the final arbiter as to whether the ranger has enough evidence to enable him to track the quarry.

Tracking Check

If the above conditions are met, the ranger can attempt to trail the quarry by making a Tracking check, using his Tracking score. The base Tracking score is equivalent to the ranger's Wisdom. Consult Tables 15-17 for other relevant modifiers; these tables may be used in place of Table 39 in Chapter 5 of the *Player's Handbook*. In non-natural surroundings, the Tracking chances are *halved*.

Table 15: Terrain Tracking Modifiers

Terrain (use only one)	Modifier
Fresh snow (clearly outlined footprints)	+6
Soft or muddy ground, loose dirt floor (good impressions of prints, but not as defined as fresh snow)	+4
Thick brush, dense jungle (broken branches, crushed weeds)	+3
Forests, fields, dusty indoor area (occasional marks of passage)	+2
Normal ground, wood floor, plains with sparse vegetation (infrequent marks of passage)	0
Desert, dry sand	−2
Swamp (spongy surface but little mud for prints, much vegetation)	−5
Rocky terrain, solid ice, stone floors, shallow water (prohibits all but the most minute signs of passage)	−10

Table 16: Illumination Modifiers

Illumination (use only one)	Modifier
Good illumination, sunny day; continual light or equivalent indoors	0
Twilight, light fog, snow, single torch in dark interior of building	−3
Night with full moon, day with moderate fog	−6
Overcast night with no moon, dense fog, blizzard, blowing sand	−10

Table 17: Special Tracking Modifiers

Situation (use all applicable)	Modifier
Every two creatures in group being tracked	+1
Every three experience levels (round down) of the ranger	+1
Each additional tracker assisting ranger (use the score of the best tracker)*	+1
Animal follower assists in tracking**	+1
Trail is in specialized ranger's primary terrain	+2
Every 12 hours since trail was made	−1
Every hour of rain, snow, or sleet since trail was made	−5
Creature being tracked attempts to hide trail (covering footprints, detouring into stream, passing through secret door)	−5
Specialized ranger being tracked in his primary terrain attempts to hide trail	−2

* Total bonus for assistance is limited to ranger level bonus; i.e. +1 per 3 levels.
** See Chapter 3. The animal follower does not count as an additional tracker for purposes of the previous bonus.

If the modified Tracking score is zero or less, the ranger is unable to track the quarry in question.

If the modified Tracking score is greater than zero, the ranger makes a Tracking check by rolling 1d20. If the roll exceeds the ranger's tracking score, or if the roll is 20, the check fails and no trail has been found, If the roll less than or equal to the ranger's Tracking score, the ranger has found the quarry's trail and may begin to follow it.

Interrupted Tracking

Once a ranger has found the trail, he may track the quarry indefinitely until any of the following situations occur:

The ranger moves too fast. The ranger must move slower than his normal movement rate in order to stay alert for signs of the trail. His movement rate limit depends on his modified Tracking score, as shown in Table 18.

Table 18: Movement While Tracking

Modified Tracking Score	Movement Rate Limit
1-6	1/4 normal
7-14	1/2 normal
15+	3/4 normal

Should the ranger exceed the movement rate in Table 18—for instance, if a monster abruptly ambushes him and he's forced to run—he loses the trail.

The modifiers change. If the trail leads to a new terrain type, night falls, or any other change occurs that requires a new Tracking modifier (as described in Tables 15-17), the ranger loses the trail. The new conditions may dictate the use of modifiers reflecting a trail that is easier to follow, not more difficult, and DMs should consider applying a bonus in such conditions. Nevertheless, the new roll must still be made.

A second track crosses the first. Crossed trails mingle the physical signs of each, making tracking difficult. The DM determines if such a situation exists. If so, the ranger's efforts fail. (If the ranger wishes to continue tracking, as described below, he must decide which of the crossed trails to follow.)

The ranger becomes distracted. An attack from a monster may interrupt the ranger's

progress. Further, the ranger may intentionally choose to stop if he needs to rest, eat, or hold a discussion with his companions. Any of these interruptions qualifies as a distraction.

When any of these conditions occur, the ranger loses the trail. To continue tracking the quarry, he must spend at least an hour exploring the immediate area for new signs of the trail. After an hour of searching, he makes a new Tracking check, based on a Tracking score calculated from the new conditions (if the illumination has changed from daylight to twilight, he must now modify his Tracking score by –3). If other trackers assist the ranger, modify the tracking check by +1 per assistant; add the bonus to the Tracking score of the most adept tracker. This bonus is limited to +1 per 3 levels of the ranger (round up). If the check succeeds, the ranger may continue following the trail as before. If he fails the check, he has lost the trail for good.

Identification Check

By noticing details that other characters might overlook—the depth of a footprint, the thickness of a snapped branch, a hair caught in barbed bush—the ranger can deduce a sizeable amount of information about his quarry. The more skilled the ranger, the more information he deduces.

Whenever a ranger makes a successful Tracking check, he may then attempt an Identification check. The Identification check uses the same score and modifiers as the Tracking check; essentially, the Identification check is a second Tracking check.

If the Identification check is successful, the DM provides the ranger with some information about the quarry based on the guidelines in Table 19. The ranger's experience level determines the type of information he receives. The information is cumulative; that is, a 6th-level ranger who makes a successful Identification check receives all types of

information available to rangers of level 6 and below.

The DM provides only general information, not exact details. At his discretion, the DM may give more precise or less specific information than suggested in Table 19. The information may be ambiguous ("The tracks resemble those of a large bird, though they could have been made by some sort of reptilian creature.") but the DM shouldn't intentionally mislead the ranger (for instance, by telling him the tracks were definitely made by a bird when in fact they were made by a reptile). The parenthetical comments in Table 19 indicate how a DM might respond to a ranger studying tracks that were made by a pair of juvenile red dragons, each with a human rider.

Table 19: Identification Check Results

Ranger

Level	Information Received
1-2	General type of creature ("*A dragon or other large reptilian creature.*")
3-4	Specific type of creature and where it was heading ("*Some kind of dragon, probably red. It appears to have been headed to the mountains to the north.*")
5-6	Probable number of creatures ("*Looks like two of them.*")
7	Approximate size and/or age ("*From the length of the prints, the dragons were probably juveniles.*")
8	Pace of creatures ("*There's no indication of haste; they were probably taking their time.*")
9	How recently the trail was made ("*The tracks were made within the last three or four hours.*")
10+	Special conditions of creatures: wounded or healthy, mounts, etc. ("*The unusual depth of the prints and the space between steps indicates the dragons had riders. A tiny scrap of cloth is similar to the material worn by soldiers in this area. The riders were probably human.*")

Covering Movement

Not only is the ranger able to track the movement of others, he's also adept at concealing his own trail. If a ranger moves at half his normal movement rate, he may cover his footprints, avoid snapping twigs, and execute similar actions necessary to conceal his trail. When other characters, rangers included, attempt to track a ranger who has concealed his trail, they do so at a –5 penalty to their Tracking scores. (If a terrain-specialized ranger concealed his trail while moving through his primary terrain, others suffer a –7 penalty to their Tracking scores.)

Hide in Shadows

By flattening his body or crouching in such as way as to blend into dark areas, and remaining perfectly still while doing so, the ranger can render himself nearly invisible in natural surroundings. This ability to hide in shadows works equally well in fields of tall grass, clumps of bushes, rocky hills, or any other wilderness area with dark or shaded terrain.

When hiding, the ranger can conceal himself from attackers and eavesdrop on his enemies. He can hide near a well-traveled road and secretly observe passersby, or conceal himself near an enemy campsite, waiting for an opportune moment to steal their treasure or supplies.

Table 8 in Chapter 1 gives the base chance for a ranger to hide in shadows, subject to the modifiers for race, Dexterity and armor (Tables 9-11). The following restrictions also apply:

- If attempting to hide in shadows on city streets, inside a building, or in any other non-wilderness setting, the ranger's chance is halved. Apply this reduction after all the other modifiers have been taken into account.
- The ranger must be unobserved while attempting to conceal himself. If an NPC or creature is watching him, the ranger can't hide successfully. If the NPC or creature becomes distracted, even momentarily, the ranger can slip into the area of concealment and attempt to hide.
- While hiding, the ranger must remain immobile, except for slow and careful movements, such as readying a weapon or sipping from a flask.
- If the area is completely dark—for instance, if there's an overcast sky in the dead of night—the ranger gains no special advantages from hiding in shadows, and can't use this ability.

If all these conditions are met, the DM rolls percentile dice as soon as the ranger has concealed himself. The DM doesn't tell the ranger the result of the roll; rather, the ranger learns if the attempt is successful from the reactions of those in the area.

If the check is less than or equal to the ranger's adjusted hide in shadows score, the ranger has successfully concealed himself. He's essentially invisible to all others in the area, including his companions. He has hidden successfully until he changes locations; an attempt to hide in shadows in a different area requires a new die roll. Characters using spells or magical items that reveal hidden or invisible objects can detect him. Likewise, creatures who use their sense of smell to locate prey or other exceptionally keen senses have their normal chance of sniffing out a ranger hiding in shadows.

If the check is greater than the ranger's hide in shadows score, he's failed to conceal himself and is as exposed as any normal character would be in the same area. This doesn't necessarily mean that others will notice him, especially if the area of concealment provides a lot of natural cover, such as a cluster of bushes or the long shadow from a tall tree. However, the ranger may not know if he's succeeded or failed until it's too late—for instance, if an NPC suddenly turns and charges.

Move Silently

Moving silently enables the ranger to move with a minimum of sound, almost as if he's walking on air. Even creatures with the sharpest ears are no more likely to detect his presence than they are to hear a feather drop. The ability works equally well in icy mountains, heavily wooded forests, or any other type of wilderness terrain.

Getting from place to place without being heard is only the most obvious application of this ability. Other uses include:

- Sneaking up on one or more opponents in order to surprise them.
- Examining the contents of a cart or a cabinet by removing the objects one by one, then replacing them in silence. (However, silent movement applies to the character's actions only; therefore, this ability would not negate the sound of a squeaking cabinet door or rusty hinge of a trunk.)
- Change armor or clothes.
- Other actions the DM allows, such as restringing a bow, or cutting a slit in the back of a tent.

Table 8 in Chapter 1 provides the base chance for moving silently, modified by the variables in Tables 9-11. If the ranger attempts to move silently inside a building or in any other non-wilderness area, his modified score is halved. Other restrictions:

- He can move no faster than ⅓ his normal movement rate when moving silently.
- He can't be observed when attempting to use this ability (moving silently isn't of much use to a ranger who's being watched).
- If he draws attention to himself either intentionally (speaking) or inadvertently (sneezing), the effects of moving silently are immediately negated.

The DM rolls percentile dice as soon as the ranger makes an attempt to move silently. If the roll exceeds the ranger's move silently score, he is as likely to be heard as any other character moving in the same terrain; snapping a twig or kicking a pebble may draw the attention of NPCs or creatures.

If the roll is less than or equal to the ranger's move silently score, he is able to move without sound. He continues to move silently until the terrain changes (for instance, if he enters an area of pebbles, shallow water, or dried leaves), or he attempts a new action that affects his ease of movement (such as carrying an unconscious companion or a large jug of sloshing water). Any such change requires a new roll.

Species Enemy

Every ranger has a particular creature for which he harbors a deep loathing. Even an otherwise pacifistic ranger has no reservations about harming this creature. In fact, he may actively seek it out for the express purpose of destroying it.

The creature that a ranger opposes above all others is called his *species enemy*. A ranger gains special combat modifiers when encountering his species enemy, reflecting both his knowledge of the creature and his intense emotions.

The player must choose his ranger's species enemy before the character advances to 2nd level.

The DM has final approval of the choice. Once the species enemy is determined, it never changes; the ranger retains the same species enemy for the duration of his career.

Though it's not required, the DM may wish to suggest or assign a species enemy based on the ranger's personal history. Conversely, the player may use a DM's choice of a species enemy to fill in some details about the character's early life. Here are a few ways a species enemy might reflect a ranger's background:

- The species enemy was responsible for a personal tragedy in the ranger's youth. The enemy may have killed a ranger's friend or sibling, or may have destroyed the ranger's village and everyone in it. The ranger has vowed to avenge himself against the hated creature.

- The ranger had an intense phobic reaction against a particular creature, perhaps as a result of a childhood trauma. When the ranger was an infant, for example, a snake may have slithered into his crib and tried to swallow him. After years of struggle, the ranger eventually overcame his phobia. In the process, the creature became his species enemy.

- A lord or king hired the ranger as a young man to rid the region of a particular creature. What began as a job became a personal vendetta, and the ranger has come to regard the creature as his species enemy.

Optional Rule: To determine a ranger's species enemy, consult Tables 20-29, rolling on the table corresponding to the ranger's primary terrain. The DM isn't confined to the creatures on the tables, and the tables can be expanded at will. At the DM's discretion, a skeleton or a wight may be an appropriate species enemy for a ranger whose primary terrain is Swamp or Mountains, and an ogre may be as appropriate in the Jungle as the Forest. The DM may also override any illogical selections; a shark, for instance, is a poor choice for an Aquatic ranger who's spent his life at a freshwater lake.

A table is given for Underdark (deep subterranean) enemies, even though no ranger has the Underdark as a primary terrain.

A ranger receives the following modifiers in regard to his species enemy:

Attack Bonus. Because of his special understanding of the species enemy's vulnerabilities and combat strategies, the ranger receives a +4 bonus to his attack rolls when fighting the creature. This bonus is in addition to any other bonuses the ranger normally receives.

Reaction Penalty. So intense is the ranger's emotional response to the species enemy that it's nearly impossible for him to conceal it. For this reason, the ranger suffers a –4 penalty to all encounter reactions with the species enemy.

Combat Preference. In most combat situations, the ranger will actively seek out his species enemy as the object of his attacks to the exclusion of all other potential opponents. If the party encounters three orcs and a troll, and the troll is the ranger's species enemy, the ranger will attack the troll and leave the orcs to his companions. If the ranger spots a troll in the wilderness, he may feel compelled to attack the troll unless his companions convince him otherwise or forcibly restrain him.

This compulsion doesn't automatically override the ranger's good judgement or sense of duty. If a species enemy accidently falls into a bottomless pit, the ranger won't jump in after it. If he hears rumors that a species enemy was sighted in a distant village, he won't abandon his party to investigate, although he may argue strongly for the party to check it out. If a companion cries for help, he will abandon his fight against a species enemy to come to the companion's aid, resuming his attacks against the species enemy when the companion is safe.

The modifiers apply wherever the ranger encounters his species enemy, not just in the ranger's primary terrain. A ranger whose primary terrain is Desert and whose species enemy is the blue dragon will receive a +4 combat bonus regardless of whether he meets a blue dragon in the desert, mountains, or anywhere else.

Further, the modifiers apply only to the specific creature (or creatures) designated as the species enemy, including any leaders, nobles, shamans, etc. If the species enemy is a blue dragon, the modifiers don't apply to black dragons, red dragons, or dragons of any other color. However, the modifiers affect blue dragons of all ages, from hatchlings to great wyrms. The ogre species

enemy includes ogre leaders, shamans, and chieftains, but not ogre mages or merrows. (As a rule of thumb, if a variant creature has a separate listing in its MONSTROUS COMPENDIUM® entry, it's not included as a species enemy). The DM is free to make exceptions to the lists in Tables 20-28 based on local conditions within the campaign. For instance, he may decide to include merrows as part of the ogre species enemy, or he may exclude advanced lizard men from the lizard man species enemy if campaign logic dictates.

Table 20: Arctic Species Enemy

D8 Roll	Enemy
1-3	Frost giant
4-5	White dragon
6	Cryohydra
7	Ice Toad
8	Verbeeg
9	Winter wolf
10	Yeti

Table 21: Aquatic Species Enemy

D10 Roll	Enemy
1	Dragon turtle
2	Koalinth
3	Kraken (may include giant squid)
4	Kuo-toa
5	Lacedon
6	Merrow
7	Pirate/buccaneer, human
6	Seawolf, lyc. (includes greater)
9	Sahuagin
10	Scrag

Table 22: Desert Species Enemy

D10 Roll	Enemy
1	Blue dragon
2	Desert brigand, human
3	Fire giant
4	Hieracosphinx
5	Jackalwere
6	Jann, evil
7	Lamia
8	Manscorpion
9	Naga, evil (may include desert snakes)
10	Sandling

Table 23: Forest Species Enemy

D10 Roll	Enemy
1	Green dragon
2	Bugbear
3	Ettercap (may include forest spiders)
4	Ghoul/ghast
5	Goblin
6	Hobgoblin
7	Kobold
8	Ogre
9	Orc (may include orog)
10	Troll (may include other types)

Table 24: Jungle Species Enemy

D10 Roll	Enemy
1	Black dragon
2	Carnivorous ape
3	Bullywug
4	Lizard man (includes advanced lizard men and lizard king)
5	Naga, evil (may include jungle snakes)
6	Slaver, human
7	Tasloi
8	Wyvern
9-10	Yuan-ti

Table 25: Hill Species Enemy

D10 Roll	Enemy
1	Red dragon
2	Brigand, human
3	Bugbear
4	Hill giant
5	Gnoll/flind
6	Hobgoblin
7	Leucrotta
8	Ogre
9	Ogre mage
10	Werewolf, lyc.

Table 26: Mountain Species Enemy

D10 Roll	Enemy
1	Red dragon
2	Cyclopskin (may include cyclops)
3	Ettin
4	Hill giant
5	Fomorian giant
6	Gnoll/flind
7	Manticore
8	Ogre
9	Orc (may include orog)
10	Troll (may include other types)

Table 27: Plains Species Enemy

D10 Roll	Enemy
1	Hill giant
2	Brigand, human
3	Gnoll/flind
4	Goblin
5	Harpy
6	Hobgoblin
7	Ogre
8-9	Orc (may include orog)
10	Troll (may include others)

Table 28: Swamp Species Enemy

D10 Roll	Enemy
1	Black dragon
2	Behir
3	Bullywug
4	Ghoul (may include ghast)
5	Goblin
6	Hydra (may include lernaean hydra and/or pyrohydra)
7	Lizard man (includes advanced lizard men and lizard king)
8	Muckdweller
9	Su-monster
10	Troll (may include other types)

Table 29: Underdark Species Enemy

D10 Roll	Enemy
1	Bugbear
2	Derro
3	Drow (includes drider)
4	Duergar
5	Gibberling
6	Illithid
7	Kuo-toa
8	Troglodyte
9	Troll (may include other types)
10	Umber hulk

Animal Empathy

Many characters regard animals as non-thinking beasts that react purely on instinct, incapable of responding to reason. The ranger, on the other hand, sees animals as emotionally complex creatures whose fears and desires may be less sophisticated than those of humans, but are no less real. This innate understanding of animal behavior gives the ranger a limited ability to influence their emotions and manipulate their behavior.

The ranger knows the meaning of a twitching tail, a cocked head, a low growl. He knows that a snarling wolf positioned in a crouch may be more frightened than hostile. If approached correctly, a hissing snake may slither away rather than strike. By calling on his animal empathy, a ranger can use soothing words and gestures to turn hostility to indifference, and indifference to friendship.

Conditions

A ranger can't influence an animal's reactions at will. The following limitations apply:

The animal must be native to the real world; natural animals. Rangers can't modify the reactions of supernatural creatures (skeletons and ghouls), magical creatures (basilisks and golems), or creatures of extra-planar origin (aerial servants and elementals). The ranger can affect giant animals.

The animal must be intelligent, but not exceptionally so. To respond to a ranger's words and gestures, the animal must be able to

comprehend them. In practice, this means that a ranger can't use this ability to influence the behavior of non-intelligent animals (those with Intelligence scores of zero) such as centipedes or barracudas. Conversely, creatures of higher intelligence, such as leprechauns, ogres, and a paladin's warhorse, resist the ranger's *animal empathy*. As a rule of thumb, rangers can only use this ability on natural animals whose intelligence ranges from Animal to Low (Intelligence score of 1 to 7).

The animal can't be the ranger's species enemy. A ranger who confronts the species enemy is too overwhelmed by intense emotions to establish the proper empathy. Therefore, a ranger can never modify the reaction of his species enemy using this ability.

The ranger must remain calm. The ranger must move towards the animal quietly, slowly, and confidently, all the while speaking soothing words and making calming gestures. Fear cannot be shown, nor a weapon wielded, nor any action taken that might frighten or enrage the animal.

The ranger be distanced from the rest of the party. If the ranger approaches with companions, the animal will react to the presence of all the characters, not just the ranger. The ranger's efforts to soothe the animal will go unnoticed. Ideally, the rest of the party will be out of the animal's sight when the ranger approaches. If this is impractical, the ranger's companions should be at least 10 feet behind him, remaining quiet and taking no actions that the animal might interpret as hostile.

The animal must be able to hear and see the ranger. The ranger must be in plain sight for the animal to size up; the ranger may not be concealed in the brush, hidden in shadows, or have erected any type of physical barrier between himself and the animal. The animal must also be able to hear the ranger, meaning that the area must be relatively quiet, free of distracting or disturbing sounds. In most cases, the ranger must be within a few feet of the animal, or close enough for the animal to see the ranger's eyes. The DM may make exceptions in special circumstances. For instance, if the ranger approaches an

animal in total darkness, the DM may rule that soothing words are sufficient to calm the animal. In situations where silence is imperative, gestures alone may suffice. However, in all cases, the ranger must still be relatively close to the animal to modify its reaction.

The ranger must soothe the animal for an uninterrupted period. A ranger can't attempt to soothe an animal that's charging or attacking; the animal must be stationary or moving only slightly (a pacing wolf, a weaving serpent). Once the ranger moves close to the animal, the creature must be soothed for 5-10 (1d6+4) uninterrupted rounds; the DM may increase this time if the animal is unusually anxious or exceptionally hostile. (This time can be lapsed by the DM if nothing else is going on.)

A ranger who meets these conditions can use animal empathy in an attempt to modify the animal's reactions. Though the game result is the same, technique differs depending whether the animal is wild or domestic.

Wild Animals

This group includes animals not normally domesticated, such as lions, snakes, and rats. It also includes domesticated animals that have been trained to attack, such as dogs.

Before the ranger attempts to soothe a wild animal, the DM must determine the animal's current attitude, taking into account its natural temperament (Is it naturally aggressive, or inclined to flee rather than fight?), immediate conditions (Did it just wake up? Is it sick or wounded? Hungry?) and pre-existing circumstances (Has it recently been harassed or befriended by characters similar in appearance to the ranger? Is it guarding its nest or lair?) The DM should then select the animal's current attitude from Table 30. The attitude should not be announced ("The wolf is Cautious."). Instead, clearly describe the animal's appearance and behavior and let the ranger come to his own conclusions ("The wolf paces back and forth, eyes darting. It begins to snarl as you approach.").

Table 30: Animal Attitudes

Attitude	Description
Frightened	Filled with panic and terror. Will flee at earliest opportunity.
Friendly	Feels warm or conciliatory toward stranger. Will not attack. May nuzzle or lick stranger to express affection.
Indifferent	Bored or unimpressed. Oblivious to stranger.
Cautious	Suspicious, guarded, nervous. Ready to defend itself if attacked.
Threatening	Openly belligerent. Growling, snapping, crouched to spring. Likely to attack if stranger doesn't withdraw.
Hostile	Aggressive, violent, enraged. Will definitely attack if stranger doesn't withdraw; may pursue even if he does.

To determine if the ranger is able to modify the reaction of a wild animal, the animal must make a saving throw vs. rods (even though the ranger's animal empathy ability isn't magical). As shown on Table 31, the ranger's experience level imposes a penalty to the creature's roll.

Table 31: Animal Empathy Modifier

Ranger Level	Modifier
1-3	–1
4-6	–2
7-9	–3
10-12	–4
13-15	–5
16+	–6

If the animal fails its saving throw, the ranger has successfully modified its behavior. The attitude of the animal shifts one category, up or down, on Table 30 as decided by the ranger. If the animal was Indifferent, it now becomes either Cautious or Friendly, and behaves accordingly. This new reaction applies only to the ranger. An animal that the ranger changed from Threatening to Cautious may still behave in a Threatening manner to other members of the party, particularly if another character decides to interfere with the ranger's efforts or otherwise draws attention to himself. However, as long as the ranger stays near the animal and continues to soothe it, the animal's attention will remain focused on the ranger, and it will remain Cautious. After the ranger leaves the area, the animal's attitude remains altered for a short time (from a few minutes to an hour, as decided by the DM) before it reverts to its original disposition.

If the animal succeeds in its saving throw, it resists the ranger's efforts and its attitude remains unchanged. The ranger notices no significant difference in the animal's behavior. An Indifferent animal continues to ignore the ranger, a Hostile animal may suddenly charge him. The ranger can't make a second attempt to modify its behavior.

Domestic Animals

This group includes animals that have non-hostile dispositions and are routinely domesticated, such as horses and dogs. It also includes formerly wild animals, such as bears and monkeys, that have been tamed and now are comfortable around people.

Such animals are presumed to be Frightened, Friendly, Indifferent, or Cautious. Regardless of their initial disposition, when a ranger approaches and soothes them, they become Friendly. No saving throws are necessary; this change is automatic. It's also permanent, so long as the ranger stays in sight of the animal. If the ranger leaves the area, the animal reverts to its original disposition a short time later (within a few minutes to an hour).

The attitude change applies to the ranger only; an Indifferent dog feels Friendly to the ranger but remains oblivious to the ranger's companions. A Cautious horse is Friendly to the ranger and will carry him on its back, but bucks furiously if anyone else attempts to mount it.

Additionally, the ranger can ascertain the general qualities of any domestic animal he befriends. By observation alone, he could determine:
- Which puppy in a litter will become the best hunter and most loyal companion.

• Which horse at a sale is the healthiest, strongest, and fastest mount.
• Which sheep in a flock will produce the highest quality wool.
• Which sow in a sty will give birth to the largest broods.

The DM should provide any information of this type that the ranger wants to know, though he should refrain from answering specific questions. For instance, the ranger can determine which horse in a corral is the fastest, but he can't tell the horse's exact speed just by observing it.

A special case occurs if an animal has been attack-trained. This is most usual in the case of dogs, horses, and hunting birds such as falcons, but might apply to other animals, such as bears or leopards. These are treated as wild animals, and receive the saving throw vs. rods to resist the ranger's empathy as described above.

Nature Lore

Though the experiences of a ranger living in an arctic wasteland may differ dramatically from one who makes his home in a jungle, both have spent many years observing the patterns of nature, and both have arrived at similar conclusions about the relationship between living things and their environment.

All rangers, then, have an inherent understanding of natural lore, encompassing a broad set of principles involving conservation, ecology, and natural order. Though not every ranger knows specific details about particular situations, all of them understand the general concepts at work. Some examples:
• The plant and animal life in any given habitat tend to be interdependent. The butterfly pollinates the flower, the flower produces nectar to feed the butterfly.

- Animals and plants adapt to natural changes in the environment. Grass becomes dormant in the winter and grows again in the spring. A wolf's fur thickens as the temperature drops, and thins when the weather becomes warmer.
- To avoid ruining the land, natural resources used by man must be replenished. If trees are harvested in a forest, new trees should be planted in their place.

A ranger's knowledge of natural lore enhances his reverence for all living things. In practical terms, it allows him to recognize ecological and environmental problems, both actual and potential. In some cases, he may be able to offer suggestions for correcting them.

There are no hard and fast rules for determining the extent of a ranger's natural lore and its application. The DM must decide how much a particular ranger knows on a case by case basis, taking into account the ranger's training, background, and primary terrain. In most situations, experience is the main factor; the higher the ranger's level, the more he's likely to know.

Table 31 provides natural lore guidelines for rangers of various levels. The information is cumulative; a 7th-level ranger also knows the information available to lower-level rangers. Keep in mind that these are generalizations; a 2nd-level ranger who was raised on a farm may know as much about the ecology of growing crops as another ranger of 10th level. By way of illustration, the parenthetical comments indicate what the ranger might know if attempting to figure out why crops no longer grow in a once-fertile farmland.

Table 32: Nature Lore

Ranger Level	Quality of Information
1-3	Knows general principles of how climate, terrain, and life forms interact. Can identify problems, but can only guess at causes. (The topsoil has eroded away.)
4-6	Can determine causes of problems. (Heavy rainfall washed away the topsoil and leached away the nutrients.)
7+	Can suggest solutions to problems. (Add fertilizer to the remaining soil. To prevent further erosion, keep land covered with grasses or trees.)

If the DM is stumped as to whether a ranger knows a particular piece of information, he may require the ranger to make a Wisdom check, adding bonuses or penalties to the roll depending on the relative difficulty of the question. For instance, knowing if a particular substance will work as a fertilizer is a relatively easy question, requiring no penalty to the roll. Knowing which specific crops the fertilizer will nourish is a more difficult question, and a penalty to the roll may be in order. In all cases, the DM should use common sense. A ranger who's never been out of the desert won't know much about the effects of a hurricane on a coastal environment, regardless of his level.

Survival

The ranger is exceptionally skilled at surviving harsh conditions associated with his primary terrain. In game terms, the ranger is considered to automatically have the Survival proficiency in his primary terrain. This skill costs no proficiency slots. A ranger can spend slots in the Survival proficiency to acquire survival skills in environments other than his primary terrain.

The ranger's survival skill helps in the following ways, all of which apply only in the primary terrain. In certain cases, the DM may require a Survival check (which is equivalent to an Intelligence check). A ranger rolling less than or equal to his Intelligence score on 1d20 succeeds in the check.

- The ranger knows the basic precautions necessary to enhance the chances of survival, and can instruct and assist any companions accordingly. For example, a ranger whose primary terrain is Mountains realizes that physical exertion in high altitudes may result in headaches and fatigue (due to low air pressure). A Desert ranger knows that in arid climates, it's better to rest in the still air than exposed to a strong wind (wind promotes evaporation from the skin, increasing the degree of dehydration). An Aquatic ranger understands that saltwater can't be used for drinking. An Arctic ranger realizes that temporary protection can be had from a bitter wind by tunneling inside a snow drift. This knowledge doesn't guarantee survival

by any means; it merely improves the odds. If the ranger wonders about any particular piece of information, the DM will decide if he knows it, requiring a Survival check if necessary.

- The ranger can stave off starvation by finding small amounts of food. A successful Survival check locates enough food to feed himself or one other character. He can locate food in this way once per day.
- The ranger can find enough water to keep himself or another character alive for one day by making a successful Survival check. This assumes that the water is there to be found.
- The ranger can interpret subtle changes in the environment to anticipate natural disasters. A Plains ranger can recognize the appearance of the sky associated with a coming tornado. A Mountain ranger can identify the rumbling sound that precedes an avalanche. The DM may require Survival checks to verify a ranger's interpretations.

Optional Rule: One way in which a DM can use the Survival ability in a "quick-and-dirty" fashion is to set up special penalties (cumulative penalties for fatigue or exposure) in especially harsh climes. A party with a ranger, or one that is properly prepared and outfitted, simply avoids the potential penalties. Those who are unprepared take the penalties until the DM decides they have acclimated to the setting, or until they take other appropriate actions determined by the DM.

Strongholds

Like fighters, rangers have the ability to build and maintain castles, forts, and strongholds. Unlike fighters, rangers are not joined by free soldiers or other special followers in doing so.

Theoretically, any ranger can build a stronghold. In practice, most rangers who build them are 9th level or higher, since rangers of lower level usually lack the necessary resources, reputation,

and skills. A DM may allow a lower-level ranger to have a stronghold under exceptional circumstances; for instance, a ranger might come into an inheritance, or a group of peasants might build a castle in gratitude for his assistance.

Some rangers acquire strongholds in cooperation with the local king or ruler. The ranger begins the process by petitioning the ruler for permission to build a stronghold in a particular area. If the ranger demonstrates good will and has a reputation for trustworthiness and strong leadership, the ruler usually grants permission. In exchange for this permission, the ranger may have to pay an annual tax, or make himself available to serve in the ruler's military forces in times of war. If the ranger meets his obligations, the ruler may loan royal forces to the ranger if his territory is invaded or his stronghold besieged.

More commonly, rangers prefer to build their strongholds in the unsettled wilderness, beyond the sovereignty of any government. Though free of obligations to a ruler, the ranger must also fend for himself in times of peril; if an army of orcs lays claim to the ranger's territory, the ranger is on his own.

Because a ranger's stronghold gains him no special followers, it tends to be significantly smaller and less elaborate than that of a fighter of comparable level. Though a fighter may receive money by selling products produced on his land, taxing settlers, or charging rent, these options are rarely available to rangers. In most cases, a ranger's stronghold generates only a modest income, if any.

Guidelines for building and maintaining strongholds are beyond the scope of this book. For more information, you might investigate the *DMRG2 Castle Guide*, which includes details of castle construction along with a number of standard floor plans.

Though most rangers prefer castles and forts made of wood and stone, these are by no means the only types available. Other possibilities include tree houses (in Forest and Jungle terrain), fortified encampments (Desert), observation platforms (Mountains), floating citadels (Swamp and Aquatic), and ice towers (Arctic).

Perhaps the ranger's most interesting ability is the chance to attract unusual followers. Unlike fighters and other character classes that acquire followers, the ranger's followers include animals and magical creatures as well as humans and demihumans. In fact, it's possible that all of a ranger's followers may be animals, which can result in unexpected benefits (strangers aren't as likely to mess with a ranger accompanied by a wolf pack) as well as unforeseen complications (ever try getting a room at an inn with a bear trotting behind you?).

Humans and demihumans (and magical creatures) are drawn to a ranger because of his sterling reputation. They serve as followers out of loyalty and respect, remaining true to the ranger so long as he treats them decently. In this way, such followers are different from normal hirelings and mercenaries who serve for pay.

The motivations of animal followers are less obvious. Animals have no conception of what constitutes a reputation, sterling or otherwise. Instead, animals bond to rangers by instinct. The nature of this bond lies somewhere between the relationship of an infant animal and its parent (picture a baby duck contentedly swimming behind its mother), and a master and his pet (think of a dog's affection for the person who provides him with companionship). If the ranger honors the bond, the follower will often remain loyal for its entire life.

It's important to keep in mind that this bond has no magical basis. The follower stays with a ranger of its own volition, not from some supernatural compulsion, and may leave if conditions become intolerable. Likewise, a ranger doesn't control the actions of his followers, though he may instruct human followers to carry out specific functions, and train animal followers to perform various tricks and tasks.

Gaining Followers

It's strictly up to the Dungeon Master to determine when a ranger receives his followers, how many he's entitled to, and the circumstances under which they appear. Though the player is free to express his preferences, the DM has the final word.

Number of Followers

As soon as a ranger reaches 10th level, the DM secretly rolls 2d6. The result indicates the maximum number of followers the ranger will receive over the course of his career. This roll is made only once, and the number is never revealed to the player. The DM should make a note of the number on a sheet of paper; he can use the same sheet to keep track of the followers as the ranger receives them to make sure he doesn't exceed his allotment. The player should also keep track of his ranger's followers; the record sheets at the end of this book are designed for this purpose.

Lost followers are not replaced. If a ranger has a limit of two followers and both are killed, he'll never receive another follower for the rest of his career.

Identity of Followers

After the DM makes the 2d6 roll to determine the number of followers, it's time to think about who or what they're going to be. He should begin by deciding the identity of the first two or three followers, so that he can make plans to smoothly introduce them into his campaign. He can determine the identities of the remaining followers later, whenever he likes.

To determine the identity of followers, the DM may roll on Table 19 in Chapter 3 of the *Player's Handbook*, use Tables 33-43 in this chapter, or simply choose any particular creature he likes. Regardless of the method preferred, the DM should keep the following restrictions and recommendations in mind:

• The type of followers should make sense within the context of the campaign. Lions and crocodiles shouldn't show up in the arctic, just as dolphins shouldn't appear in the desert.
• The use of powerful creatures as followers should be kept to a minimum, so as not to overshadow the efforts of the ranger and other player characters. It's difficult to design challenging encounters for a ranger with a dozen giants at his beck and call! Such creatures should be introduced with care and pacing; it is more fun for the player to have a chance for a powerful ally in his ranger's future.

- A species enemy can't be a follower. The ranger's antagonism for his species enemy makes bonding impossible.
- Generally, the follower will not be a poisonous creature. Rangers do not use poisons, and their followers tend to follow suit. Occasionally a ranger may find himself with an intelligent and poisonous follower; remember that poison use is not a good act, and that to some extent the ranger is responsible for his followers. This can beused by the DM as a special hindrance or to encourage role-playing.
- Certain character kits have specific follower requirements or limitations which take precedence over other considerations. See Chapter 4 for details.

Using the Follower Tables

The DM may find the Follower Tables (Tables 33-43) especially useful for determining followers, as they provide a variety of types associated with specific terrains. To use the tables, select a terrain and roll 1d100. Some explanations:

- If the result has an asterisk (*) and the ranger already has a follower of this type—or if he's had a follower of that type and lost it—ignore the result and roll again.
- If more than one species of a particular animal is given in parentheses, the DM can choose whichever species he likes. For example, if the result on Table 33 is a herd animal, the DM can choose either a caribou, reindeer, or musk ox.
- If the result is "Human/demihuman," roll again on the Human/Demihuman Followers Table (Table 43). See the Humans and Demihumans section at the end of this chapter for further guidelines.
- The Trainability column indicates an animal follower's aptitude for learning tricks and tasks; these notations are explained in the Training Followers section later in this chapter.
- Statistics for some creatures not found in core MONSTROUS COMPENDIUM® collections are in the Helpful Statistics section.

The DM isn't confined to the creatures listed on the tables. New entries can be drawn from the MONSTROUS COMPENDIUM volumes and other sources. New tables can be created, based on

unique terrain and cultural demographics of a campaign; the Aquatic Followers Table, for instance, may be subdivided into Saltwater and Freshwater Tables.

The DM must also choose which tables to use for each ranger. He may decide to use only the table corresponding to the ranger's primary terrain (for instance, a ranger whose primary terrain is Desert receives followers only from the Desert table), use the table corresponding to the ranger's current location in the campaign, or focus on the primary terrain table with occasional use of the other tables (most of the Desert ranger's followers come from the Desert table, but he receives a few from the other tables as well).

There are advantages and disadvantages to each method. For instance, if you're only using the primary terrain table, a Desert ranger is likely to end up with a collection of creatures he's comfortable with, but he may have a hard time acquiring any followers at all if the campaign keeps him out of arid environments. Using the local table ensures that a ranger will have regular access to followers, but he may end up with a bizarre menagerie (imagine a Desert ranger with a merman, skunk, and baboon!). Regardless of which method you prefer, it's best to settle on one at the outset of a campaign and use it throughout.

How and When Followers Appear

To give the DM maximum flexibility for introducing followers into his campaign, no fixed rules exist for determining exactly when they show up. Once the appropriate level is attained, followers should trickle in, one at a time, throughout the course of the ranger's career. As a rule of thumb, assume that a new follower makes an appearance no more than once every few months.

Keep the terrain in mind when deciding how often animal or special followers appear. Regions heavily populated with animals, such as dense jungles or lush forests, are more likely to generate such followers than barren mountains or bleak arctic landscapes. As seen in Tables 33-43, certain types of followers tend to show up in particular areas; for instance, a ranger is more likely to acquire a camel follower in the desert than in the jungle. But exceptions abound; a ranger might

encounter a camel that accidently wandered into the plains, or encounter one on display in a zoo in the mountains. As long as the DM creates an explanation, animal and special followers can show up in a surprising variety of places.

Regardless of when and where followers show up, the DM should strive to work their appearance into the events of a campaign. Here are a few situations that may result in a new follower:

Use of Proficiencies, Special Abilities, or Spells. After the successful use of the animal handling or animal training proficiency, the affected creature might take a liking to the ranger and offer itself as a follower. This may also occur after a ranger uses his animal empathy ability. Likewise, an animal enchanted by a spell such as *animal friendship* might linger in the area after the magical effects wear off. In any case, the effects of the proficiency or spell no longer apply; the animal in question has decided of its own accord to stick around.

Planned Encounters. As part of an adventure, the DM may decide to stage one or more encounters featuring potential followers. For instance, the party may need to explore a cave containing a curious bear, search for a sunken treasure chest surrounded by friendly dolphins, or navigate a jungle filled with mischievous baboons. Assuming that the ranger doesn't inadvertently sabotage the encounter—he kills the bear or avoids the treasure chest—this is one of the most dependable methods for introducing new followers.

Hunting or Shopping. When shopping for a new mount, a ranger may be surprised to find one of the horses in the stable noses its way to the front, as if presenting itself for purchase. When hunting for the evening meal, the ranger might suddenly notice that a deer or other game animal is following *him.* Perceptive rangers may realize that these animals are offering themselves as followers.

Character Interaction. The ranger spares a foe, only to be adopted by the grateful creature. An NPC youth of long acquaintance (perhaps one rescued on a previous adventure) decides to take ranger training with the PC as a mentor.

Abrupt Appearance. For no apparent reason, an creature may present itself to the ranger. Hiking through the woods, the ranger becomes aware of a brownie sauntering behind him. The ranger wakes up with a sleeping fox curled up on his chest. A pseudodragon flutters from the sky and perches on the ranger's shoulder. From a purist's point of view, this is the least satisfying option for introducing followers, as it doesn't arise directly from the events of the story. But it's an acceptable method when all else fails.

Acquiring Specific Followers

Clearly, some types of followers are more desirable than others. Most rangers will find a horse to be more useful than a rabbit, a dog more advantageous than a mouse. Even in the best of situations, a snake or scorpion follower may be more trouble than it's worth.

There's not much a ranger can do to ensure he gets the type of followers he wants. Becoming a follower is essentially a choice made by the animal or NPC, not the ranger. Though the ranger can influence animal behavior to a certain degree, a ranger can't force a particular creature to become a follower against its will.

However, a ranger can increase his chances of acquiring specific followers in several ways. The easiest and most obvious way is to go where the animals live. A ranger who wants a polar bear follower should go to arctic. Farms and market places are good sources of domestic animals, while zoos and carnivals may stock a wide variety of exotic creatures.

The frequent use of the animal training or animal handling proficiencies, as well as the *animal empathy* special ability, brings the ranger in close contact with potential followers. Spells such as *locate animals or plants* can lead him to particular species, while the *call animal follower* spell (described in Chapter 6) may successfully summon a follower.

Note that such efforts don't guarantee the arrival of a follower in any way. In many campaigns, however, extra efforts made to locate followers increases the likelihood of their appearance.

Recognizing Animal Followers

A good DM tries to capture the behavior of real animals, and doesn't just announce to the ranger that an animal follower just presented itself. Instead, the DM describes the actions and behavior of the animal and

allows the ranger to come to his own conclusions.

How does a ranger know if a particular animal is indeed a follower? Here are some signs:

- The animal doggedly follows him. If the ranger climbs a steep mountain, the animal struggles to keep up. If he goes swimming, the animal waits on the shore.
- The animal shows signs of affection. A lion rubs against the ranger's legs, a wolf licks his face, a horse nuzzles him.
- The animal is uncharacteristically docile. A tiger sits peacefully in the grass while the ranger has dinner. A wild dog yawns when the ranger approaches, but growls when the ranger's companion comes near.

A day or two spent observing such actions should convince even the most skeptical ranger that he's acquired a follower. The DM may verify this conclusion, but is under no obligation to do so. If doubt remains in the ranger's mind, he may be able to ask a companion to use *speak with animals* or a similar spell to verify the animal's status.

Human and demihuman followers tend to express their admiration openly and unambiguously, fawn over the ranger's every utterance, gazing admiringly at him, or offer their assistance at every opportunity. Unless he's exceptionally suspicious or just plain dense, a ranger should have much less trouble recognizing human and demihuman followers.

Table 33: Arctic Followers

D100 Roll	Follower	Trainability
01-07	Animal, herd (caribou, reindeer, musk-ox)	Low
08-15	Avian (penguin, tern, snowy owl)	Low
16-25	Bear (polar)	Med.
26	Elephant (mammoth, mastodon)*	Med.
27	Elephant (oliphant)*	High
28-30	Great cat (snow leopard)	Med.
31-32	Great cat (giant lynx)*	High
33-34	Great cat (smilodon)*	Med.
35-37	Dog (wild, war)	Med.
38-43	Mammal, small (ermine, snow hare)	Low
44-45	Remorhaz*	Low
46-49	Seal	Med.
50-52	Selkie	–
53-54	Toad (ice)*	High
55-56	Walrus	Med.
57-62	Wolf (common, dire)	Med.
63-66	Wolverine (normal, giant)	Med.
67-70	Yeti	–
71-00	Human/demihuman	–

Table 34: Aquatic Followers

D100 Roll	Follower	Trainability
01-12	Avian (gull, duck, osprey, parrot, pelican)	Low
13-14	Crab, giant	Neg.
15-18	Crocodile (common)	Neg.
19-20	Eel (electric, giant, weed)	Neg.
21-22	Fish, giant (pike, catfish)	Low
23-24	Frog, giant	Neg.
25-32	Dolphin	High
33-34	Hippocampus*	High
35-36	Locathah*	–
37-41	Mammal, small (beaver, sea otter, giant otter)	Low
42-43	Merman	–
44-45	Nixie*	–
46-47	Octopus, giant*	Neg.
48-50	Seahorse, giant	Med.
51-54	Sea lion	Med.
55-58	Selkie	–
59-60	Triton*	–
61-00	Human/demihuman	–

Table 35: Desert Followers

D100 Roll	Follower	Trainability
01-08	Avian (falcon, hawk, owl, vulture)	Low
09-13	Camel	Low
14-23	Dog (wild, war)	Med.
24-25	Dog, moon*	High
26-28	Griffon*	Med.
29-35	Horse (medium, light, wild)	Med.
36-40	Jackal	Med.
41-42	Jann*	–
43-44	Lizard (giant)	Neg.
45-50	Mammal, small (jackrabbit, kangaroo rat, prairie dog)	Low
51-52	Scorpion (large)	Neg.
53-55	Snake (poisonous)	Neg.
56-58	Thri-kreen	–
59-60	Toad (fire, giant)	Neg.
61-00	Human/demihuman	–

Table 36: Forest Followers

D100 Roll	Follower	Trainability
01-04	Animal, herd (deer, stag)	Low
05-12	Avian (falcon, hawk, owl)	Low
13-14	Badger (common, giant)	Low
15-16	Bat (common, giant)	Low
17-28	Bear (black, brown)	Med.
29-31	Boar (wild, giant)	Med.
32-34	Centaur, sylvan	–
35-41	Mammal, small (ferret, fox, squirrel, raccoon, rabbit, woodchuck, chipmunk)	Low
42	Pegasus* (if ranger is female, 50% chance for unicorn*)	–
43	Pixie*	–
44-45	Porcupine (black, brown, giant)	Low
46	Pseudodragon*	–
47	Satyr*	–
48-49	Skunk (normal, giant)	Low
50	Treant*	–
51	Voadkyn*	–
52-54	Weasel (wild, giant)	Low
55	Werebear*	–
56-60	Wolf	Med.
61-00	Human/demihuman	–

Table 37: Hill Followers

D100 Roll	Follower	Trainability
01-05	Animal, herd (deer, goat, sheep)	Low
06-07	Aurumvorax*	–
08-17	Avian (falcon, hawk, owl)	Low
18-19	Badger (giant, common)	Low
20-21	Bat (common, large)	Low
22-32	Bear (black, brown, cave)	Med.
33-36	Boar (wild, giant)	Med.
37	Brownie*	–
38	Draconet (firedrake)*	Med.
39	Hippogriff*	Med.
40-43	Horse (medium, light, pony, wild, mule)	Med.
44-46	Lizard (minotaur)	Neg.
47-54	Mammal, small (fox, mouse, rabbit, squirrel)	Med.
55	Pegasus*	High
56-59	Wolf	Med.
60	Wereboar*	–
61-00	Human/demihuman	–

Table 38: Jungle Followers

D100 Roll	Follower	Trainability
01-05	Animal, herd (zebra, giraffe, antelope)	Low
06-07	Ape, carnivorous*	High
08-15	Avian (parrot, cockatoo, toucan)	Low
16-17	Bat (common, large)	Low
18-19	Boalisk	Low
20-21	Boar (warthog)	Med.
22	Couatl*	–
23-24	Faerie dragon*	–
25-26	Elephant	Med.
27-36	Great cat (lion, tiger, jaguar, leopard)	Med.
37-38	Grippli	Med.
39-40	Lizard man (advanced)	–
41-47	Mammal, small (ferret, monkey, mouse)	Low
48-50	Primate (baboon, orangutan)	High
51-52	Rhinoceros*	Low
53-56	Snake (normal constrictor, giant constrictor, jaculi)	Neg;
57-58	Weretiger*	–
59-60	Tabaxi	–
61-00	Human/Demihuman	–

Table 39: Mountain Followers

D100 Roll	Follower	Trainability
01-03	Aarakocra*	–
04-11	Animal, herd (goat, deer, sheep)	Low
12-21	Avian (wild eagle, falcon, hawk, owl)	Low
22-24	Badger (giant, common)	Low
25-36	Bear (black, brown, cave)	Med.
37	Dragonet (firedrake)*	–
38-39	Eagle, giant*	High
40	Galeb duhr*	–
41-45	Great cat (mountain lion)	Med.
46-47	Griffin*	Med.
48-50	Hippogriff*	Med.
51-53	Lizard (minotaur)	Neg.
54-60	Mammal, small (fox, mouse, squirrel, beaver)	Med.
61-65	Wolf	Med.
66-00	Human/demihuman	–

Table 40: Plains Followers

D100 Roll	Follower	Trainability
01-06	Animal, herd (deer, goat, buffalo, sheep, cattle, antelope)	Low
07-18	Avian (falcon, hawk, owl, pigeon, crow, raven)	Low
19-21	Badger (common, giant)	Low
22-24	Boar (wild, giant)	Med.
25-26	Brownie*	–
27-32	Dog (wild, war)	Med.
33-35	Dog, blink*	High
36-42	Mammal, small (mouse, fox, chipmunk, rabbit, wild pig, gopher, hamster)	Low
43-44	Cat, small (domestic, wild)	Med.
45-49	Horse (heavy, medium, light, pony, wild, mule)	Med.
50-51	Hyena	Low
52-53	Rat (common, giant)	Med.
54-55	Wemic	–
56-00	Human/demihuman	–

Table 41: Swamp Followers

D100 Roll	Follower	Trainability
01-08	Avian (owl, heron, loon, raven)	Low
09-11	Badger (common, giant)	Low
12-14	Bat (normal, large)	Low
15-17	Boar (wild, giant, warthog)	Med.
18-22	Crocodile (common)	Neg.
23-25	Frog (giant)	Neg.
26-28	Lizard (giant)	Neg.
29-32	Lizard man (advanced)	–
33-39	Mammal, small (ferret, fox, otter, mouse, muskrat)	Low
40-41	Naga (water)*	–
42-44	Porcupine (black, brown, giant)	Low
45-47	Rat (common, giant)	Med.
48	Shambling mound*	Low
49-60	Snake (constrictor, giant constrictor)	Neg.
61-63	Toad (giant)	Neg.
64-65	Werebear*	–
61-00	Human/demihuman	–

Table 42: Underdark Followers

D100 Roll	Follower	Trainability
01-06	Bat (normal, large)	Low
07-18	Bear (cave)	Med.
19-21	Beetle (fire, boring)	Low.
22-24	Crocodile (common)	Neg.
25-26	Doppleganger*	–
27-34	Lizard (giant—subspecies)	Med.
35-38	Lizard (subterranean)	Neg.
39-40	Mimic (common)*	High
41-48	Mongrelman	–
49-51	Myconid*	Low
52-53	Otyugh*	Med.
54-59	Owlbear	Low
60-62	Rat (common, giant)	Med.
63-65	Spider (giant—steeder)	High
66-00	Human/demihuman	–

Subspecies: This assumes a subspecies native to the Underdark that is more intelligent or trainable than the standard species.

Table 43: Human/Demihuman Followers

D100 Roll	Follower
01-02	Bard
03	Bard (half-elf)
04-06	Druid
07-08	Druid (half-elf)
09-14	Cleric
15	Cleric (elf)*
16	Cleric (half-elf)
17-23	Fighter (elf)
24-28	Fighter (gnome)
29-33	Fighter (halfling)
34-51	Fighter
52	Fighter/Cleric (half-elf)
53-54	Fighter/Mage (elf)*
55	Fighter/Illusionist (gnome)*
56-67	Ranger (half-elf)
68-92	Ranger
93	Ranger/Cleric (half-elf)
94-95	Thief (halfling)
96-97	Thief
98	Thief (gnome)
99-00	DM's Choice

* If ranger has had a follower of this type, roll again.

Sea Ranger: Any full elf follower is 80% likely to be an aquatic elf.

Mountaineer: Replace any full elf with mountain dwarf. Any full elf fighter/mage is replaced by a gnome fighter/illusionist.

General Behavior of Followers

This section pertains to animal followers, as
do the three sections which follow—Training
Animal Followers, Follower Loyalty, and Parting
Company. Information relevant to human and
demihuman followers can be found in the last
section of this chapter.

What exactly does an animal follower *do*, any-
way?

At first, animal followers do little more than
that—they follow. While an avian follower may
perch on the ranger's shoulder for a few miles or a
dog may scout up ahead, for the most part, followers linger behind, keeping perhaps 10-20 feet
between themselves and the ranger.

In general, an animal follower attempts to
accompany the ranger wherever he goes. If the
ranger enters a cave, the follower goes in after
him. If the ranger paddles a canoe, the follower
attempts to swim alongside. If the follower can't
swim, it waits on shore for the ranger to return. If
the follower is too big to squeeze through an
underground passage, it may surface and wait for
the ranger outside.

Likewise, if a ranger moves at a pace faster than
the follower can maintain, the follower will
attempt to pursue as best it can. When a ranger
interrupts his travels—for instance, if he stops to
camp—he may give the lagging follower enough
time to catch up. If a follower is unable to rejoin
the ranger because of a lost trail (the animal hasn't
seen the ranger in several days and can no longer
track him), physical barriers (the animal is incapable of following the ranger across a vast river)
or inhospitable terrain (a seafaring ranger has left
for the shore, abandoning a water-breathing follower), the follower is considered to be released;
see the Parting Company section below for details.

Routine Activities

For the most part, an animal follower can take
care of itself. Assuming there's an adequate supply of game or edible vegetation in the area, the
animal will hunt or graze as necessary to keep
itself fed. It will find its own water, keep itself
groomed, and rest when tired. If the ranger

marches by day and rests by night, nocturnal animals will either reverse their normal sleeping patterns and sleep when the ranger sleeps, or sleep by day and catch up with the ranger in the evening.

In extreme circumstances, an animal follower may depend on the ranger for routine care. If an animal follower accompanies a ranger into a city or other area where it's unable to hunt, the ranger will probably have to supply food. In a hot desert, a ranger may need to share his water. Wounded or ailing animals sometimes require medical attention. If an animal fails to receive adequate care, it may abandon the ranger (see the Parting Company section).

As an animal becomes more attached to a ranger, it may require extra attention or reassurance. Usually, an animal lets the ranger know when it needs attention by rubbing against him, frolicking in front of him, or whining incessantly. Usually, a ranger can soothe an anxious animal follower by playing with it for a few minutes, offering some comforting words, or stroking its fur. If the ranger makes a habit of ignoring a follower, it may abandon him.

Procreation

Most healthy animals have a powerful instinct to procreate. On occasion, a follower will disappear into the wilderness to seek a mate. Usually, the follower returns in a few hours, or at most, a few days. However, so strong is the urge that the follower may abandon the ranger altogether if it has to travel long distances to find a suitable partner. Also, the quest for a mate is not without risk; a male follower may die while fighting a rival for the attentions of a desirable female (which may account for why some followers mysteriously disappear and never come back). But more often than not, a follower will complete its liaison without incident, rejoining its ranger unharmed and content.

Should a female animal follower give birth, the offspring don't automatically become followers. Initially, offspring are considered "followers" of the parent, as their relationship with their mother more or less parallels the mother's relationship with the ranger. As the offspring mature, they may wander away to start lives of their own, or

they may stay and become followers, as decided by the DM. Offspring who become followers count against the ranger's normal limit.

Combat

Animal followers will rarely defend their rangers against attack unless trained to do so (see the Training Followers section below), especially if the opposition is supernatural or uses fire. In general, a follower is mainly concerned with its own safety, fighting only when necessary to protect itself. An exceptionally violent animal may relish any opportunity to attack, and some will stand guard over or attempt to drag away their incapacitated ranger, but most of the time, a follower is more likely to take cover or retreat than engage in combat. The DM determines the combat reactions of a follower just as he would for any animal in the game.

Communication

When a ranger acquires an animal follower, he gains no special way of communicating with it. Unless the ranger trains the creature to respond to specific vocal sounds or physical signals, the follower passively accompanies the ranger on his travels, oblivious to his commands.

Reactions to Others

Animal followers feel loyal and friendly to their rangers. Most animal followers would no more harm their rangers than they would their own mothers. A follower would be unlikely to retaliate violently if the ranger mistreated it; instead, the follower would simply leave.

The ranger's presence has a calming influence on wild animal followers which tempers their reactions to the ranger's other companions. The animal followers will generally leave other player characters alone, so long as the PCs keep their distance and don't antagonize them. However, if a PC comes too close to a lion, tiger, or other wild animal follower, the follower may respond with a warning snarl or even a swipe of the paw. If the PC doesn't get the message, the follower may attack. Such an attack continues until the PC withdraws or the ranger

intervenes. If the ranger has trained the follower to attack only when ordered, fellow PCs won't have to worry about assaults. Otherwise, the ranger's companions are advised to keep their distance. Even a ranger will not approach a predatory follower just after it has made a kill.

Naturally docile animals, such as sheep and mice, pose no threat to the party. Neither do domesticated creatures, such as farm animals and pets. Unless a trained animal is responding to its ranger's commands, the DM will decide how docile followers react, exactly as he does for followers that are wild animals.

Wild animal followers respond to non-player characters in much the same way as they do the ranger's companions; that is, they ignore NPCs who keep their distance and make no hostile actions, but may attack NPCs who get too close or threaten them. Docile animals respond timidly to unfamiliar NPCs, possibly cowering behind the ranger or seeking cover.

A ranger's calming influence also extends to followers who would normally consider each other predator and prey. If a deer and a lion are both among a ranger's followers, they co-exist harmoniously so long as they remain with the ranger. Though it's unlikely the pair would cuddle up together to go to sleep, neither would the lion eat the deer. At the same time, the lion follower would consider all other deer fair game, hunting them as necessary to satisfy its hunger. Should the ranger abandon or dismiss his lion and deer followers, the animals would shortly revert to their natural states, and the deer might stand a good chance of becoming the lion's next meal.

Disadvantages

Animal followers provide many benefits to rangers, but there can be drawbacks as well. Here are a few typical complications, which the DM can use to add color to a campaign, serve as story springboards, or enliven an otherwise routine encounter.

- Some animals attract predators. A rat follower could attract a giant snake, or a boar follower might lure a hungry dragon. The ranger and his companions could be ambushed along with the followers.

- Certain followers may be sought by hunters and collectors. A weasel follower with lustrous ivory fur might prove irresistible to unprincipled sportsmen. A renegade wizard could target the party to get her hands on the feathers of a black owl follower, which she needs for a spell component. Rustlers might assault a party just to steal a ranger's horse follower.

- The presence of unusual followers may make NPCs less likely to deal with the party. A traveler may hesitate to share information when a growling bear lurks in the background. A giant eagle fluttering overhead could discourage a merchant from trading with the PCs. The DM may modify an NPC's reaction by as much as –4 when disconcerting, threatening, or obnoxious animal followers are present.

- Some animals have habits which can make life uncomfortable, if not downright miserable, for the ranger and his companions. A filthy hyena follower might smell so bad that it makes the PCs' eyes burn. A parrot follower may insist on keeping the party up all night with its incessant chatter. A curious squirrel follower could pick the pocket of a slumbering wizard, steal a crucial spell component, then bury it in the forest.

Training Animal Followers

Rangers can train their animal followers to perform a remarkable variety of tricks and tasks. Because of the ranger's unique rapport with his animal followers, he can teach them more efficiently than other characters are able to train normal animals. And because of the followers' eagerness to please, they learn their tricks and tasks more quickly.

Two methods are provided for representing this special relationship with animal followers. The Standard method is the simplest and most straightforward, but treats all animals more or less the same. The Alternative method requires extra bookkeeping, but is a bit more realistic, as it takes into account the learning capacities of different species. Both methods are similar to and compatible with the animal training proficiency (the animal training proficiency itself isn't used to train

followers). Whichever method you prefer, it's best to stick with it throughout the entire campaign.

Before examining the training methods, let's clarify what is meant by tricks and tasks. These definitions apply to the animal training proficiency as well as the training methods described below.

A *trick* is a specific action performed in response to a specific stimulus, such as a command, a sound, or a gesture. The action involves only a single step and requires no independent decision-making. In every instance, the animal performs the action exactly as taught, without improvisation of any kind. The stimulus must be unambiguous and precise ("Stay"); any variance in the stimulus ("Don't move") is likely to be misinterpreted, resulting in a failure to perform the trick as intended.

A *task* is general sequence of actions performed in response to a stimulus. The action may involve multiple steps and require some independent decision-making. Completion of the task may require a certain amount of improvisation. The stimulus may be non-specific (for instance, if taught the task of tracking, the follower is able to track a variety of animals, not just one particular species). Obviously, tasks are more difficult to master than tricks.

The Standard Method

This training method uses essentially the same rules as the animal training proficiency described in Chapter 5 of the *Player's Handbook*. The ranger announces the trick or task he wishes to teach a particular follower (examples of tricks and tasks are given below). The DM may disallow the trick or task if he decides the follower is incapable of performing it; a reptile, for instance, may be too dull to come on command, or a chipmunk may lack the attention span needed to track. If the DM approves, the ranger proceeds. It takes the ranger 2d4 weeks to teach a trick to a follower and two months to teach a task.

When the training period ends, the ranger makes a Wisdom check (using his own Wisdom score). If the check succeeds, the animal has mastered the trick or task. If the check fails, the ranger can make another attempt to teach the follower the same trick or task by expending the same time and effort. He then makes another Wisdom check. If it succeeds, the animal learns the trick or task. If it fails, then the animal cannot be trained to perform that trick or task. A follower can learn a maximum of 2d4 tasks or tricks, in any combination of the two.

A ranger can train up to three followers at the same time. As all followers are naturally cooperative with the ranger, he doesn't need to prepare "wild" animal followers by taming them (unlike the requirement given in the animal training proficiency).

Successful training assumes the ranger works with the followers for short periods on a regular basis; the amount of time spent is less important than working with the follower *every* day. If the ranger fails to maintain a regular schedule—say, if he skips a full week or so of training—he must start over, investing another two months for a task or 2d4 weeks for a trick.

The DM should write down the number of tricks and tasks a particular follower is able to learn. The player should also note the tricks and tasks on his ranger's record sheet as the followers learn them. Additionally, when teaching a follower a new trick or task, the player should keep track of how many weeks have passed for each training period.

The Alternative Method

The Alternative method involves the use of a *trainability rating*, a general indication of a follower's capacity to learn. The higher the trainability rating, the more tricks and tasks an animal can know and the faster it can master them. The trainability rating is primarily based on the animal's Intelligence score, but also takes into account its fondness for humans and demihumans, its willingness to learn, and its eagerness to please. Trainability ratings apply *only* to a ranger's followers and have no bearing on the relationships between animals and other character classes or on the animal training proficiency.

Tables 31-42 give trainability ratings for a variety of animal followers. The DM can use the trainability ratings in these tables as guidelines for assigning ratings to species not listed, should he

decide to modify or expand the tables.

The DM may also make exceptions for animal individuals. He may decide, for instance, that a particular squirrel is smart enough to merit a Medium rating rather than the Low rating given on Table 34. Likewise, he may rule that an exceptionally dull wolf deserves no better than a Low rating. In any case, the DM should make such a determination as soon as the follower arrives. A follower's trainability rating should not change once it has been assigned.

The four ratings—Negligible, Low, Medium, and High—are discussed in detail below. Each describes the types of animals encompassed by the rating, the time required to learn tricks and tasks, and the maximum number of tricks and tasks that followers with the rating can learn. For convenience, Table 44 summarizes this information.

Additionally, each description lists several tricks and tasks associated with the rating. The lists don't include all possible tricks and tasks, but a general sample; the DM should use the lists as a basis to determine the difficulty of any other trick or task that the ranger wishes to teach a follower. A follower can learn tricks and tasks associated with all lesser ratings, as well as those associated with its own rating; a Medium trainability follower, for instance, can learn tricks and tasks associated with Negligible, Low, and Medium ratings.

In all other respects, the Alternative method uses the same rules as the Standard method. Only the types and numbers of tricks and tasks, along with the training times, are different.

Negligible Trainability

This category includes animals with little aptitude for learning, such as fish, insects, arachnids, and reptiles. Most of these creatures have Intelligence scores of 0. Followers with negligible trainability can learn only the simplest tricks, such as those requiring movement towards or away from a stimulus. They can't learn tasks. Since some of these creatures are unable to discern sound, the ranger may need to use a bright light (such as a torch) or a broad gesture (a sweep of the hands) instead of a vocal command to get the follower to respond.

A follower with negligible trainability can learn no more than a few (1d4) tricks, though the DM may decide that a particular animal is not capable of learning *any* tricks. Training time is 2d6 weeks per trick.

Sample tricks:

Withdraw. The follower moves away from the ranger at maximum speed for 1-4 rounds, then stops.

Come. The follower advances toward ranger at maximum speed, stopping when it comes within a few feet.

Stay. The follower stays in place for 2-12 rounds, after which it resumes its normal activity.

Attack. The follower aggressively attacks any creature indicated by the ranger. The attacks persist until the ranger breaks the command. Whether a follower fights to the death is up to the DM; in many cases, a follower in danger of losing its life (an animal that has lost half of its hit points) will withdraw. If the ranger commands such an animal to continue its attacks, a morale check may be in order (see the Parting Company section below). Animals that have been attack-trained usually have a base morale of at least 11.

Attack-trained animals get a save vs. rods against another ranger's *animal empathy* ability.

Low Trainability

Animals in this category have an average but unexceptional aptitude for learning. They can learn a wide range of tricks, but few tasks. The category includes herd animals, small mammals, and birds, most of which have Intelligence scores of 1. The majority of animals either belong to this category or the Medium trainability category.

A follower with Low trainability can learn 2-8 (2d4) tricks and tasks, of which half or less can be tasks. Training time is 2-8 (2d4) weeks per trick and 10 weeks for tasks.

Sample tricks:

Heel. The follower remains within a few feet of the ranger, mimicking his movement. The follower tries to move as fast as the ranger, stop when he stops, and stay with him until the ranger breaks the command. This type of movement is distinct from the follower's normal movement, as the follower remains at the ranger's side at all times, rather than lurking in back of the party. Mastery of the Come and Stay tricks usually precedes the learning of this trick.

Sit. The follower sits on its haunches until the ranger breaks the command, at which time the follower resumes its normal actions. Variations include Standing, Rearing, Rolling Over, Playing Dead, and other simple physical feats, all of which are distinct tricks and require individual training periods.

Speak. The follower growls, barks, chirps, or makes any other natural sound on command.

Fetch. The follower retrieves a specific object and brings it to the ranger. Typical objects include coins, balls, bones, or sticks. In order for the follower to execute the command, the ranger must first show the object to the follower before throwing it or hiding it. The follower won't search indefinitely; if the ranger tosses the object in a field of high grass, for instance, the follower may search for 10-30 minutes before giving up and returning to the ranger. Note that the Fetch trick doesn't allow the follower to hunt for and recognize objects belonging to a general category; that is, a follower can't enter a building and look for hidden gems or other treasure items.

Carry Rider. This assumes the animal is physically able to carry a rider. It obeys simple movement commands from the rider, such as turning left and right, stopping, and trotting. However, the follower can't execute any of the maneuvers associated with the Stunt Riding task explained in the Medium trainability section below. This does not replace riding proficiency; any maneuvers performed by the rider, such as using the mount as a shield or leaping from the steed's back to the ground, require the riding proficiency checks.

Sample tasks:

Retrieve. The follower can locate and bring back a specific type of item from a general location. Such items might include coins, jewelry, weapons, or food; a general location might be the interior of a building, a grove of trees, or a shallow stream. The ranger must show the follower a sample similar to the desired item, and must also indicate the area which the follower is to search. The follower won't search indefinitely; if unable to find an item, it usually will return empty-handed (or empty-mouthed) within an hour.

Bodyguard. The follower protects the ranger or a designated friend from attacks by keeping opponents at bay or by attacking them directly, as commanded by the ranger. The follower will fight alongside the ranger, making its own decisions which enemies to attack (it may, for instance, attack an unnoticed opponent sneaking up behind the ranger). The Attack trick must be learned before this task.

Medium Trainability

Exceptionally bright animals belong to this group, including those commonly found as pets, trained for circuses, or used in warfare. These animals will tend to have Intelligence scores in the 2-4 range.

A follower with medium trainability is able to learn 4-10 (2d4+2) tricks or tasks in any combination. Training time is 2d3 (2-6) weeks for tricks, and 8 weeks for tasks.

Sample tasks:

Track. The follower can follow the trail of an animal, human, or demihuman; in general, only followers capable of tracking prey by scent are eligible to learn this task. The follower must be familiar with the creature being tracked, or the ranger must provide a sample of the scent (a piece of clothing, a scrap of hide). It can retrace its path to lead the ranger to the creature. If the follower assists the ranger in tracking, the ranger adds +1 to his Tracking proficiency checks (see Chapter 2). If the follower is tracking by itself, it makes Tracking checks independently of the ranger. Assume that the base Tracking score of a wolf, lion, or similar predator ranges from 13-16. A hunting dog's score may be as high as 19, while a young badger's score as low as 11; the DM makes the call.

Stunt Riding. An animal follower with this proficiency can ride, performing all of the feats associated with the airborne and land-based riding proficiencies (as appropriate to the follower's size and species). For airborne mounts, animal's Stunt Riding score is the same as the ranger's Wisdom score, with a –2 penalty. For land-based mounts, the Stunt Riding score is equal to the ranger's Wisdom score, with a +3 bonus. Therefore, a ranger with Wisdom 14 who wants his stunt-riding dog to balance on a horse leaping a gap wider than 12 feet must roll his Riding score of 17 or less (14 for his Wisdom, +3 for a land-based mount).

High Trainability

Only a handful of followers, such as dolphins and certain primates, qualify for this category. Animals with high trainability can reason, weigh options, and arrive at their own conclusions. Their ability to learn tasks rivals that of some humans and demihumans. Their Intelligence scores begin at 5 and go up.

A follower with high trainability can learn 6-12 (2d4+4) tricks or tasks, or any combination of the two. Training time is 1d4 weeks for tricks, and 6 weeks for tasks.

Sample tasks:

Lookout. As directed by the ranger, the follower stands watch or scouts ahead, keeping alert for signs of trouble. If the follower perceives a threat, it unobtrusively alerts the ranger. This training includes a special signal the follower can give for the ranger's species enemy.

Complex Chore. The follower can perform a complex chore requiring decision-making or a rel-atively detailed series of steps. Such chores include building a fire, washing dishes, or grooming a horse. Learning each chore requires a separate training period.

Weapon Use. The follower wields a sword, dagger, or other simple weapon, using it when attacking. Each weapon requires its own training period, and opposable thumbs are needed in most instances. This task is most useful when the follower has already mastered the Attack trick or Bodyguard task, described above.

Not Applicable (–)

Creatures who can communicate with spoken language and whose Intelligence scores are on par with those of humans don't have trainability ratings. To determine their behavior as followers, consult the guidelines in the Humans and Demi-humans section below, along with the relevant information in their *Monstrous Compendium*® entries.

Table 44: Follower Training Table

TR	TT (Tricks)	TT (Tasks)	Max. Number
Neg.	2d6 weeks	-	1d4–1
Low	2d4 weeks	10 weeks	2d4*
Med.	2d3 weeks	8 weeks	2d4+2
High	1d4 weeks	6 weeks	2d4+4

* Up to half of these can be tasks

Abbreviations:
  TR: Trainability Rating
  TT: Training Time (time required to learn trick or task)
  Max. Number: Maximum number of tricks and tasks (in any combination) the follower may learn

Success of Tricks and Tasks

Followers perform most tricks and simple tasks automatically; no die rolls or success checks are necessary. If the outcome of a particular task is uncertain (a follower taught to pull a wagon has a heavy load to haul) the DM may require an ability check if the relevant ability score is known (the follower pulls the wagon if a Strength check succeeds), or he can assign a percentile chance based on his assessment of the situation (the load is exceedingly heavy; the DM sets the chance of success at 20%).

The DM should adjudicate the Attack trick, the Bodyguard task, and similar combat-oriented tricks and tasks just as he would for normal combat situations, determining attack and damage rolls as required.

Parting Company

If a ranger treats his followers well, they'll remain with him indefinitely. If the ranger has not neglected the well-being of his followers, or violated their trust, loyalty checks for them are rarely necessary.

When a Follower Abandons a Ranger

However, there is a limit as to how much abuse a follower will tolerate. The actions—or inaction—of the ranger may necessitate morale checks, as determined by the DM. Should a morale check succeed, the follower remains with the ranger. Should a check fail, the follower goes its own way, in most cases never to return. Followers who permanently abandon their ranger are considered lost and are not replaced.

Here are some situations that may result in a follower abandoning its ranger. It's up to the DM to decide when a given situation becomes stressful enough for the follower to require a morale check.

Inhospitable Terrain. An animal may hesitate to enter an environment radically different from its own. A hawk follower native to the mountains probably won't resist following a ranger into a forest or plain, but it may balk at entering an arctic region. Even if an animal follows a ranger into hostile terrain, it may not remain there for long; for example, a hawk may tolerate the freezing climate of the arctic for no more than a day or two.

Reckless Endangerment. Followers trained for combat willingly participate in encounters that may result in injury or even death. However, if the ranger forces an animal to participate in an unrelenting series of battles, resulting in serious damage or chronic fatigue, the follower may rebel and leave. Likewise, if a ranger regularly compels an animal to follow him into caverns, ruins, and similarly dangerous places, the animal may flee.

Starvation. Though followers usually find their own food, in certain situations they may depend on their rangers for nourishment. If a ranger neglects to keep a follower fed, the follower may decide to look for greener pastures.

Mistreatment. Most followers won't stand for beatings, whippings, or other physical mistreatment. (Being of noble character, most rangers won't administer such punishments, but exceptions do occur.) If the ranger persists in this behavior, abandonment is inevitable.

Inattention. Some followers, particularly dogs and other domestic animals, have emotional as well as physical needs. A ranger who consistently ignores or withholds praise and affection from his followers risks losing them.

Mating Season. An animal's urge to mate may overwhelm its loyalty to its ranger. An animal may disappear during mating season and never return, particularly if it has trouble finding a suitable partner. Morale checks usually aren't applica-

ble in these situations; instead, the DM may take advantage of mating season to restore balance to the game by eliminating a powerful follower, or getting rid of a cumbersome follower that's proving to be too much of a burden to a ranger.

Impending Death. When certain followers reach the end of their days, due to illness or old age, they may abandon their ranger to die alone (an aged elephant journeying to an elephant's graveyard). Morale checks aren't usually necessary. Instead, the DM may engineer a poignant scene where the ranger realizes that death is near for his loyal companion, and must come to terms with the loss.

When a Ranger Abandons a Follower

Situations may arise where the ranger wants to rid himself of a particular follower. A follower with negligible trainability may prove to be more annoying than helpful. A filthy or frightening follower may make the party uncomfortable. A follower may eat too much, move too slowly, or scare off too many NPCs. Whatever the reason, the ranger has two options for abandoning a follower, either of which he can exercise any time he likes.

Release. This is a form of temporary abandonment. Using commanding gestures and a firm voice, the ranger lets the follower know that he wants it to remain behind. Because of the special bond between the follower and the ranger, the follower instinctively understands what the ranger is telling it, and responds by reluctantly wandering away into the wilderness. Should the ranger return to the general area where he released the follower, and call out to the follower or otherwise make his presence known, the released animal may show up again, ready to resume its role as a follower. (The DM decides if a released follower returns; generally, if the ranger attempts to locate the follower within a few months of its release, the animal will show up within a day or so. Otherwise, the ranger should assume that the released follower has died or relocated.)

Dismiss. This is a form of permanent abandonment. As with release, the ranger communicates his desire to dismiss a follower through a series of gestures and vocal commands. The dismissed follower moves away into the wilderness, never to be seen again. A dismissed follower will not return to the ranger. A ranger can't replace dismissed followers; they still count against his normal limit.

Other Options

A ranger who doesn't want to release or dismiss an unwanted animal follower has a host of other options, limited only by his imagination and the DM's approval. He can arrange for a farmer, a zoo keeper, or other NPC to care for the follower (making sure, of course, the caretaker is of good alignment). He can keep it in his stronghold, asking a human or demihuman follower to care for it. He can also give it to a friendly NPC as a gift (again, presuming the NPC is of good alignment; failure to do so may be taken as a sign of betrayal by the ranger's remaining followers).

Humans and Demihumans

Humans and demihumans become followers for different reasons than animals. Drawn to a ranger's reputation for honor and integrity, humans and demihumans serve as followers out of respect, admiration, and hero-worship. They remain loyal so long as their basic needs are met, and the ranger doesn't betray their trust.

Trainability doesn't apply to human and demihuman followers. Instead, they will perform any duties or functions within reason. Typically, such followers serve as soldiers, but they may also work as guards, servants, or personal aides.

Human and demihuman followers accompany the ranger as long as their basic needs are met and their are fairly treated. Some may serve with the understanding that the ranger will teach them the ways of the wilderness. It's up to the ranger to determine the needs and expectations of each new follower when he arrives.

A ranger's human and demihuman followers aren't confined to a stronghold. They may accompany him on his travels or undertake independent missions. In other respects, a ranger's followers adhere to the guidelines given in Chapter 12 of the *Player's Handbook.* The DM should prepare a character sheet with all relevant statistics for each new follower. The DM, not the player, controls the

actions of the follower.

Restrictions. In general, human and demihuman followers should be of 1st to 4th level when they appear; a 15th-level fighter has better things to do than tag along after a 10th-level ranger. Additionally, the follower should be of good alignment; except in rare cases, rangers won't tolerate neutral or evil followers.

Followers can be of either sex. The age of the follower is also unimportant, although because of their low levels, most followers will be relatively young.

Personalities. Impressionable youths, curious scholars, impulsive vagabonds, and orphaned wanderers all make good followers. Interesting quirks or personal problems make followers more fun for the players, and also provide springboards for adventures. Chapter 12 of the *DUNGEON MASTER Guide* offers suggestions for creating NPC personalities, which are also suitable for followers.

Abandonment. Just as he may do with animal followers, the ranger may dismiss or release his human and demihuman followers. Released followers may rejoin the ranger at a later time. Human and demihuman rangers who are dismissed or otherwise lost can't be replaced.

Human and demihuman followers may also abandon their rangers. Situations that may trigger abandonment include reckless endangerment, continual verbal abuse, or inattention to the follower's needs. If the ranger commits an act of cowardice or otherwise violates his code of honor, a follower may become disillusioned and abandon the ranger in disgust. The DM might make morale checks to determine if a follower stays or goes, he may resolve the situation by role-playing (the follower requests an explanation for the ranger's cowardly behavior; the follower stays if the ranger offers a reasonable justification), or in extreme cases, he may have the follower simply disappear without explanation.

Notes on Falconry

The principle of training hunting birds is that all food comes from the trainer, otherwise they are likely to fly off. They will be very dependent on the trainer; failure to feed them for 24 hours is pushing their limits. If more than 36 hours pass, the birds will likely die.

Birds should be flown and exercised daily. Their health will deteriorate if they are not flown once at least every 3-4 days.

Flying multiple birds at once is nearly impossible, as species dominance instincts take over; the higher status bird will let the lower status bird do the dirty work, then come in and steal the kill. Rarely, a species will hunt in family groups—one main hunter and several others to flush out the prey. A real-world example of this behavior is the Harris hawk.

No falconer will fail to wear a heavy leather gauntlet on his catching arm (the "off" arm, usually the left). The gauntlet will not be metal, which is uncomfortable for the bird. It will cover the forearm, perhaps extending as far as the elbow. Carrying birds like this is tiring, so a perch of some sort (as on a staff) is desirable.

Hunting birds are *never* carried on the shoulder. Their natural instinct is to take out an eye or ear (which they can do with unbelievable speed) and their training reinforces the instinct. Even a well-trained bird cannot be trusted so close to the face.

Owls can be flown as hunting birds. They are much harder to train than hawks or falcons (comparable to the independent feline versus the eager-to-please canine). Unlike other birds, owls can be flown in the dark; however, their instinct is to strike stationary targets. They will not attack while a target is moving, but only when it pauses, stops, or hunkers down. Owls will kill hawks and falcons; the two types of birds cannot be flown together.

Although they share similar abilities and philosophies, no two rangers are quite alike. But how do you make one different from another?

This chapter offers a convenient solution in the form of *character kits*. Character kits are structured collections of proficiencies, traits, benefits, and limitations that help define different rangers as unique individuals. A kit can serve as a basis for a ranger's personality, background, and role in a campaign.

Character kits are entirely optional—ranger characters can get along without them just fine. But they're a lot of fun, adding color and depth to a campaign, as well as making rangers more interesting to play. We'll take a look at a number of kits in detail, and explain how to use them. We'll also give some tips on designing new kits from scratch.

Acquiring Kits

Players choose character kits for their rangers as part of the character creation process. Only one kit can be chosen for a particular ranger.

When creating a new ranger, begin by determining his ability scores (*Player's Handbook*, Chapter 1), race (*PH*, Chapter 2) and alignment (*PH*, Chapter 4). At this point, select a character kit, recording the pertinent information on the character sheet (the record sheets at the end of this book are designed for character kits; permission is granted to copy these pages for personal use). In accordance with the kit information, flesh out the character by determining other relevant details, such as character proficiencies (*PH*, Chapter 5; and Chapter 5 of this book) and equipment (*PH*, Chapter 6; and Chapter 7 of this book).

A player chooses a character kit at the outset of his ranger's career. It's possible, however, to incorporate the character kit rules into an existing campaign, providing the DM agrees that the kit is appropriate. A kit must be compatible with a ranger's personal history, his background, and his established personality traits. For example, the Mountain Man kit doesn't make sense for a ranger who's never been to the mountains. On the other hand, the Sea Ranger kit is a logical choice for a ranger who's spent most of his life at sea.

DM Decisions

Before players create their characters, the DM should examine each of the kits and consider the following questions:

Is this kit appropriate to the campaign? Not all kits fit with every campaign, and the DM is free to exclude any he feels are inappropriate. If the campaign takes place entirely on land, for instance, players may be barred from choosing the Sea Ranger kit. Before the players create their characters, the DM should tell them which kits are allowed and which are forbidden.

Do the players need additional information about any kit? Any campaign details relevant to a particular kit should be explained to the players before they create their characters. For example, the DM may announce that an army of orcs have allied with a group of stone giants and declared war against all Giant Killers, or that the local king has levied a hefty tax on anyone charging for guide services, Pathfinders included.

Are there changes in any kit? The parameters for each kit aren't engraved in stone, and the DM is free to make any changes he likes. He may decide that only female Guardians are allowed in his campaign world, or that all Justifiers must be members of a particular military order. All such changes should be made clear to the players before they create their characters.

Kit Subsections

All character kits described in this chapter consist of the following elements:

Description: This section describes the features that distinguish a character associated with this kit, including his cultural background, duties, manner, and appearance.

Requirements: Any special racial, ability score, or alignment requirements are listed here. Characters can't take the kit if they don't meet the listed qualifications. "Standard" means that no special racial or ability requirements apply to this kit. A good alignment is assumed.

Primary Terrain: Certain kits tend to be associated with specific environments. *Required* indicates that a character taking the kit must take the

indicated primary terrain; if more than one type is listed, the player may choose whichever type he prefers. *Recommended* means that a character taking this kit is advised to use one of the listed primary terrain types, but isn't required to do so. *Any* means that there are no required or recommended types for this kit; the player may use any primary terrain he likes.

Role: The character's role in society and in a campaign is detailed here. Typical motivations, personality, and beliefs are examined, along with common relationships with other people, reasons for joining an adventuring party, and usual function within a party. Note that these traits don't necessarily apply to each and every character associated with this kit; players may shape the personalities of their characters based on these suggestions, or they may disregard them entirely and create personalities of their own design.

Secondary Skills: If you're using the rules for secondary skills from Chapter 5 of the *Player's Handbook*, the character is restricted to the choice of skills listed in this section, or "no skill."

Weapon Proficiencies: If you're using the weapon proficiency rules, a kit may require the character to take specific weapon proficiencies or choose from a restricted list. Alternately, the character may have the option of choosing from a list of recommended weapons.

Nonweapon Proficiencies: Although nonweapon proficiency rules are technically optional, they're strongly recommended when using ranger kits. However, if you're using secondary skills, you shouldn't use nonweapon proficiencies.

Bonus proficiencies are received free of charge; they cost no proficiency slots. A *required* proficiency must be taken and does cost slots. *Recommended* proficiencies are skills typical for the kit. They cost the normal number of proficiency slots. It's a good idea for a beginning player to spend all or most of the ranger's initial slots on recommended proficiencies. *Barred* proficiencies cannot be taken initially, though they can be taken during play.

An asterisk (*) indicates a new proficiency described in Chapter 5.

Armor/Equipment: Some character types tend to use specific equipment, while others have limitations on the items available to them. Requirements and recommendations are given here, along with any style preferences associated with the kit. Unless indicated otherwise, a character must buy the required equipment, including weapons, from his initial funds. Like all members of the warrior group, a ranger begins with 50-200 (5d4 × 10) gp. If he lacks the funds to buy all of his required equipment, he should buy as much as he can, then pick up the rest as soon as he gets the money.

Species Enemy: A particular species enemy may be required or recommended. If the enemy is *required*, the character has no choice; he must take the indicated creature as a species enemy. If more than one creature is listed as a required enemy, the character can pick the one he prefers. *Recommended* enemies are only suggestions; the character may choose one if he likes, or ignore the recommendation. *Any* means that a ranger should choose his species enemy normally, as described in Chapter 2.

Followers: As with the species enemy entry, this section may include either required or recommended followers. The DM should make sure that at least one of each *required* type shows up as a follower some time in the ranger's career (depending on there being enough slots available). *Recommended* followers show up at the DM's option. *Any* means that the character has no special follower restrictions or recommendations.

Special Benefits: All kits give special benefits that aren't normally available to other characters. Typical benefits include improved abilities, special relationships with followers, and reaction bonuses. All benefits are received free of charge, and don't count against the normal limitations of the ranger class.

Special Hindrances: To balance their special benefits, kits also carry special hindrances. Hindrances may include reaction penalties, cultural restrictions, or ability limitations. All special hindrances are in addition to any disadvantages normally associated with the ranger class.

List of Kits

Beastmaster

Description: A wanderer, the Beastmaster has a natural affinity for animals; in fact, he has a limited form of telepathic communication with them. This is often the result of a magical bond with the Animal Kingdom, formed either at the time of his birth or upon reaching young adulthood. Unlike other adventurers, the Beastmaster does not command, train, or control his animal companions, rather they are his friends and comrades-in-arms. Misunderstood and feared by nobles and common folk alike for his unnatural abilities with animals, the Beastmaster seldom stays in one place for long, nor is he comfortable in civilized lands.

Requirements: Standard.

Primary Terrain: Any outdoor land.

Role: Beastmasters tend to walk alone, accompanied only by the fierce natural beasts that are their friends and allies. Traveling the fringes of settled lands, the Beastmaster has small use for the trappings of civilization, but even less for the minions of evil, particularly those of a magical or priestly nature. Thus, a Beastmaster will often find himself aiding the oppressed or enslaved, and pitted against the cruelties of evil priests or wizards and their allies.

Secondary Skills: Hunter, Fisher.

Weapon Proficiencies: A Beastmaster is initially limited to weapons that he can make himself: axe (any), club, dagger, dart, javelin, knife, quarterstaff, sling, or spear.

Nonweapon Proficiencies: *Bonus:* None, but see Special Benefits. *Recommended:* Agriculture, Bowyer/Fletcher, Endurance, Hunting, Leather working, Running, Swimming, Weather Sense. *Optional:* See Weaponsmithing (Crude) in the Mountain Man section).

Barred: Armorer, Etiquette, Heraldry, Navigation, Weaponsmithing.

Armor/Equipment: The Beastmaster starts only with leather armor and weapons he has made.

Species Enemy: Standard.

Followers: None, but see Special Benefits.

Special Benefits:

Stealth: The Beastmaster has a +5% chance to hide in natural surroundings.

Animal Henchmen: Although a Beastmaster receives no special followers at high level, he can acquire normal or giant animals as henchmen. He may acquire them at any level, and their number depends on his Charisma. If these animals are slain or driven away, they can be replaced by new animals without penalty (though this may take some time).

Animal Telepathy: The Beastmaster can establish telepathic communication with any normal or giant animal within 30', if he does nothing else in the round. The animal must have a minimum Intelligence of 1. This has the following benefits:

• The Beastmaster can communicate to the creature that he desires its friendship. If the offer is sincere (and the animal will be able to sense if it isn't), the creature can be calmed and will not attack or flee unless it is attacked.

• The Beastmaster can recruit an animal he has befriended as a henchman if he is not at his limit and if the creature fails a saving throw vs. rods. The saving throw is penalized by –1 for every three levels of experience the Beastmaster has earned. At the DM's option, animals may present themselves for recruitment in the same way that followers appear to other rangers.

Animal Bonding: The Beastmaster forms a mental bond with any animal he recruits as a henchman. There is no distance limit, but this ability does not cross planar boundaries. This bond has the following effects:

• The Beastmaster can communicate directly with any animal henchman to which he has a bond. This gives him the ability to directly explain tricks or tasks he wishes the animal to attempt, or to communicate needs and desires. Conversely, the animal can also communicate its needs and desires to him.

• He can see through the eyes of the animal by concentrating on the mental link. He can see through the eyes of one creature in a round (himself included).

• He has the animal lore proficiency with respect to the bonded animal. Furthermore, if he is mentally linked to the animal, success with the proficiency is automatic.

• Every time the Beastmaster gains a level, all of his current animal henchmen gain an additional hit point.

Animal Horde: At 9th level, the Beastmaster can summon a horde of wild animals to fight for him. They must come from a land that he controls, and it takes one week to gather them.

They can be brought together only for some great purpose that can be explained simply. Up to 100 Hit Dice of animals per level of the Beastmaster will come. For every 10 animals, there will be a pack leader with one additional Hit Die and maximum hit points. The horde will stay together for one week for each level of the Beastmaster. There is no record of a Beastmaster summoning more than one horde in a year.

> *Optional Rule:* The Beastmaster can split his experience award, giving up to half of his earned experience to any or all of his animal henchmen that played a role in the adventure. Such henchmen advance on the Fighter Experience Table, receiving +1 to attack rolls and +3 hit points for every level gained.

Special Hindrances:

Empathic Shock: The Beastmaster feels pain when one of his henchmen is wounded, suffering a –2 penalty to all rolls in the next round. If he is mentally linked with a henchman when it is killed, he suffers a –2 penalty to all rolls for the next 24 hours.

Unruly Allies: The Beastmaster's animal henchmen are free to come, go, or act as they will. Any attempt to arbitrarily restrict or regulate their freedom, or habitually ignoring their needs and desires, will result in resentment, sulkiness, and possible abandonment.

Outcast: The Beastmaster suffers a –1 penalty to reaction rolls by common NPCs, and a –2 when dealing with a civilized aristocracy. Further, his maximum effective Charisma when dealing with his own race is 15.

Limited Funds: The Beastmaster starts with 1d4 × 10 gp.

No Fortress: At no time will the Beastmaster build a fortress. At 9th level, he may establish himself as the protector of an area of land equivalent to a barony.

Explorer

Description: The restless spirit of the Explorer makes him the most nomadic of all rangers. His travels take him around the world, as he continually seeks new lands to investigate and new cultures to study. No region is too remote, no society too primitive to pique the Explorer's interest. An expert in communication, survival, and anthropology, the Explorer's skills are invaluable for safely navigating uncharted terrain and negotiating with suspicious natives.

Requirements: An Explorer must have a minimum Intelligence score of 12.

Primary Terrain: Any (no specialization; use for followers and species enemy only).

Role: Motivated as much by curiosity as money, the Explorer spends more of his time planning expeditions than looking for employment. Still, Explorers are in high demand as guides, mapmakers, and scouts. A reputable Explorer can demand a high price for his services. However, rumors of a lost civilization are more likely to intrigue an Explorer than the promise of treasure, and he chooses his jobs accordingly.

Though a Pathfinder (discussed elsewhere in this chapter) or similarly skilled guide plays a crucial role in leading an expedition through unexplored territory, it's often an Explorer who's actually in charge. The Explorer decides when it's best to forge ahead and when to rest. He knows that small parties travel better than large ones, as each additional member increases the likelihood of delays from injury and disease. Above all, he understands the relationship between safety and self-restraint. He discourages his companions from taking unnecessary risks whenever possible.

An Explorer balances his natural impulsiveness with healthy doses of caution and common sense. More of a scholar than a brawler, he is usually a reluctant combatant, resorting to violence only when all other options fail. But when attacking, he fights with a single-mindedness that can border on savagery. A seasoned Explorer counsels his companions to follow two rules vital to wilderness survival, particularly where primitive civilizations are suspected to exist: (1) negotiating is usually preferable to attacking; and (2) if you intend to attack, then attack to kill.

Secondary Skills: Fisher, Forester, Hunter, Navigator, Trader/Barterer, Trapper/Furrier.

Weapon Proficiencies: Because an Explorer favors lightweight, easy-to-use weapons, his weapon proficiencies are confined to the following choices: short bow, light crossbow, dagger, dart, knife, sling, short sword.

Nonweapon Proficiencies: *Special Bonus:* Survival; the Explorer receives the benefits of this proficiency in *all* terrain types. Assigning additional slots to this proficiency does not enhance its use in any way. *Required:* Cartography*, Reading/Writing. *Recommended:* Ancient History, Bowyer/Fletcher, Camouflage*, Direction Sense, Distance Sense*, Endurance, Fire-building, Fishing, Foraging*, Herbalism, Hunting, Languages (Ancient and Modern), Mountaineering, Navigation, Rope Use, Signaling*, Swimming, Trail Marking*, Trail Signs*, Weather Sense.

Armor/Equipment: An Explorer has no special armor or equipment requirements. However, he rarely wears armor heavier than leather and most Explorers find shields awkward and confining.

Species Enemy: Any.

Followers: An Explorer has the normal 2d6 career limit (however, see Special Hindrances).

Special Benefits:

Languages: An Explorer has the capability of learning twice the normal number of languages allowed by his Intelligence score (see Table 4 in Chapter 1 of the *Player's Handbook*). For instance, an Explorer with an Intelligence score of 12 can learn six languages instead of the usual three. All languages still cost a proficiency slot each.

Find the Path: The Explorer can use this ability to sense the correct direction that will eventually lead to a desired geographical locale, which must be in an outdoor setting. The Explorer must have some clue, map, information, or body of research about the locale in order to use this ability. It can be used once per week, providing a day's worth of guidance (hence it is of greatest use on an expedition of weeks or months duration).

Culture Sense: This ability allows the Explorer to acquire general knowledge about the laws and customs of a tribe, village, or settlement. Once per week, the Explorer may attempt to use this ability by touching a member of the tribe or village. The villager must have the knowledge the Explorer wishes to gain; for instance, the villager can't be an infant or mentally deficient. Cooperation of the villager isn't required; touching an attacking or sleeping villager works as well.

The villager must make a saving throw vs. spells. If the throw succeeds, the Explorer learns nothing. If the throw fails, the Explorer acquires an instant understanding of the villager's laws and customs, including those applicable to related clans or tribes (such as the social etiquette pertaining to all aarakocra in the region, not just this particular group). Information learned through this ability might include local laws (no one is allowed on the village streets after dark without written permission), accepted courtesies (strangers bow to all children), and cultural taboos (hats and other head coverings are considered offensive). Successful use of this ability also gives the Explorer a +1 reaction adjustment when encountering any other members of the tribe, village, or settlement.

The DM may limit the quality and amount of information in any way he sees fit. The knowledge acquired through this ability doesn't ensure proper conduct; the Explorer's behavior (and the player's decisions) will ultimately determine the reaction of all villagers.

Special Hindrances:

Limited Animal Empathy: Because he spends little time in one place, and much of his time is spent on native cultures and geographical studies, an Explorer does not develop animal empathy to the degree of other rangers. When dealing with wild or attack-trained animals, the animal's saving throw vs. rods has a +2 bonus. Further, the Explorer must make a successful Wisdom check when trying to calm or befriend domestic animals.

Few Followers: The Explorer would travel lightly, unencumbered by followers that require his attention. Thus, he will have no more than two followers at the same time. If he already has two followers, a new follower won't arrive until one of his current followers is dismissed, lost, or killed.

No Fortifications: An Explorer has little interest in the responsibilities associated with property ownership. He will never build a castle or any other fortification.

Falconer

Description: The Falconer is an expert in the handling and training of falcons, birds of prey capable of learning an impressive range of tricks and tasks. Under the direction of a skilled Falconer, a falcon can be taught to snatch a coin purse from a victim's belt, bring down game birds in mid-flight, and fight effectively against creatures many times its size. In addition to his expertise as a bird trainer, the Falconer excels as a hunter and outdoorsman.

Requirements: Standard.

Primary Terrain: Required: The Falconer must choose a primary terrain where falcons are most commonly found: Desert, Forest, Hill, Mountain, or Plains.

Role: Many Falconers serve as retainers of kings or nobles. Others freelance as guides and mercenaries. Some stage public performances in rented halls or on street corners, demonstrating their birds' remarkable stunts for appreciative crowds. Regardless of how they make a living, Falconers are held in high regard by most people, who never fail to be impressed by the Falconer's amazing rapport with his birds.

As falcons are extremely sensitive creatures, most Falconers by necessity must be even-tempered, patient, and self-assured. These traits also make the Falconer a valuable asset to an adventuring party. The Falconer's comrades will usually find him dependable and supportive, though perhaps a bit preoccupied with the needs of his bird. Sometimes falconers will have traits much like their birds—fierce, swift, and observant.

In combat, the Falconer fights aggressively, he and his falcon generally conducting their attacks against the same opponent. If his falcon and a human companion are both threatened, the Falconer will often choose to defend his falcon. To prevent misunderstandings, an honorable Falconer will make it clear where his loyalties lie before he joins an adventuring party.

Secondary Skills: Bowyer/Fletcher, Forester, Groom, Hunter, Leather worker, Trader.

Weapon Proficiencies: *Required:* A Falconer must take two of his initial weapon proficiency slots in any of the following: bow (any), crossbow (light), dagger, knife, sling, spear. The remaining slots, as well as all subsequent slots, can be used for any weapon of the Falconer's choice.

Nonweapon Proficiencies: *Bonus:* Falconry*. *Recommended:* Alertness*, Bowyer/Fletcher, Endurance, Hunting, Leatherworking, Veterinary Medicine*.

Armor/Equipment: A Falconer has no special armor or equipment requirements. However, each falcon he trains requires a set of falconry training equipment (see Chapter 7).

Species Enemy: Any.

Followers: Unlike other rangers, a Falconer receives an allotment of 3d6 followers, determined at 1st level. The falconer immediately receives a falcon follower at this time, which counts against his allotment. This falcon will be exceptionally strong and able. The DM may use the statistics in the Falconry proficiency description (see Chapter 5) for the initial falcon follower, as well as for any subsequent falcon followers.

Until 10th level, a Falconer can only have one follower, and that follower must be a falcon. If the falcon follower dies or is otherwise lost, a new falcon follower will arrive in accordance with the guidelines in Chapter 3. The new falcon counts against the 3d6 allotment.

A Falconer becomes eligible to receive followers other than falcons when he reaches 10th level. At 10th level and beyond, the Falconer may have more than one falcon among his followers, depending on the circumstances of the campaign and decision of the DM.

Important Note: Remember that a Falconer's follower will be a bird of rare and remarkable characteristics and loyalty. The Falconer can also train lesser birds for himself or others, using the standard training rules.

Special Benefits:

Enhanced Training: If a normal falcon has failed to learn a trick or task and become untrainable, the Falconer can try again after gaining a level.

Attuned Follower: Under certain conditions, a Falconer is able to establish an exceptionally strong bond with a falcon follower. The bond enables the falcon to learn more efficiently, and enhances communication between the falcon and the Falconer.

Whenever a Falconer acquires a new falcon follower, including the falcon he receives at 1st level,

the falcon may be trained as a normal follower (see Chapter 3). However, once the Falconer begins to train the falcon (using either the Standard or Alternate method), the falcon cannot become attuned.

Otherwise, the Falconer can forego training until he attempts to become attuned to the new falcon. The attuning attempt takes six weeks. For at least an hour each day, the Falconer talks to the bird, strokes its feathers, and engages in other nurturing behavior. The bird learns to respond to the Falconer's voice, though the Falconer refrains from teaching it any specific tricks or tasks during this time. (In combat encounters which take place in this period, the falcon will fly to safety at the first sign of trouble, then return to the Falconer's shoulder when all's clear).

At the end of the six-week period, the Falconer makes a Wisdom check. If the check fails, the attuning attempt has likewise failed. The falcon continues its relationship with the Falconer as a normal follower. The Falconer may begin to train the falcon according to either the Standard or Alternate method described in Chapter 3. The Falconer can't make a second attempt to attune the falcon.

If the check succeeds, the falcon is attuned. Normally, the Falconer can teach the attuned falcon a task or trick each time he gains a level, at the same time he undergoes his own level training. The Falconer may also use the normal training rule, either the Standard or Alternative method. Training time is half that given in the falconry proficiency (see Chapter 5). Regardless how it is trained, an attuned falcon can learn tricks or tasks in any combination, up to one per level of the falconer. An attuned falcon never becomes untrainable.

Additionally, once a falcon becomes attuned, it receives a one-time hit point bonus equal to twice the Falconer's level. For example, if a falcon becomes attuned to a 3rd level Falconer, the falcon receives a bonus of 6 hit points. This bonus remains the same, even if the Falconer later advances in level.

The following benefits apply only to a Falconer and an attuned falcon.

Fearless Falcon: When fighting on behalf of a Falconer or under a Falconer's direction, an attuned falcon never needs to make a morale check.

Falcon Species Enemy: An attuned falcon has its own species enemy. When a falcon follower becomes attuned, determine its species enemy, either by rolling on the appropriate table in Chapter 2 (Tables 20-27), or by the DM choosing a particular enemy. The falcon and ranger may share the same species enemy. The falcon has all of the species enemy bonuses and penalties described in Chapter 2.

Attack Bonus: An attuned falcon receives a +2 bonus to all attack rolls, except when fighting its species enemy (when it receives a +4 bonus).

Speak With Falcon: A Falconer who reaches 10th level acquires the ability to speak with an attuned falcon follower. The ability is similar to the 2nd level priest spell *speak with animals,* except it requires no components or casting time, and the Falconer can do so at will.

Mental Communication: At 15th level, the Falconer can communicate mentally with an attuned falcon follower. Both the Falconer and attuned falcon can send and receive thoughts at will, up to a distance of 100 yards per level of the Falconer. Walls or other physical boundaries have no effect on this ability.

Special Hindrances: If an attuned falcon dies, or is lost for any other reason, the Falconer succumbs to grief and despair for 1-4 weeks. During this period of mourning, the Falconer makes all attack rolls and ability checks at a –2 penalty. Additionally, during this period, no new followers can be acquired, nor can the Falconer use the *animal empathy* ability.

Feralan

Description: What happens to children who wander into the wilderness and are never recovered? Or worse, children who are abandoned by their families, left in the woods to fend for themselves? Sadly, most of them eventually succumb to the dangers of the wild. But a fortunate few are taken in by animals, raised as part of a lion's brood or a wolf's litter. Cut off from civilization, they gradually take on the characteristics of the creatures who adopted them. In the process, they become Feralans, beings who combine the savagery of a beast with the intellect of a man.

The Feralan may look like a human, but for the most part, he acts like a wild animal. He speaks the language of animals and lives in their lairs. He leads them on hunts, defends them against predators, and considers them his family. Yet, the Feralan retains vestiges of his own race, characterized by his agile mind and an unshakable curiosity about human civilization. Many Feralans have picked up enough human language to communicate with them, albeit on a limited basis.

Despite his bestial tendencies, the Feralan's moral principles are not so different from other rangers. He values the well-being of his followers as much as his own. He avoids needless killing and considers himself the nemesis of hunters who stalk game for sport. Greed and jealously are as unknown to the Feralan as they are to the creatures of the forest.

Familial Species: At the beginning of his career, the player should choose a familial species for his Feralan, representing the type of animal that raised him. A Feralan can have only a single familial species, which never changes. The familial species must share the Feralan's primary terrain and is subject to the DM's approval. Animals suitable as familial species include wild dogs, bears (any), wolves, great cats (any), and primates (any). The DM may augment this list with additional choices if he likes; familial species can't be human, demihuman, humanoid, or of magical or supernatural origin.

Requirements: Feralans must have a minimum Constitution of 15 and a minimum Strength of 14. They cannot be of lawful alignment.

Though some humans and demihumans raised by wild animals have neutral or evil outlooks, only those with good alignments qualify as Feralans. Because Feralans have little use for the laws and regulations of the civilized world, most are chaotic good.

Primary Terrain: The vast majority of Feralans have Forest or Jungle as their primary terrain. Arctic, Hill, Mountain, Plains, and Swamp are possible but less common.

Role: Many people fear Feralans, wrongly considering them to be ferocious wildmen or savage werecreatures. Those who befriend Feralans, however, come to know them as trustworthy, noble, and even gentle. Still, Feralans remain wary of most humans and demihumans, finding their actions unpredictable and often incomprehensible.

Feralans rarely volunteer to join adventuring parties. However, because Feralans are fervent animal advocates and protectors of the wild, they are inclined to cooperate with parties who share their concerns.

While a Feralan's human companions may admire his courage and respect his instincts, they may find his beast-like behavior offensive at best, frightening at worst. After a hunt, a Feralan may drag the carcass of his prey back to the party's campsite and eat it raw, tearing off chunks with his familial followers. Personal hygiene is rarely among a Feralan's priorities, though he may occasionally lick himself clean. He grooms his animal friends by picking bugs from their fur, then cuddles up with them to go to sleep. When disturbed, he may snarl like a wolf. To celebrate victory over a predator, he may howl at the moon. He communicates in grunts, growls, and sentence fragments. He may disconcert new associates by sniffing them.

Secondary Skills: Fisher, Forester, Hunter, Trapper/Furrier. The secondary skills reflect talents that Feralans have picked up in the wild; therefore, all skills have wilderness applications only. A Fisher Feralan, for instance, may know how to swim and catch fish, but won't be able to operate a boat.

Weapon Proficiencies: *Required:* club, knife. A Feralan's remaining slots must be spent on primitive weapons: blowgun (rare), dagger, short bow, dart, hand axe, sling, spear.

Nonweapon Proficiencies: *Bonus:* Hunting or Fishing; Trail Signs*. His remaining initial proficiencies must be chosen from these: Alertness*, Animal Handling, Animal Lore, Blind-fighting, Direction Sense, Endurance, Fire-building, Fishing, Foraging, Hunting, Rope Use, Running, Set Snares, Survival, Swimming, Veterinary Healing*, Weather Sense.

Armor/Equipment: Feralans adorn themselves in crude smocks or loincloths made of furs and hides. They wear only what is necessary to keep themselves warm and comfortable.

A Feralan wears no armor, nor does he carry a

shield. His main weapons—the ones associated with his weapon proficiencies—he makes himself from bones, branches, rocks, and other natural materials. If he loses or breaks one of these weapons, he can come up with a replacement in few hours, assuming suitable materials are available. He can use weapons other than those he makes, but prefers not to.

Species Enemy: Any.

Followers: Unlike other rangers, the Feralan begins to receive followers at 5th level. At least half (rounded up) of his followers will be of his familial species. A Feralan will receive at most *one* human, demihuman, or humanoid as a follower, and this only at 10th level or higher.

Special Benefits:

Stealth: The Feralan receives a +10% chance to hide in natural surroundings and a +10% chance to move silently.

Feral Rage: During melee combat, the initial wounding of an opponent may impel the Feralan into a frenzy of blood lust, increasing his fighting effectiveness. A Feralan can make one attempt to become enraged at any particular opponent. After the first round in which a Feralan inflicts damage on an opponent, the Feralan has the option of making a saving throw vs. death magic. If the roll succeeds, the Feralan goes into a feral rage for the next 2d6 rounds. During that time, the rage gives the Feralan a +2 bonus to all attack and damage rolls, and his base Armor Class improves by 2 (an unarmored Feralan's AC is temporarily raised to 8). However, all attacks must be made against the designated opponent and the Feralan must attack in every round he's able; he can't voluntarily break off an attack, or choose to attack a different opponent.

An enraged Feralan must continue to attack the designated opponent until the feral rage wears off, or the opponent dies or escapes. If the rage wears off, the Feralan may continue to attack normally, or take any other action; however, the Feralan can't attempt to become enraged again against the same opponent. If the opponent dies, the feral rage automatically ends. If the opponent flees, the Feralan will pursue for the duration of the rage.

Climbing: The Feralan has a base climbing success rate of 60%. This allows tree climbing at the Feralan's normal movement rate (cliff climbing instead if the primary terrain is Arctic, Desert, or Mountain). This ability is much more limited than the thief ability to climb walls. The climbing modifiers discussed in Chapter 14 of the *Player's Handbook* apply in all situations other than those given.

Speak with Animals: The Feralan can use this ability at will with animals from his familial species. The ability is similar to the 2nd level priest spell *speak with animals,* but requires no components or casting time.

Familial Rapport: The familial followers of a Feralan will generally do what they're asked, assuming they're physically capable of doing so, when the Feralan speaks to them in their own language. Mistreated familial followers may still abandon a Feralan, as detailed in the Parting Company section of Chapter 3.

Animal Training: The Feralan may train non-familial followers (use guidelines in Chapter 3).

Call of the Wild: When in his primary terrain, the Feralan may attempt to summon familial species animals by howling at the top of his lungs for 1-6 rounds. The DM then secretly rolls percentile dice. If the result is less than or equal to the Feralan's Wisdom score plus his level (a 5th level Feralan with Wisdom 15 has a base chance of 20%), 1-4 familial animals show up within the next hour. Once they arrive, these animals act as followers for the next 1-4 hours. During this time, the Feralan may command them with his *speak with animals* ability. At the end of the 1-4 hour period, the summoned animals disappear into the wilderness. A Feralan can attempt *call of the wild* once per day.

Special Hindrances:

Limited Magic: Because of his mental predisposition and animalistic tendencies, a Feralan can only learn and cast a limited number of spells. He has access only to spells of the animal sphere and can't cast spells any higher than 2nd level. Table 41 show the Feralan's spell progression.

A Feralan may use any magical item normally allowed a ranger.

Table 45: Feralan Spell Progression

Feralan Level	Casting Level	Priest Spell Level*	
		1	2
1-7	-	-	-
8-9	1	1	-
10-11	2	2	-
12-13	3	2	1
14-15	4	2	2
16+	5	3	2

* Animal sphere only

Limited Money: A Feralan has little interest in money or gems, which for the most part are as worthless to him as rocks. He keeps only enough funds to cover training costs, equipment replacement, and basic living expenses. He usually allows fellow party members to divide the remainder of his share of treasure as they wish. (However, the Feralan still receives all experience points due him for finding treasure and fellow party members receive no experience point benefit for the Feralan's share.)

No Fortifications: Lacking extensive resources but mainly lacking the inclination, a Feralan will not build a castle or any other type of fortification at any point in his career.

Reaction Penalty: The rough manner and appearance of the Feralan inflicts a –3 penalty when encountering human, demihuman, or humanoid NPCs, including other Feralans.

A Feralan will seldom, if ever, develop any close relationship with politically powerful human, demihuman, or humanoid NPCs.

Forest Runner

Description: Wherever a corrupt or oppressive regime holds power, there's bound to be a Forest Runner. Forest Runners rise in opposition to such regimes, living on the fringes of society, usually one step ahead of the law. They're criminals only in a technical sense, as they adhere to a personal code that compels them to wage war against greedy aristocrats and unjust rulers. While the powers-that-be view the Forest Runner as a lawless troublemaker, commoners see him as hero, perhaps their best hope against a tyrannical government.

Constantly on the move, Forest Runners live by their wits and have learned to make do with minimal resources. They excel in combat and make formidable opponents. Ever active and brimming with self-confidence, Forest Runners delight in harassing authority figures, particularly the pompous and well-to-do. Many a hapless aristocrat has been left bound, gagged, and penniless after a humiliating roadside encounter with a Forest Runner.

Any time after reaching 4th level, the Forest Runner will acquire a *personal nemesis*. This is an NPC of near equal level whose campaign goal is to capture or kill the Forest Runner.

Requirements: A Forest Runner must have a Charisma score of at least 12.

Primary Terrain: Most Forest Runners hail from civilized regions in Forest, Hill, Plains, Mountain, or Jungle. However, no terrain type is excluded, providing it contains a reasonably sized and sufficiently corrupt settlement. (A Forest Runner from a primary terrain other than Forest, modifies the name accordingly, such as Mountain Runner, Swamp Runner, and so on.)

Role: The Forest Runner is usually selfless, resourceful, and roguishly charming. A loner by circumstance and not by choice, a Forest Runner readily allies with adventuring parties who share his outlook. As a champion of underdogs everywhere, the Forest Runner doesn't necessarily feel bound to his homeland, and may journey anywhere in the world to promote justice. Occasionally, he may join a party to acquire treasure for distribution to the needy. If the local authorities are putting the heat on, he may accompany a party simply to disappear for a while.

Secondary Skills: Bowyer/Fletcher, Forester, Farmer, Hunter, Leather worker, Teamster, Weaponsmith.

Weapon Proficiencies: The Forest Runner receives a bonus weapon proficiency slot, above and beyond those he's normally allowed. The bonus slot must be filled with one of the following weapons: long bow, quarterstaff, long sword, or dagger. He must then fill three of his first six slots with the remaining weapons on this list. Once he's met this requirement, he may fill subsequent slots with any weapons of his choice.

Nonweapon Proficiencies: *Required:* Bowyer/Fletcher. *Recommended:* Alertness*, Blacksmithing, Camouflage*, Disguise, Endurance, Leatherworking, Persuasion*, Riding (Land-based), Rope Use, Weaponsmithing.

Armor/Equipment: Standard.

Species Enemy: A Forest Runner's species enemy should have some association with the corrupt regime he opposes. It may be the king's pet (such as a wolf or tiger), an evil race with which the monarchy has aligned itself (goblins or ogres), a symbol of the government (a snake or a hydra) or a creature the opposed officials have used in war (a dragon or a giant).

Followers: Any.

Special Benefits:

Stealth: The Forest Runner has a +5% chance to hide in natural surroundings and a +5% chance to move silently.

Inspire: Once per day, prior to making an attack, a Forest Runner may spend 2-5 (1d4+1) rounds boosting the morale of his companions with flattering words and expressions of confidence. He can influence a number of companions equal to his level. If the Forest Runner makes a successful Charisma check afterwards, the companions enjoy a +2 bonus to their morale for the next 3-12 (3d4) rounds. Each companion also receives a +1 bonus to his first attack roll. The inspiring speech doesn't affect animals, other Forest Runners, or himself. The Forest Runner can't attempt to inspire his companions in the midst of battle or while they're occupied in any other activity.

Disguise: The Forest Runner can take the Disguise proficiency for one proficiency slot.

Reaction Bonus: In his homeland or any region where his reputation precedes him, a Forest Runner can count on food and shelter at no charge for himself and his companions from supportive commoners. A Forest Runner also receives a +1 reaction modifier from peasants of good or neutral alignment of all cultures.

Special Hindrances: Forest Runners will rarely develop a close relationship with any NPC with political power. Additionally, a Forest Runner runs a constant risk of arrest by authorities of his homeland, as well as from other regimes with which his homeland has extradition agreements. Law-enforcement authorities may plague a Forest Runner through his entire career.

Giant Killer

Description: The Giant Killer is a skilled combatant, often from humble beginnings, trained to the specific purpose of slaying giants. He has mastered combat techniques designed to fell giants, and has become an expert in their behavior and habits. A Giant Killer is nothing if not confident; a giant's immense size merely means he makes a good target.

For the purposes of this kit, giants include true giants, such as: cloud giants, fire giants, frost giants, hill giants, stone giants, and storm giants. Also included are giant-kin, such as cyclops, ettins, firbolg, fomorians, verbeeg, and voadkyn. The DM may augment this list with other giants relevant to his particular campaign.

Requirements: A Giant Killer must have a minimum score of 15 in both Strength and Dexterity.

Primary Terrain: Any terrain is acceptable, so long as some type of giant calls it home.

Role: Giant Killers have keen minds, strong bodies, and unshakable egos. Most Giant Killers tirelessly promote their own skills and accomplishments, boasting of their latest triumphs to anyone who'll listen. Not surprisingly, their reputations precede them in most civilized regions. However, reactions among residents vary. For every person who reveres the Giant Killer as a hero, there's another who dismisses him as a blowhard. But when giants plague a community, everyone welcomes a Giant Killer with open arms.

Even when their services are desperately needed, Giant Killers rarely exploit their position. Most charge only modest fees, or settle for a medal or other token of appreciation in lieu of payment. As often as not, Giant Killers seek no remuneration of any kind, fighting giants for the sheer pleasure of it.

Unsurprisingly, the mere promise of an encounter with a giant is reason enough for most Giant Killers to join an adventuring party. For the most part, a Giant Killer leaves decision-making to others. Though in principle, he may share the party's fervor for the expedition at hand, he's usually more concerned with finding giants. He may become impatient and surly if the party goes for too long without meeting one.

The Giant Killer relishes violent encounters

of all kinds, if only to exercise his combat skills. Of course, he comes into his own when fighting giants, and it's a wise party that follows his lead in such situations.

Secondary Skills: Bowyer/Fletcher, Forester, Groom, Hunter, Tailor, Weaponsmith.

Weapon Proficiencies: Because the Giant Killer faces tall adversaries, he must become proficient with missiles and hurled weapons. The first weapon slot, and every odd slot (third, fifth, and so on), must be a missile weapon: bow (any), crossbow (any), sling, staff sling, or any melee weapon that can be hurled. The even-numbered slots may be filled with any weapons of the Giant Killer's choice.

Nonweapon Proficiencies: Giant Killers pursue their interest in giants with such single-mindedness that they have little time left to master other skills. Therefore, a Giant Killer is allowed only one nonweapon proficiency at first level. This must be selected from the following: Bowyer/Fletcher, Cobbler, Cooking, Hunting, Pottery, Riding (Land-based), Running, Tailor, Swimming, Weaving.

Armor/Equipment: Giant Killers have no special equipment requirements. They often carry shields decorated with medals and ribbons awarded them from grateful communities for slaying troublesome giants. Though such shields can be used normally, they're mainly for show; Giant Killers generally put them aside before engaging a giant in battle.

Species Enemy: None; however, see Special Bonuses against giants.

Followers: Normal (but see optional rule).

Special Benefits:

Attack Bonuses: A Giant Killer has all the following bonuses when attacking giants:

- **Giant Killers inflict bonus damage against giants, +1 point of damage for every level of the Giant Killer.** For example, if a 7th level Giant Killer makes a successful attack with a spear, the giant suffers 1-8 points of damage from the spear, plus 7 for the Giant Killer's level.
- **Giants have a base –4 to hit when attacking Giant Killers.** A giant with a THAC0 of 10 needs a 14 to hit a Giant Killer with AC 0.
- **Giant Killers can dodge giant attacks.** If a giant with initiative attacks and hits, the Giant Killer may give up his action to dodge. If the Giant Killer saves vs. death magic, the giant's attack misses. If the Giant Killer has initiative, he can dodge instead of attacking for the round.

Infuriate: A Giant Killer can goad a giant into making careless and ill-conceived attacks. To infuriate a giant, the Giant Killer spends two rounds darting between the giant's legs, waving his hands, and hollering insults. The Giant Killer cannot make attacks or take any other actions while attempting to infuriate the giant; if interrupted (to dodge, for example), he must start over. During this time, the giant can attack the Giant Killer; however, because of the Giant Killer's erratic movement, the giant's attacks are made at an additional –2 penalty.

At the end of this period, the giant makes a saving throw vs. spells. If the throw succeeds, nothing special happens. If the throw fails, the giant becomes enraged for the next 2-12 (2d6) rounds. During that time, the giant directs all of his attacks against the Giant Killer; the giant's attacks are made at an additional –4 penalty. The Giant Killer may attack normally while the giant is infuriated.

Optional Rule: Follower Infuriation

A Giant Killer may enhance his chances of infuriating a giant by using an animal follower that has been trained to infuriate. The follower, which must be a bird or other flying creature of small size (S), learns this trick in accordance to the Training Followers rules in Chapter 3. The trick counts against the follower's normal limit of tricks and tasks. Only a Giant Killer can train a follower to infuriate.

While the Giant Killer is executing his infuriating routine, the follower may also infuriate the giant by swooping around his head and screeching. The giant's saving throw against the infuriation is reduced by a –2 penalty for the infuriating follower. This effect is not cumulative with additional followers. An infuriated giant might direct its attacks at the infuriating follower in addition to the Giant Killer. If the giant tries to attack an infuriating follower, the follower successfully dodges the blow unless the attack roll is a 19 or 20. A follower can't attempt to infuriate alone. A follower can only augment the infuriating attempts of the Giant Killer.

Giant Lore: If a Giant Killer discovers a footprint, lair, campsite, or any other physical evidence of a giant, a successful Wisdom roll enables him to learn some general information about the giant in question. Such information may include the giant's type, approximate size, and companions. He may also learn how recently the giant was in the area and in what direction the giant traveled. The DM decides the quality and amount of information the Giant Killer receives.

Special Hindrances:

Tracking Limitation: Unlike other rangers, the tracking ability of the Giant Killer is limited to tracking giants. A Giant Killer who selects a general Tracking proficiency can track other creatures as non-ranger character.

Because Giant Killers seldom make an effort to conceal their identities, they're often singled out for harassment. Insecure villagers may challenge Giant Killers to duels to impress their friends, or bullies may ambush Giant Killers to demonstrate their toughness.

To avenge the death of a companion, some giants may target Giant Killers for assassination. Giant tribes occasionally offer bounties for proof of a Giant Killer's death, making the Giant Killer a prime candidate for attacks.

Greenwood Ranger

Description: The rarest and certainly the most unusual ranger, the Greenwood Ranger, or Limbant, combines characteristics of both humans and plants. The Greenwood Ranger begins life as a normal human, but through resolute appeals to the gods, he gradually acquires plant-like qualities that enhance his relationship with the vegetable kingdom and endow him with remarkable powers.

A Greenwood Ranger resembles a normal human covered from head to toe with a layer of thick brown bark, similar to that of an oak tree. The bark on the back of his head and the backs of his hands and arms is tinged with green; the green bark enables him to absorb nutrients directly from the sunlight (see the Special Benefits section below). He has no body hair, no teeth, and his tapering fingers and toes look like gnarled branches. Tangles of short roots grow from his feet and ankles.

Aside from these physical differences, the Greenwood Ranger moves, speaks, and behaves much like an ordinary human. As his human qualities are dominant, he has a +2 bonus when saving against *hold plant, charm plant,* and similar plant-related spells. Otherwise, the Greenwood Ranger makes saving throws, attack rolls, and ability checks as a normal human ranger.

Becoming a Greenwood Ranger: A ranger must make the commitment to become a Greenwood Ranger at 1st level, even though the Greenwood Ranger's special abilities are not acquired until 4th level. From 1st through 3rd level, he is considered to be a latent Greenwood Ranger. A latent Greenwood Ranger operates as the standard ranger described in the *Player's Handbook*, though following the Secondary Skill, Weapon Proficiency, and Nonweapon Proficiency restrictions described below (and receiving the indicated Bonus Proficiencies). He may wear any armor allowed a normal ranger. He does *not* have any of the Greenwood Ranger's special benefits or hindrances at this time.

During this latency period, the ranger must spend a minimum of three hours per week in silent prayer, petitioning the gods to transform him into a Greenwood Ranger. It isn't necessary for the player to keep track of the hours spent in prayer; presumably, the character will set aside enough spare time to meet this requirement. The gods may tolerate an occasional lapse—for instance, the ranger may be too sick to pray in a particular week—but the ranger is otherwise expected to keep up with his prayers. If the ranger intentionally neglects his prayers on a regular basis (as determined by the DM), the gods will inform the ranger in a dream that he's no longer eligible to become a Greenwood Ranger. The ranger is forced to abandon the kit, and may *not* take another.

When the latent Greenwood Ranger reaches 4th level, the gods give him a simple task to complete, involving the protection or support of plant life. Typical tasks include assisting a treant, replanting an area of forest devastated by fire, and teaching a primitive tribe how to grow and harvest their own crops. A latent Greenwood Ranger who fails to complete this task within a month must spend an additional 1-4 months praying, at which time the

gods will grant a new task.

A latent Greenwood Ranger who completes the task then locates an isolated area of forest or jungle, lies on the ground, and covers himself with leaves and branches. He then falls asleep for a full day. If disturbed before 24 hours elapse, the transformation is interrupted; the ranger may try again at another time. Otherwise, upon awaking, the ranger will have transformed into a Greenwood Ranger. Once transformed, the Greenwood Ranger *cannot* abandon this kit, although actions that would normally cost a ranger his class result in the loss of spell use and other penalties determined by the DM.

Requirements: A Greenwood Ranger must be human. Otherwise, the ability requirements are the same as those for a normal ranger.

Primary Terrain: *Required:* Forest or Jungle.

Role: Because he must sacrifice a portion of his humanity to become a Greenwood Ranger, a human drawn to this kit usually has only a tenuous link with formal society. He is an outsider, with few close friendships or family ties, capable of walking away from the civilized world without regret. Orphans, social outcasts, and eccentric personalities are good candidates to become Greenwood Rangers.

Greenwood Rangers live deep in the forest or jungle, far from urban centers. Most people tend to shun Greenwood Rangers, repulsed by their appearance or fearful of their strange powers. But their distrust is unwarranted. Greenwood Rangers are gentle-natured, thoughtful souls to whom all life is precious. A Greenwood Ranger will mourn the loss of a favorite shade tree as much as the passing of a human companion. To the Greenwood Ranger, the wilderness is a glorious, sacred place. If necessary, he will risk his life to preserve it.

In most cases, a Greenwood Ranger will align with any adventuring party who shares his affinity for nature, providing he agrees with their cause. A Greenwood Ranger tends to keep to himself, offering his opinion only when asked and deferring to the party's leader in most situations.

Secondary Skills: Bowyer/Fletcher, Farmer, Forester, Woodworker/Carpenter.

Weapon Proficiencies: A Greenwood Ranger's weapon proficiencies are limited to the following choices: axe (any), bow (any), crossbow (any), dagger, knife, quarterstaff, sling, spear, long sword, short sword.

Nonweapon Proficiencies: *Bonus:* Herbalism. *Required:* Agriculture. *Recommended:* Carpentry, Endurance, Foraging*, Swimming, Trail Marking*, Weather Sense. *Barred:* Armorer, Blacksmithing, Fire-building, Engineering, Leatherworking, Mining, Mountaineering, Navigation*, Riding (Land-based and Airborne), Seamanship, Spelunking*, Stonemasonry, Weaponsmithing.

Armor/Equipment: A Greenwood Ranger can't wear armor. However, his bark-like skin provides comparable protection. At 4th level, the Greenwood Ranger's skin gives him an Armor Class of 5. For every level thereafter, the AC increases by 1; an 8th level Greenwood Ranger, for example, has an AC of 1. At 15th level, the Greenwood Ranger reaches his maximum AC of –6.

Normally, Greenwood Rangers don't wear clothing aside from a cloth loincloth or simple smock. Thanks to their tough feet, shoes are unnecessary. Some Greenwood Rangers are fond of decorative pins made of gems or colorful minerals. Greenwood Rangers wear such pins by attaching them directly to their skin.

Species Enemy: Any.

Followers: A Greenwood Ranger will have at least one treant follower at some point career.

Special Benefits:

Speak with Plants: The Greenwood Ranger can *speak with plants* at will. This ability is similar to the 4th level priest spell, except it requires neither components nor a casting time.

Photosynthesis: Unlike a normal human, the Greenwood Ranger has no need to drink or eat. He receives nourishment directly from the sun. So long as he is exposed to sunlight at least an hour per day, he stays healthy. He suffers 1-2 points of damage every day he goes without exposure to the sun. Overcast days are sufficient to nourish a Greenwood Ranger.

A Greenwood Ranger satisfies his thirst by dipping his feet in any pool or puddle of fresh water for 10 minutes every other day. Exposure to a light rain or soaking his feet in a bucket will also suffice. If he goes without water for 48 hours, he begins to suffer damage at the rate of 1-2 points per day.

Buoyancy: A Greenwood Ranger requires oxy-

gen like any other human and is subject to drowning and suffocation. However, because the Greenwood Ranger's woody skin makes him naturally buoyant, he can't drown unless he's physically held underwater.

Rooting: Upon reaching 8th level, a Greenwood Ranger can accelerate healing by *rooting*. He may attempt this once per week. To use this ability, the Greenwood Ranger must bury his feet in the earth (not sand or snow; the soil must be capable of supporting plant life) up to his ankles. He must stand stationary and silent for 1-4 hours, taking no other actions during that time. If interrupted, the rooting fails; he may try again the following week. If uninterrupted, tiny roots sprout from his feet and bury themselves into the ground, absorbing healing nutrients from the soil. At the end of the rooting period, the roots withdraw, and the Greenwood Ranger has recovered 3-12 (3d4) points of damage.

Limbing: Under certain circumstances, a Greenwood Ranger can grow an extra limb. The limb grows from the center of the Greenwood Ranger's chest and functions as a normal arm.

Only Greenwood Rangers of 10th level or higher can attempt *limbing*. A Greenwood Ranger may make an attempt once a month by lying on the ground and covering himself with leaves, branches, and earth. For the next 24 hours, he enters into a state of suspended animation, similar to that caused by a *temporal stasis* spell. If the Greenwood Ranger is disturbed during this time, the enchantment is broken and *limbing* will not occur. The Greenwood Ranger can try again the following month.

If the Greenwood Ranger is undisturbed, he awakens in 24 hours with a new limb extending from his chest. The new limb may be useful to the Greenwood Ranger in several ways:

• The Greenwood Ranger can wield three weapons at the same time. Attacks made with the third weapon suffer a –2 penalty. The Greenwood Ranger's reaction adjustment (based on his Dexterity) modifies this penalty, although it can't result in a positive modifier. The Greenwood Ranger gains only two additional attacks per

round, regardless of the number of attacks he's normally allowed. Therefore, a Greenwood Ranger able to attack 3/2 with one weapon (once in the first round, twice in the second) can attack 7/2 when using three weapons (three times in the first round, four times in the second).

- The Greenwood Ranger with a third limb receives a +3 bonus when punching, wrestling, or overbearing.
- A Greenwood Ranger with a third limb can swim at 150% of his normal swimming speed. He receives a +20% modifier to all climbing attempts.
- The extra limb helps the Greenwood Ranger perform ordinary activities more efficiently. For instance, he can carry three buckets of water at the same time or wash dishes in half the normal time.
- The third limb improves the Greenwood Ranger's performance when using certain nonweapon proficiencies involving the hands. For example, when using the juggling proficiency to catch items, he makes an attack roll vs. AC 2 instead of AC 0. When using the weaving proficiency, he can create three square yards of material per day instead of two. The DM determines the extent of the improvement depending on the particular proficiency and the attempted task.

The Greenwood Ranger's new limb withers and falls off in 1-4 days. A Greenwood Ranger can't have more than one extra limb at a time.

Special Hindrances:

Stiff Limbs: The Greenwood Ranger has a –5% penalty when trying to move silently. He gets no Dexterity bonus to his armor class.

Vulnerability to Fire: If an opponent attempts any normal or magical fire-based attack against a Greenwood Ranger, he qualifies for a +4 bonus to his attack roll and a +1/die bonus to his damage roll. The Greenwood Ranger suffers a –4 penalty to all saving throws involving fire-based attacks. Any fire-based attacks that hit inflict +1 hit point per die of damage.

Vulnerability to Extreme Climates: Though his skin provides protection in most environments, the Greenwood Ranger risks damage from prolonged exposure to extreme temperatures. After any full day spent in a climate where the temperature is below freezing, or averages 100 degrees or more, a Greenwood Ranger must make a Constitution check. Failure results in the loss of 1-4 hit points.

Limited Magic: A Greenwood Ranger can only learn and cast spells from the plant sphere. He uses the ranger's normal spell progression (given in Table 5 in Chapter 1).

Reaction Penalty: Because of his bizarre appearance, the Greenwood Ranger suffers a –3 reaction adjustment penalty when encountering any NPCs, with the exception of learned nobles, sages, and other high level characters of good or neutral alignment. Such worldly characters aren't intimidated by his appearance.

Guardian

Description: The Guardian is a self-appointed protector of the wilderness. Compelled by a strong sense of duty, he has assumed responsibility for an unsettled tract of land, doing his utmost to maintain it in its natural state and protect its animal occupants. Though he feels kindly towards woodsmen, elves, and others who share his respect for nature, he has little patience for those who would exploit the wilderness for gain or spite.

A Guardian constantly monitors the region he has sworn to protect. He scrutinizes the activity of strangers, advises travelers, and intercepts careless hunters. He keeps an eye out for fires, floods, and other natural disasters, and does what he can to comfort animals in times of crisis.

Domain: All Guardians have a specific region that they protect. The DM should establish the boundaries of a Guardian's domain at the beginning of his career. There are no fixed rules for assigning domains, but in general, a 1st level Guardian's domain shouldn't exceed a few square miles. The domain expands by several square miles each time the Guardian increases in level. By 5th level, a Guardian's domain might encompass a region about 20-25 miles across. By 15th level or higher, the domain might comprise an area the size of a small country.

A Guardian's domain should correspond to his primary terrain. The domain is typically located in an uncivilized part of the world, such as a remote mountain range or unexplored jungle. Two or more Guardians may share an especially large domain, but such cases are rare.

Requirements: Standard.

Primary Terrain: Forest, Hill, Jungle, Mountain, or Plains.

Role: A Guardian operates of his own volition, having no official sanction or title. He carries out his custodial duties as he sees fit, taking whatever steps he deems necessary to protect his domain. Despite his independence, he usually maintains good working relationships with officials of bordering lands. The relationship benefits both parties. The Guardian notifies the officials of approaching armies or other potential threats, while the officials may provide help for problems the Guardian can't handle alone. Though many governments would jump at the chance to have such able warriors in their employ, Guardians resist all such offers, and steadfastly maintain their autonomy.

An adventuring party entering a Guardian's domain has a good chance of encountering the Guardian himself. A Guardian will usually agree to guide a party through his domain and—presuming the party's intentions are compatible with the Guardian's philosophy—assist them in their efforts. Though a Guardian is reluctant to leave his domain, he may do so if presented with a compelling reason, such as the ravaging of a pristine wilderness or a threat to the ecology in another land.

Guardians tend to be self-sufficient, clear-headed, and conscientious. They make excellent leaders. Though a Guardian may develop deep friendships with other party members, he always parts company at the end of an adventure, returning to his domain as soon as he can.

Secondary Skills: Bowyer/Fletcher, Farmer, Fisher, Hunter, Trapper/Furrier, Woodworker/Carpenter.

Weapon Proficiencies: *Recommended:* Bow (any) or crossbow (any), dagger, javelin, knife, quarterstaff, sling, spear, staff sling.

Nonweapon Proficiencies: *Bonus:* Hunting or Fishing. *Recommended:* Agriculture, Bowyer/Fletcher, Fire-building, Fishing, Foraging*, Herbalism, Hunting, Riding (Land-based), Rope Use, Set Snares, Swimming, Veterinary Healing*, Weather Sense.

Armor/Equipment: Standard.

Species Enemy: Any.

Followers: A Guardian acquires at least one human or demihuman follower at some point in his career. There are no other restrictions or recommendations.

Special Benefits:

Bonus Sphere: The Guardian has miner access to the Protection sphere.

Bonus Spells: A Guardian can cast certain spells within the boundaries of his domain. These are *detect evil* (three times per day), and *bless* and *commune with nature* (once per week each).

Revive Plants: This ability enables the Guardian to revitalize any type of natural plant life suffering from drought, disease, insect infestation, or other forms of non-magical trauma. Dead plants can't be affected, nor can the Guardian invigorate plants beyond their normal limits (for instance, a Guardian can't cause an apple tree to blossom in the winter).

The process requires 8 hours and can affect a square area whose sides are 10 yards times the Guardian's level (a 5th level Guardian can revive all of the plant life within a 50 yd. × 50 yd. square). The Guardian can use this ability once per month.

Special Hindrances: If a Guardian leaves his domain for any length of time, he must make arrangements for someone else to assume his duties. He may hire a caretaker, or assign temporary custody of his domain to a human or demihuman follower. There are no fixed penalties for a Guardian who fails to do this. However, should a Guardian abandon his responsibilities for more than a few days, the gods may deny him the use of the special benefits associated with this kit. If he's absent for longer periods—say, a few weeks—the gods may also deny him the use of all spells. The Guardian recovers use of his special benefits and spells as soon as he returns to his domain.

Justifier

Description: Some expeditions are so demanding and some foes so dangerous that they require the attention of a highly trained specialist whose combat skills far exceed those of the typical ranger. Enter the Justifier, a master tactician whose military instincts, fighting versatility, and steely nerves places him in the first rank of elite warriors.

Though the Justifier specializes in neutralizing monsters, his skills qualify him for a wide range of adventures. He may organize guerilla forces and lead them into hostile territories. He may stage reconnaissance operations to gather information concerning enemy strength and logistics. He may execute strikes against monster lairs, rescue hostages, or eliminate tribal leaders or spell casters. For a determined Justifier, no job is too difficult, no enemy too formidable.

Requirements: Justifiers must have minimum scores of 14 in Strength and Dexterity. They must be human and of lawful good alignment.

Primary Terrain: Any.

Role: Justifiers boast extensive training in weapon use, scouting, warding, and outdoor survival. Some learn these skills in a regular standing military, others are trained by military orders. A few highly motivated individuals are self-taught. Justifiers are in high demand by rulers as army officers, as well as by private individuals who use them as bodyguards. Many hire themselves out as mercenaries or volunteer for causes that further their own ideals.

As Justifiers thrive on action, most are eager to join adventuring parties. On occasion, freelance Justifiers may demand a retainer from a party or a guaranteed percentage of any treasure found. But more often than not, a freelance Justifier will join a party without remuneration if their task is just and promises him the chance to exercise his combat skills.

A Justifier's companions will find him disciplined, focused, and unyielding in his determination to accomplish his objectives. He socializes little, preferring instead to keep his body strong with punishing exercise and his mind sharp with quiet meditation. A natural leader in combat situations, he fights with grim intensity and fearless perseverance.

Secondary Skills: Armorer, Bowyer/Fletcher, Forester, Hunter, Trapper/Furrier, Weaponsmith.

Weapon Proficiencies: *Recommended:* Bow (any), crossbow (any), dagger, sling, spear, sword (any). See Special Bonuses.

Nonweapon Proficiencies: *Bonus:* Survival; in addition to having this proficiency in his primary terrain, the Justifier receives the proficiency in an extra terrain of his choice (see also, Special Hin-

drances). *Recommended:* Alertness*, Blind-fighting, Bowyer/Fletcher, Camouflage*, Endurance, Falconry*, Hunting, Mountaineering, Navigation, Riding (Land-based), Rope Use, Running, Set Snares, Swimming, Weaponsmithing.

Armor/Equipment: A Justifier has no special armor or equipment requirements. Though most Justifiers prefer light armor, such as leather, they can wear any type of armor and still hide in shadows and move silently. Refer to Table 13: Optional Armor Adjustments in Chapter 1 for adjustments to success chances.

Species Enemy: Any. A Justifier is more respected by his enemies than other rangers, and therefore suffers only a –2 penalty on encounter reactions with his species enemy, and no penalty if there is a formal truce.

Followers: Any.

Special Benefits:

Weapon Specialization: Because of his extensive combat training, the Justifier must use some of his initial proficiency slots to take one weapon specialization (see Chapter 5 of the *Player's Handbook*). The weapon of specialization is taken from the list of recommended weapons.

Stealth: The Justifier receives a +5% bonus to his chance of hiding in natural surroundings and to his chance of moving silently.

Tactical Advantage: This ability allows the Justifier and his companions to gain a combat advantage by studying the enemy and exploiting their weaknesses. The Justifier must spend at least a full, uninterrupted turn secretly observing an enemy or group of enemies prior to making an attack. At the end of this period, the Justifier makes a Wisdom check. If successful, the Justifier has correctly assessed the enemy's weaknesses and is able to maximize the timing of an attack. The Justifier and his party automatically surprise the enemy and gain the initiative for the first round. A Justifier can attempt to gain a tactical advantage only once in a particular encounter.

Unarmed Combat Expertise: When fighting with his bare hands, the Justifier inflicts 1-4 points of damage on a successful attack roll. If the Justifier throws an unmodified 20 on his attack roll, the victim suffers 1-4 points of damage and must also make a saving throw vs. paralyzation. If the throw fails, the victim is stunned for 1-6 rounds.

Coordinated Attack: The Justifier can use this ability, in conjunction with a trained animal follower, to inflict maximum damage on an opponent. The animal follower must have been trained to attack on command (see the Training Followers rules in Chapter 3).

To attempt a coordinated attack, the Justifier and the animal both make a single attack on the same enemy in the same round (even if one or both are normally allowed multiple attacks; the animal will use its most damaging attack). If either roll misses, then that attacker automatically loses initiative in the next round. If both rolls hit, each attack causes twice the normal amount of damage. A coordinated attack involves only one follower. A coordinated attack may be attempted at any time during a combat, but only once against any particular opponent during an encounter.

Special Hindrances:

Limited Proficiencies: The Justifier's mastery of weapons and combat comes at the expense of learning other skills. For this reason, he receives only one nonweapon proficiency slot at 1st level (in addition to his Survival bonus). He acquires additional proficiency slots at the normal rate.

Limited Spell Use: Because the Justifier devotes less time to the study of magic than to the military arts, he has less access to spells than other rangers. The Justifier doesn't acquire spells until he reaches 10th level. Table 46 shows the Justifier's spell progression.

Table 46: Justifier Spell Progression

Justifier Level	Casting Level	Priest Spell Level		
		1	2	3
1-9	-	-	-	-
10	1	1	-	-
11	2	2	-	-
12	3	2	1	-
13	4	2	2	-
14	5	2	2	1
15	6	2	2	2
16+	7	3	2	2

Mountain Man

Description: Some people find the lure of the wild irresistible. Having tasted the pleasure of life in its purest, most primitive state, these hardy souls reject the trappings of civilization and wholeheartedly embrace the challenges of the untamed wilderness. These Mountain Men (and Women) spend their lives in relative isolation, enduring uncertain climates, hostile creatures, and chronic shortages of food and other vital supplies. They couldn't be happier.

The typical Mountain Man is robust, courageous, and uncomplicated. Book learning and formal schooling mean far less than self-reliance and common sense. Though uneducated by conventional standards, the Mountain Man has mastered all the skills needed to survive. He can manufacture his own weapons from the crudest materials, brew potent medicines from wild herbs, and doggedly persist in strenuous physical labor when others have long since succumbed to exhaustion. While hunting wild game and navigating dangerous terrain may be daunting to an outsider, it's all in a day's work for the Mountain Man.

Requirements: A Mountain Man must have a minimum Strength of 14 and a minimum Constitution of 15. The Mountain Man cannot be a full elf.

Primary Terrain: *Required:* Mountains.

Role: Mountain Men value privacy more than comfort. Accordingly, they make their homes in secluded caves or crude shacks hidden in remote mountain ranges. Many are nomadic, wandering from place to place with their possessions strapped to their backs, or carried by a bear or other loyal animal follower. They have little need for money, but occasionally procure goods from traveling salesmen or small town merchants, bartering with fur or hides.

Even the most stubbornly independent Mountain Man hankers for human companionship now and then, which is one of the reasons he might agree to hook up with an adventuring party. Faced with a problem too formidable for him to tackle alone—such as an encroachment from an enemy army or an infestation of powerful monsters—a Mountain Man may seek out an agreeable party to lend him a hand.

The Mountain Man speaks his mind openly and directly, regardless of who he might offend. Etiquette is hardly his strong suit, nor is personal hygiene. While some party members may find the Mountain Man's straightforward approach to life refreshing, or even endearing, most will probably view him as an unsophisticated brute, gruff and ill-mannered. Some Mountain Men have a crude sense of humor that compels them to play adolescent practical jokes, such as leaving bear droppings in a companion's sleeping bag. The Mountain Man has little interest in art or philosophy, but is a natural storyteller and loves to tell outlandishly embellished tales—often of his own exploits. He approaches combat much as he does the other elements of his life, attacking with vigor.

Secondary Skills: Bowyer/Fletcher, Fisher, Forester, Hunter, Miner, Trapper/Furrier.

Weapon Proficiencies: A Mountain Man must choose his initial weapon proficiencies from among the following: axe (any), bow (any), crossbow (any), club, dagger, dart, javelin, knife, quarterstaff, spear, staff sling, warhammer.

Nonweapon Proficiencies: *Bonus:* Mountaineering. *Required:* Hunting. *Recommended:* Alertness*, Endurance, Fire-building, Foraging, Mining, Running, Set Snares, Signaling*, Trail Marking*, Trail Signs*, Weather Sense. *Barred:* Agriculture, Armorer, Blacksmithing, Boating*, Bowyer/Fletcher (included in the special Weaponsmithing bonus, described below), Charioteering, Engineering, Etiquette, Falconry*, Heraldry, Navigation, Reading/Writing, Seamanship, Spellcraft.

Special Bonus: The Mountain Man also receives Weaponsmithing (Crude) as a bonus proficiency. He is restricted to making the weapons listed in Table 47, and can only make weapons in which he is proficient. He uses stones, wood, and other naturally available materials, so these weapons are made at no cost. This proficiency can't be improved; that is, assigning additional slots to Crude Weaponsmithing has no effect.

Optional Rule: If a weapon made of stone or bone scores a hit, roll 1d6. A stone weapon shatters on a roll of 1; a bone weapon shatters on a roll of 1 or 2 (as per *The Complete Fighter's Handbook*).

Table 47: Crude Weaponsmithing (Mountain Man)

Weapon	Construction Time
Arrows	7/day
Axe, Battle	4 days
Axe, Hand	1 day
Axe, Throwing	6 days
Bow, Long*	15 days
Bow, Short	12 days
Dagger	2 days
Dart	3/day
Javelin	1 day
Knife	2 days
Quarterstaff	1 day
Spear	2 days
Staff Sling	3 days
Warhammer	5 days

*Seasoning the wood takes 1 year.

Armor/Equipment: A Mountain Man begins his career with any two weapons in which he has a weapon proficiency. He receives these weapons at no charge. These weapons are handmade. Once his career is begun, the Mountain Man may manufacture additional weapons in accordance with the rules for his Crude Weaponsmithing proficiency. He may also use weapons he obtains from his companions or other sources.

A Mountain Man normally doesn't wear armor. Instead, he wears a handmade suit of leather and fur which gives him an Armor Class of 8. A Mountain Man often decorates his suit with dyed porcupine quills or strings of colorful pebbles. He sometimes adds bone necklaces, elaborate leather fringes, or a hat made of beaver or raccoon skin.

Though not strictly forbidden from wearing metal armor, a Mountain Man is so uncomfortable when doing so that he suffers a –2 penalty to all attack rolls.

Species Enemy: Any.

Followers: A Mountain Man has only a 20% chance of attracting human, demihuman, or humanoid followers. Treat a roll of 81-00 as a bear (type determined by DM: usually black, brown, or cave). Any followers rolled as full elves will be dwarves instead (except for full elf mages, who will instead be gnome illusionists).

Special Benefits:

Will to Live: Where others would submit to death, the hardy Mountain Man clings to life ferociously. This ability manifests itself in the following ways:

- If missing a saving throw vs. death magic would be fatal, the Mountain Man receives a +2 saving throw bonus.
- If a damage roll would reduce the Mountain Man to zero hit points or less, the Mountain Man makes a Constitution check. If the check succeeds, he is reduced to 1 hit point. A Mountain Man cannot use this ability if he has only 1 hit point remaining.
- If an encounter results in the death of a Mountain Man, he may not die immediately. If he makes a *system shock* roll, he fights on for another 1-4 rounds or until he suffers damage below –10 hit points equal to his level, whichever occurs first. He then drops dead.

Brew Healing Elixir: When a Mountain Man reaches 7th level, he gains the ability to brew a special healing elixir. He must spend 1-4 hours gathering the necessary fresh herbs and mosses, usually available in any forest, jungle, or mountain region (as determined by the DM). It takes an hour to brew the elixir, which remains potent for 24 hours. The elixir acts as one dose of a *potion of healing*. The Mountain Man may brew the healing elixir once per day.

Special Hindrances:

Limited Stealth: The Mountain Man has a –5% chance to hide in natural surroundings and a –5% chance of moving silently.

Limited Magic: A Mountain Man lacks the patience and discipline to wield magic effectively. He memorizes fewer spells than other rangers and doesn't acquire them until he reaches 10th level (see Table 48).

Table 48: Mountain Man Spell Progression

Mountain Man Level	Casting Level	Priest Spell Level		
		1	2	3
1-9	–	–	–	–
10-11	1	1	–	–
12-13	2	2	–	–
14-15	3	2	1	–
16+	4	2	2	–

No Fortifications: A Mountain Man has no interest in fortifications and will never build one.

Limited Money: Other than his weapons and clothing, a Mountain Man may own only a single item worth 15 gp or more. The total value of all of his other possessions, including money and treasure, save training costs, cannot exceed 100 gp. Excess treasure and possessions are given away as the Mountain Man sees fit. (However, the Mountain Man still receives all experience points due him for finding treasure and fellow party members receive no experience point benefit for the gifts from a Mountain Man.)

Reaction Penalty: The Mountain Man's crude manner and ungainly appearance make strangers uncomfortable. He suffers a –1 reaction adjustment from all NPCs.

The Mountain Man suffers a –2 reaction penalty when encountering nobles, aristocrats, and other cultural elite, as they find him particularly unpleasant.

Pathfinder

Description: The Pathfinder has an uncanny knack for blazing trails, a skill that allows him to find the easiest routes, reduce travel time, and avoid natural hazards. His acute sense of direction minimizes his chance of getting lost. He can estimate the number of miles he's covered with startling accuracy. The Pathfinder makes an invaluable guide, helping to ensure safe and efficient passage.

Though Pathfinders come from all walks of life, most have homelands in sparsely settled or exceptionally hostile terrains where learning to find one's way can mean the difference between life and death. A Pathfinder usually demonstrates an aptitude for trailblazing early in life, but diligent practice is required to refine his skills. Often, a young Pathfinder exercises his skill by asking a companion to blindfold him, lead him into an unexplored area in the wilderness, then abandon him. The Pathfinder must find his way home using only his wits. Experienced Pathfinders occasionally engage in this game to brush up on their technique or to impress potential clients.

Requirements: Same as standard ranger.

Primary Terrain: Forest, Hill, Jungle, Mountain, or Plains.

Role: Though some Pathfinders are retainers of kings or lords, most operate independently. Pathfinders are generally regarded as honest, although their services are rarely inexpensive.

Being characters of high principle, Pathfinders often offer their services to parties undertaking adventures to promote the common good. Rarely will a Pathfinder join a party purely for gain, though he may consider such an arrangement when business is slow.

As a member of an adventuring party, the Pathfinder usually finds himself in front, scouting the terrain ahead to ascertain the best route and spot potential hazards. Unless the Pathfinder has organized the party himself, he usually leaves the leadership role to someone else while he concentrates on trailblazing.

Secondary Skills: Farmer, Forester, Groom, Hunter, Navigator, Trapper/Furrier.

Weapon Proficiencies: A Pathfinder must fill an initial weapon slot with the machete (see Chapter 7), hand axe, or sword; such weapons are useful for cutting away brush and clearing paths. Subsequent slots may be filled with any weapons of his choice (see also Special Benefits).

Nonweapon Proficiencies: *Bonus:* Direction Sense, Distance Sense*, Trail Marking*. *Required:* Alertness*. *Recommended:* Camouflage*, Endurance, Fire-building, Foraging*, Mountaineering, Navigation, Signaling*, Trail Signs*, Weather Sense.

Armor/Equipment: Because he spends a lot of time on foot, the Pathfinder favors light armor, such as leather or padded. He seldom carries a shield. Otherwise, the Pathfinder has no particular preferences or requirements.

Species Enemy: Any.

Followers: All species are eligible, though the Pathfinder is likely to attract followers with higher movement rates (12+), as he tends to have little patience with creatures that can't keep up with him.

Special Benefits:

The first two benefits, *trail sense* and *overland guiding*, apply only when the Pathfinder leads the party. At least 20 feet must separate the Pathfinder from the rest of the party; the proximity of others distracts the Pathfinder, making him unable to take advantage of these benefits.

Trail Sense: The Pathfinder's chance of getting lost in any outdoor land setting is reduced by 10%. Furthermore, his base chance of getting lost in his primary terrain (i.e. the Surroundings column of Table 81 in the *DUNGEON MASTER Guide*) will not exceed 20%. This is not cumulative with other benefits, such as the one for the direction sense proficiency.

Overland Guiding: A Pathfinder is able to find the optimum trail through rough terrain, increasing the party's movement rate when traversing long distances. To determine terrain costs for overland movement when a Pathfinder leads the party, use Table 49 in this book in place of Table 74 in Chapter 14 of the *DUNGEON MASTER Guide*. The movement costs indicate points of movement spent per mile of travel; when moving through the various terrain types, subtract the points from the total movement available to the party for that day. (Note that less rugged terrain types are relatively unaffected, as the optimum paths are usually obvious, even without the help of a Pathfinder.)

Table 49: Terrain Costs for Pathfinders

Terrain Type	Movement Cost
Barren, wasteland	1
Clear, farmland	1/2
Desert, rocky	1
Desert, sand	2
Forest, light	1
Forest, medium	2
Forest, heavy	3
Glacier	1
Hills, rolling	1
Hills, steep (foothills)	3
Jungle, medium	4
Jungle, heavy	6
Marsh, swamp	6
Moor	3
Mountains, low	3
Mountains, medium	4
Mountains, high	6
Plains, grassland, heath	1
Scrub, brushland	1
Tundra	2

Marksmanship: Owing to his steady hand and acute vision, the Pathfinder has a +1 bonus to the

attacks made with a favorite missile weapon. It must be one in which he has proficiency and selected as a weapon of choice.

Recognize Trail Hazard. By observing subtle changes in the terrain, the Pathfinder is able to recognize natural hazards, enabling him and his companions to avoid them. Typical hazards include quicksand, sinkholes, slippery slopes, and thin ice. A Pathfinder has no special ability to recognize man-made hazards, such as pit traps or dangerous bridges, nor does he have any special talent for anticipating encounters with hostile natives or animals.

A Pathfinder's chance of recognizing a hazard is 10% per experience level; to a maximum chance of 90% at ninth level. If the DM determines that the Pathfinder is approaching an area containing a natural hazard, he secretly rolls percentile dice. If the roll is equal to or less than the Pathfinder's chance, the Pathfinder recognizes a potential hazard. (Optionally, the DM might only describe an unusual aspect of the terrain and let the Pathfinder come to his own conclusions. For example, if the Pathfinder is approaching a pool of quicksand, the DM might say that the ground feels exceptionally spongy. If the Pathfinder nears a patch of thin ice, the DM might point out that the ice ahead is discolored and laced with tiny cracks).

Special Hindrances: By moving ahead of the party, the Pathfinder places himself in a position of risk. Separated from his companions, the Pathfinder is more likely to be the victim of enemy attacks. He runs a greater risk of drawing fire from snipers, and is more susceptible to ambushes from hostile creatures. If he fails to recognize a hazard, he'll probably be the first to become a victim.

Sea Ranger

Description: Though most rangers live and work on land, the Sea Ranger makes his home at sea. Whether sailing the ocean in a mighty galleon or riding a river's currents in a handmade raft, the Sea Ranger finds the world's waters an endless source of wonder. A sailor and an adventurer, he guards his watery domain with vigilance, and counts many of its creatures among his friends and allies.

He has an extensive understanding of weather patterns at sea and of the behavior of marine animals. He specializes in combat, both on and under the water. He may be a member of a formal navy, an independent operator, or a mercenary. He may be charged with enforcing naval laws. Some Sea Rangers protect ports or fishing territories. Others serve as escorts for trade fleets.

Aquatic Terrain: For the purposes of this kit, Aquatic terrain includes oceans, lakes, ponds, and rivers, as well as coastlines, beaches, and small islands.

Requirements: Because a Sea Ranger must master a wide range of knowledge he requires a minimum Intelligence score of 12. Because few elves and half-elves have the temperament for the seaman's life, virtually all Sea Rangers are human (though being human isn't a strict requirement).

Primary Terrain: *Required:* Aquatic.

Role: Sea Rangers have reputations as dedicated, sharp-minded professionals. As such, they are often sought by adventuring parties in need of their special skills, particularly when an adventure takes them to aquatic environments or they expect to face opponents of oceanic origin. Though Sea Rangers generally prefer to remain at sea, they travel on land as necessary to achieve the goals of their party. As many of a Sea Ranger's followers are waterbound, he obviously has less access to them when adventuring on land, a handicap he endures graciously but without enthusiasm.

The environment has a profound effect on a Sea Ranger's attitude. On land, his party companions will find him hesitant and uncertain, following orders without comment and reluctant to offer advice. In an aquatic setting, however, he becomes a different person—confident, assertive, and commanding. Only the most stubborn or foolish parties will decline a leadership role to a Sea Ranger in watery terrain.

Secondary Skills: Fisher, Navigator, Sailor, Shipwright, Trader/Barterer, Weaver.

Weapon Proficiencies: *Recommended:* Dagger, knife, harpoon, sword (any), pole arm (any), trident; *Optional:* Belaying pin, cutlass, gaff/hook.

Nonweapon Proficiencies: *Bonus:* Boating* or Seamanship; Swimming. *Recommended:* Cartography*, Direction Sense, Distance Sense*, Endurance, Fishing, Navigation, Riding (Sea-based)*, Rope Use. *Barred:* Agriculture, Blacksmithing, Charioteering, Falconry*, Mining, Mountaineering, Rid-

ing (Land-based), Spelunking*, Stonemasonry.

Armor/Equipment: Because heavy armor interferes with swimming and makes moving around a ship uncomfortable, most Sea Rangers wear armor with an AC of 8 or less.

Species Enemy: Any aquatic creature is eligible as a species enemy.

Followers: The primary terrain of all animal followers must be Aquatic. Any full elf follower is 80% likely to be an aquatic elf.

Special Benefits:

Sea Tracking: Because of his knowledge of prevailing winds, currents, and other general aquatic conditions, the Sea Ranger can effectively track waterborne craft and aquatic creatures. This is not so much a reading of physical signs as an instinctive deduction of the probable course and destination of the quarry. For purposes of general play, the Sea Ranger uses the normal Tracking proficiency check rules.

Land Scent: When at sea, the Sea Ranger can smell the presence of land (including islands) within 50 miles. Further, if the Sea Ranger has ever been to that land before, he has a 10% chance per level of identifying it precisely.

Sea Legs: The Sea Ranger has a fine sense of balance, which comes into play when he must fight on a narrow beam (such as a yardarm or boarding plank) or a pitching deck. Not only is he sure-footed under such conditions (avoiding any attack penalties for them), but any saving throws or Dexterity checks made to maintain his balance are made at a +2 bonus.

Aquatic Combat: A Sea Ranger suffers no penalties to his attack rolls when in water; otherwise he follows the standard rules for underwater combat given in Chapter 9 of the *DUNGEON MASTER Guide*.

Parliament of Fishes: When a Sea Ranger reaches 12th level, he may attempt to call a *parliament of fishes*. He may use this ability once per week. If successful, the Sea Ranger can demand a service of the school. Typical services include the location or recovery of small items, the provision of edible water plants, information about local monsters or

conditions, and perhaps transport across a small body of water if the parliament members are large enough. Once a month this can be the equivalent of a *commune with nature* spell.

To call a *parliament of fishes*, the Sea Ranger locates a pond, lake, or any other body of water containing aquatic life. Sometime between sunset and dawn, he kneels beside the body of water and concentrates for a full turn. An attack or interruption in any other way during this time will break his concentration, and he can't attempt to call a *parliament of fishes* until the following week.

Otherwise, at the end of 10 rounds, 10-100 (10d10) fish or other aquatic creatures (as appropriate to the body of water) surface and stare expectantly at the Sea Ranger. The Sea Ranger must then toss an offering into the water; the gift may be food, a coin, or any other object of the ranger's choice.

The DM then rolls 1d10 and consults Table 50. If the offer was reasonably generous, increase the result by +1. If the offering was exceptionally valuable, increase the result by +2. If the offering was meager (a copper piece or a chunk of bread), decrease the result by –1. If the offering was essentially worthless (a bone or a chunk of rock), decrease the result by –2. The result can't be decreased below 1 or raised above 10.

Table 50: Parliament of Fishes Results

D10 Roll	Results
1-2	The fish immediately submerge; the offer is rejected. From dawn to sunrise the following day, the ranger suffers a –1 penalty to all attack rolls and ability checks.
3-7	The fish swim listlessly in circles for a few moments, then submerge; the offer is neither rejected nor accepted. The ranger is unaffected.
8-10	The fish dive and splash excitedly for a few moments, then submerge; the offer is accepted. The parliament grants the ranger a boon within their power.

Special Hindrances:

Tracking Limitation: A Sea Ranger's chance of tracking in non-Aquatic terrain is *halved*.

Move Silently/Hide in Shadows: The Sea Ranger has neither of these abilities, replacing them with Sea Legs and Aquatic Combat.

Seeker

Description: Devoted to spiritual awareness and self-enlightenment, the Seeker's deep beliefs affect him more than any other elements of his life. The Seeker seeks fulfillment by following the tenets of his faith and striving to understand the relationship between himself and the natural world. He views animal followers as fellow travelers on his spiritual journey.

Seekers can come from any culture, but typically originate from societies placing a premium on religion and scholarship. Many Seekers begin their spiritual quests as students of priests. Others are self-taught philosophers or restless academicians hungry for knowledge that can't be learned from books. Regardless of their background, all Seekers have felt compelled to embark on a wilderness pilgrimage that may last the rest of their lives.

No particular religion is common to all Seekers. Some worship specific gods, while others venerate nature itself as an unknowable but all-encompassing force. All Seekers, however share a reverence for life and a philosophy that embodies discipline, and personal responsibility, and self-sacrifice.

Requirements: A Seeker must have a Wisdom score of 15 or more. A particular religion may impose additional requirements, as determined by the DM.

Primary Terrain: Any.

Role: Good people of all cultures tend to look favorably on Seekers. At worst, Seekers are dismissed as useless but harmless eccentrics. More often, they're regarded as sensitive seekers of truth, admired and respected for their devotion. Priests of compatible alignment are especially deferential to Seekers; even if such a priest follows a different belief system, he recognizes that the Seeker shares his veneration of a higher power.

Though Seekers generally prefer solitude, they constantly seek opportunities to broaden their outlook and stimulate spiritual insight. For these reasons, they may join adventuring parties solely

for the promise of new experiences. Moral considerations also motivate Seekers; parties can sometimes recruit Seekers by appealing to their sense of justice.

Typically, the companions of a Seeker will find him amiable, thoughtful, and comforting. Seekers aren't proselytizers—rarely are they interested in converting others to their beliefs—but they enjoy nothing more than debating philosophical issues. A companion who engages a Seeker in such a discussion may find himself listening to a detailed, scholarly discourse that may last the better part of the day.

Though Seekers usually decline to make decisions for the party, they often serve as counselors and advisors to the leaders. Non-aggressive by nature, Seekers avoid combat whenever possible, but fight fearlessly to thwart attacks against their followers or comrades. A Seeker is reluctant to take the life of another creature except to protect a companion, a follower, or himself, or to destroy his species enemy.

Secondary Skills: Farmer, Forester, Groom, Mason, Scribe, Tailor/Weaver, Woodworker/Carpenter.

Weapon Proficiencies: A Seeker receives only a single weapon proficiency at first level. This proficiency must be spent on one of the following weapons: club, light crossbow, dagger, dart, knife, quarterstaff, or sickle, sling. He cannot ever use a sword of any type.

Nonweapon Proficiencies: *Bonus:* Religion. *Recommended:* Agriculture, Ancient History, Artistic Ability, Astrology, Carpentry, Cobbling, Etiquette, Languages (Ancient), Pottery, Reading/Writing, Spellcraft, Veterinary Healing*, Weaving. The Seeker can take clerical proficiencies at the listed (non-doubled) costs.

Armor/Equipment: In most cases, Seekers have no special equipment restrictions beyond those normally associated with rangers. However, Seekers worshipping particular gods or adhering to strict religious doctrines may have additional restrictions, as determined by the DM. Certain Seekers, for example, may be forbidden from using any bladed weapon or wearing any type of armor. Such restrictions should be made clear at the outset of the Seeker's career.

Seekers have little interest in material possessions. After keeping enough money to meet their basic needs, they typically give away the rest of their gold and treasure to the poor.

Species Enemy: The species enemy must be evil. Alternately, a specific evilly-aligned religious group or cult may be taken, in which case members and minions of the group are considered the species enemy. Other common species enemies include ghouls (and other undead), evil dragons, death dogs, evil humanoids, etc.

Followers: All creatures are eligible as followers, except the species designated as a sacred animal (see the Special Hindrances section).

Special Benefits:

Increased Access to Spells: Unlike other rangers, the Seeker acquires spells when he reaches 6th level. He can also cast 4th level spells. Table 51 shows the Seeker's spell progression.

The Seeker has access to spells from an extra sphere in addition to those of plant and animal. When reaching 6th level, he chooses an extra sphere from the following options: divination, healing, protection, weather. This extra sphere remains the same for the rest of his career.

Magical Staff Use: The Seeker can use any magical staff that can be used by a druid.

Table 51: Seeker Spell Progression

Seeker Level	Casting Level	Priest Spell Levels			
		1	2	3	4
1-5	-	-	-	-	-
6	1	1	-	-	-
7	2	2	-	-	-
8	3	2	1	-	-
9	4	2	2	-	-
10	5	2	2	1	-
11	6	3	2	1	-
12	7	3	2	2	-
13	8	3	3	2	1
14	9	3	3	3	1
15	10	4	4	3	1
16+	11	4	4	3	2

Special Hindrances:

Mediation: A Seeker must spend a full hour each day in silent meditation. This hour must

always occur at the same time of day, such as the first hour of dawn or at high noon; once decided, it can never be changed. If a Seeker neglects to mediate or is interrupted more than once (for more than a total of two rounds), he suffers a –1 penalty to all ability checks and attack rolls the following day.

Sacred Animal: Every Seeker has a sacred animal that symbolizes his ideals. A Seeker's sacred animal at the same time he is determined at the same time as the species enemy. The player selects the sacred animal from the options listed in Table 52, subject to the DM's approval; for example, if the Seeker's primary terrain is Arctic, his sacred animal might be the polar bear, the snow leopard, or the seal. A Seeker retains the same sacred animal throughout his career. He cannot acquire a follower of the same species as his sacred animal. The player may choose a sacred animal other than those listed in Table 52, so long as it's different from the Seeker's species enemy.

Table 52: Sacred Animals

Primary Terrain	Species
Aquatic	Dolphin, whale, or giant turtle
Arctic	Polar bear, snow leopard, or seal
Desert	Camel, owl, or hawk
Forest	Bear (brown or black), wolf, or small mammal (raccoon, fox, squirrel, or rabbit)
Hills	Bear (black or brown), elk, or wolf
Jungle	Elephant, lion, or chimpanzee
Mountains	Wild eagle, giant eagle, or bear (black or brown)
Plains	Falcon, horse, or raven
Swamp	Owl, raven, or small mammal (fox, otter, or mouse)

In compliance with his religious principles, the Seeker has vowed to protect his sacred animal in the following ways:
- He is forbidden from intentionally or unintentionally inflicting harm on his sacred animal, or standing by while others do.
- He is required to care for injured or ailing sacred animals.
- He must liberate captive sacred animals held against their will. This requirement excludes followers of other rangers, or domesticated animals serving as pets or mounts. However, it includes farm animals that are being raised for consumption.
- He must protect his sacred animal from hunters, trappers, and predators.

If the Seeker violates any of these requirements, as determined by the DM, he is consumed with guilt and remorse, preventing him from casting spells of any kind for the next week. If his action or inaction directly results in the death of a sacred animal, he is unable to cast spells for a full month. If he benefits from an *atonement* spell cast by a sympathetic priest, the one week suspension is reduced to four days, and the month suspension is reduced to two weeks.

Stalker

Description: At first glance, this soft-spoken, rather nondescript character seems hopelessly out of place in an adventuring party, looking instead like an town dweller who's wandered into the wilderness by mistake. But the drab demeanor is only a facade, concealing keen senses, a shrewd mind, and remarkable insight. Only his closest friends realize the extent of his expertise in intelligence-gathering. And that's just the way he likes it.

Stalkers serve as spies, informants, and interrogators. Unlike other rangers, Stalkers are comfortable in both wilderness and urban settings. A Stalker may covertly observe a bandit camp to inventory their supplies and hostages, or eavesdrop in the corridors of an evil wizard's castle. A few innocuous questions enable him to distinguish friend from foe, and fact from fiction. His mastery of stealth makes him a deadly opponent.

Requirements: A Stalker must have a minimum Intelligence score of 14. Stalkers must be human.

Primary Terrain: Any; in addition, the Stalker's primary terrain can be Urban (see Special Benefits).

Role: Stalkers tend to be introspective and reflective, valuing intellect over physical prowess. They avoid drawing attention to themselves, seldom speaking unless directly addressed, then responding succinctly and without elaboration. They avoid small talk and

socializing, instead preferring the company of a good book or an hour spent examining an unusual footprint. Stalkers tend to suppress their emotions so their decisions aren't colored by what they consider to be irrelevancies.

Though most people respect Stalkers, they are also wary of them. The Stalker's stealthiness and secrecy make many people uneasy, as these are traits usually associated with thieves and sneaks. But Stalkers value honor as much as any ranger, and nobles rarely hesitate to hire one in times of crisis. A hired Stalker can be trusted to focus on the job at hand, complete it efficiently, make his report, then go his own way without comment.

Adventuring parties often hire Stalkers on retainer, though occasionally, a Stalker will join a party with no assurance of monetary reward if the adventure presents an intriguing challenge. Stalkers rarely are party leaders, though they express their opinions freely when invited to do so. In combat, most Stalkers are brave but cautious, waiting for tactical opportunities to present themselves rather than charging into the fray. They prefer to surprise their opponents, striking silently and quickly.

Secondary Skills: Any.

Weapon Proficiencies: Stalkers become proficient only with weapons they can easily conceal. Their weapon proficiencies are limited to blowgun, dagger, dart, knife, short sword, staff, and sling. *Optional:* garrote, rapier (walking stick), stiletto.

Nonweapon Proficiencies: *Bonus:* Alertness*, Camouflage*. *Recommended:* Blind-fighting, Etiquette, Modern Languages, Persuasion*, Signaling*, Trail Marking*, Trail Signs*.

Armor/Equipment: A Stalker prefers to carry no more gear than he can comfortably strap to his back. He wears well-made but unpretentious clothing, similar to that of a laborer or peasant, that allows him to blend in with crowds. Though he can wear any type of armor (see Special Benefits) he favors leather. Stalkers almost never carry shields, finding them awkward and restrictive.

At the beginning of his career, a Stalker receives a free "terrain suit" (see Chapter 7). The terrain suit corresponds to his primary terrain (night black for Urban).

Species Enemy: Any. Optionally, the Stalker can declare a specific thieves' guild or assassin's guild as his enemy.

Followers: Because a Stalker prefers to work unhampered, his followers are limited in number, species, and size. Though he receives a career total of 2d6 followers like other rangers, a Stalker has only one follower at a time. A new follower won't appear until the Stalker's current follower dies or is dismissed. A Stalker won't acquire a new follower even if he releases his current follower or arranges for its care elsewhere; he must sever all ties with the old follower before another will arrive.

A Stalker never accepts human or demihuman followers. Nor will he accept followers whose intelligence compares favorably with that of humans, such as pixies or aarakocra, as he fears such beings are undependable and may cause unnecessary distractions. Because he wishes to minimize the chances of attracting attention, all animal followers must be less than four feet tall (size "S" or "T").

Special Benefits:

Tracking: A Stalker has normal ranger tracking abilities in outdoor land settings. In addition, he has full (not half) tracking capabilities in urban settings.

Stealth Abilities:

- A Stalker has a +10% bonus to his base chance to hide in shadows/hide in natural surroundings and a +10% bonus to his chances to move silently.

- A Stalker has the full (not half) chance for success when attempting to hide in shadows or move silently in urban settings or in non-natural constructions such as crypts or dungeons.

- Stalkers can hide in shadows and move silently when wearing armor of AC 6 or less (see Table 13: Optional Armor in Chapter 1).

- When a Stalker successfully uses his move silently ability to sneak up on a opponent to surprise him, the opponent suffers a –3 penalty to his surprise roll. The Stalker must be 90' or more from party members without similar silent movement abilities.

Interrogation: When interrogating an NPC for any reason, a Stalker can acquire special knowledge about the NPC in one (but not both) of the following ways:

- By making a successful Intelligence check (use half the Intelligence score, rounded up), the Stalker can determine the general alignment of the NPC. If successful, the Stalker learns the good-evil component of the NPC's alignment (good, neutral, or evil).
- The Stalker can ascertain the NPC's honesty. The DM secretly makes an Intelligence check for the Stalker. If the check fails, the DM tells the Stalker nothing about the honesty of the NPC. The Stalker must make up his own mind about the NPC's reliability based on the NPC's responses.

If the check succeeds and the NPC is being honest with the Stalker, the DM tells the Stalker that the NPC is telling the truth to the best of his knowledge. A successful check in no way compels the NPC to reveal any information to the Stalker. The NPC may refuse to cooperate, but the Stalker is assured of the truthfulness of anything the NPC decides to share (note that the NPC may still pass along unreliable information that he believes to be true).

If the check succeeds, and the NPC is being dishonest with the Stalker, the DM tells the Stalker that the NPC may be lying. It's up to the Stalker to separate the truth from the lies; a successful check only tells him that he shouldn't take everything the NPC says at face value.

Photographic Memory: When a Stalker reaches 10th level, he acquires a limited photographic memory, enabling him to recall details about anything he's seen or heard since achieving 10th level. He can recall a fragment of a conversation, conjure up a mental image of a place he's visited, or remember words on a printed page. To use this ability, the DM secretly makes a Intelligence check for the Stalker, with a –2 penalty. If the roll fails, the memory is too vague to be of any use to the Stalker. If the roll succeeds, the DM tells the Stalker what he wishes to remember. If the roll is a natural 20, the DM gives the Stalker intentionally misleading information about whatever he's trying to remember (a room, for instance, is incorrectly recalled as having a locked window or mysterious claw marks on the walls). Because of the mental stress involved, this ability can be used only once per day.

Special Hindrances: Neither lawbreakers nor outlaws appreciate snoops. Typically, the harshest possible penalties are reserved for captured Stalkers. Should a band of orcs or goblins realize that a Stalker is in their midst, they're likely to chase him down and beat him mercilessly. A Stalker caught lurking in private residence will probably be prosecuted to the fullest extent of the law. An otherwise friendly NPC may be less likely to cooperate with the party if he recognizes one of the members as a Stalker.

Warden

Description: The Warden works for a noble, king, or wealthy land-owner, and is charged with managing and protecting a tract of land owned by his overlord. He keeps his overlord's land free of monsters, guards against spies and trespassers, intervenes when natural disasters occur, and sees to the welfare of the animal population. While a Warden may operate alone, making decisions as he sees fit, he ultimately answers to a higher authority.

Areas overseen by Wardens vary by size and geography, depending on their overlords' holdings and interests. A Warden may be in charge of a game reserve or oversee a parcel of farmland. He may supervise a private park, or be responsible for undeveloped property in the mountains or desert. The size of a guarded land may range from a few square miles for Wardens just beginning their careers, to vast estates for high-level Wardens. Generally, as a Warden's experience increases, so do the boundaries of the land he supervises.

Requirements: As a representative of a greater lord, a Warden is required to deal diplomatically with a variety people from all walks of life. Therefore, a Warden must have a minimum Charisma of 12. A Warden cannot be of chaotic alignment.

Primary Terrain: Any, though Forest and Plains are the most common. The primary terrain should correspond to the area the Warden is first assigned to supervise.

Role: In most societies, Wardens occupy positions of modest status, comparable to those of mid-level bureaucrats or well-to-do merchants. Some are members of the military, but more often, they're aides to government officials or

affluent civilians. Wardens tend to hold the same job for life.

A Warden serves his lord with the loyalty of a good soldier. He tends to be fastidious in his behavior and strictly law-abiding, which also makes him a bit inflexible. To most Wardens, rules are rules, and there's not much middle ground.

When an adventuring party enters a Warden's guarded area, he may agree to assist them for the sake of expediency; the sooner the party leaves his area, the sooner things will get back to normal. Conversely, a Warden may seek out a party to help with a particularly difficult task, such as ridding the guarded area of destructive creatures or locating a treatment for a crop disease. Depending on the circumstances, a Warden may journey anywhere in the world; he is not bound to remain in his guarded area. However, a Warden will not undertake any adventure without direct orders from, or with the express permission of his overlord.

Other members of an adventuring party may find a Warden to be cordial but distant. A Warden's loyalties lie primarily with his overlord, not with his companions, and this can create stress for party members who insist on comradeship. Some Wardens are also prone to homesickness; the further an expedition takes him from his guarded area, the more anxious and sullen he may become.

Nevertheless, a Warden's dedication and professionalism can only enhance a party's effectiveness. Many comply unwaveringly with orders from the party leader, offer pointed advice when needed, and fight courageously on the battlefield.

Secondary Skills: Armorer, Bowyer/Fletcher, Farmer, Forester, Groom, Weaponsmith, Woodworker/Carver.

Weapon Proficiencies: *Recommended:* Bow (any), crossbow (any), quarterstaff, pole arm (any), spear, sword (any).

Nonweapon Proficiencies: *Recommended:* Agriculture, Carpentry, Engineering, Etiquette, Falconry*, Heraldry, Hunting, Languages (Modern), Reading/Writing, Riding (Land-based), Stone Masonry.

Armor/Equipment: Wardens have no special armor or equipment requirements. Depending on the affluence and generosity of the overlord, Wardens may have access to the finest equipment money can buy, such as gem-studded shields and onyx-tipped arrows. As a rule, Wardens take meticulous care of their gear, spending much of their free time honing their blades to razor-edge sharpness, and polishing their armor until it gleams like silver. Wardens affiliated with the government may wear elaborate uniforms emblazoned with medals, ribbons, and other service commendations.

Species Enemy: Any, though the species enemy is often a creature that plagues the Warden's guarded land or torments his overlord (in human lands, this is likely to be brigands).

Followers: Any.

Special Benefits:

Stipend: A Warden in good standing with his overlord receives a monthly stipend commensurate with his responsibilities and experience. Warden salaries average 30-50 gp per month, plus a monthly bonus of 10 gp times the Warden's level.

Expenses: When undertaking an expedition on behalf of his overlord, the Warden may receive a small stipend to cover his expenses. A typical stipend ranges from 100-500 gp, depending on the length of the expedition, the level of the Warden, and the generosity of the overlord. The Warden may spend these funds only on goods and services directly relating to the success of the expedition. In lieu of money, the Warden may receive loan of a mount, weapons, or equipment necessary for the undertaking.

Annual Boon: Once per year, the Warden can ask the overlord for a boon. It is traditional that this be granted insofar as the resources of the overlord (and the judgement of the DM) allow, although exceptionally greedy or ill-considered requests will reflect badly upon the Warden.

Reaction Bonus: When representing his overlord, a Warden receives a +2 bonus to his reaction checks with all good and neutral characters of high social status (including aristocrats, government officials, and affluent citizens), regardless of their culture or whether he's met them before.

Special Hindrances:

Accountability: A Warden is held fully account-

able for any actions that may reflect badly on his overlord. Should the Warden break the law, insult a noble, or otherwise behave improperly, his overlord will demand an explanation. An unsatisfactory explanation will result in a reprimand at best, and termination of his job at worst. A terminated Warden is forced to abandon this kit, suffering all of the penalties described in the Abandoning Kits section elsewhere in this chapter.

If a Warden receives expenses (as detailed in his Special Benefits), he must make a full accounting of his expenditures and return any excess funds at the conclusion of his expedition. Should a discrepancy be discovered, the Warden may be fined or imprisoned. If he's been given special equipment instead of or in addition to a expenses, all items must be returned in good condition. Otherwise, money may be deducted from the Warden's stipend to replace them, or the overlord may confiscate an equivalent amount of the Warden's goods.

Overlord Demands: A Warden is always subject to orders from his overlord. Some orders are critical, others trivial, but all must be followed in order for the Warden to remain in good standing. Failure to comply with an order may result in a variety of penalties, ranging from fines to termination of employment.

An overlord may require the Warden to carry out a special order in conjunction with his primary assignment, or a Warden may receive burdensome duties as part of his regular job. In all cases, the DM decides when the overlord makes a special demand, the type of demand, and the penalties for violation. Some sample demands of a Warden:

- When an expedition takes the Warden far from home, he must take along a young relative of the overlord who wants to see the world. The Warden accepts responsibility for the relative's safety and behavior.
- While on an expedition to a distant land, the Warden must make contact with a long-lost friend of his overlord and extend an invitation to visit.
- At all times and wherever he goes, the Warden must display a banner bearing the insignia of his overlord.
- In times of austerity for the overlord, the Warden must turn over some or all of the treasure he collects on an adventure.

Abandoning Kits

Once a kit is chosen for a ranger, it can't be exchanged later in the game for a different one. However, unless otherwise specified, it can be abandoned entirely, the character continuing the game as a standard ranger; that is, a ranger as described in the *Player's Handbook* without any of the benefits or hindrances associated with a particular kit.

Why would a player want to abandon a kit? Maybe recent campaign events have made the kit less fun to play (the king has declared amnesty for all Forest Runners). Perhaps the player feels limited by the kit restrictions (he wants more spells than those allowed to the Greenwood Ranger). Or maybe he's just tired of it (the Sea Ranger is fed up with life on the water). Whatever the reason, the DM should honor a player's request to abandon his kit. The abandonment may take place gradually, if the DM's wishes to work the change into an adventure, or immediately, if the DM doesn't see the change as significantly affecting the story line of his campaign.

A character who abandons a kit undergoes the following modifications:

- All of the kit's bonuses and benefits are lost. All penalties and hindrances are ignored.
- The character may use any weapons and armor normally available to the ranger.
- Should the character acquire new weapon proficiency slots, they may be spent on weapon proficiencies of the player's choice.
- The nonweapon proficiencies associated with the kit, including requirements and recommendations, no longer apply.
- Bonus proficiencies *aren't* forfeited. Instead, they are set aside (written down but not used) until the character acquires new nonweapon proficiency slots. The new slots must be spent paying for the former bonus proficiencies, in an order determined by the player. The player must pay for all former bonus proficiencies before he can choose any new nonweapon proficiencies.

Creating New Kits

Players aren't restricted to the ranger kits described in this chapter. If a player is interested in a certain type of character not discussed here, he can design a new kit from scratch, using the above examples as guidelines.

Before going to all the trouble of designing a new kit from the ground up, study the existing kits to see if any of them can be modified to fit the archetype you have in mind. If not, copy the Ranger Kit Record Sheet in the back of this book. Begin by filling out the description of the new kit, then write down the information needed in each section. Refer to the Kit Subsections descriptions at the beginning of this chapter if necessary.

When you've finished filling out the Record Sheet, let your DM look it over. He may make some adjustments to ensure that characters taking the new kit aren't too powerful or that the kit is sufficiently different from existing kits. The DM reserves the right to make additional adjustments after he sees how it works in the context of a campaign.

Stuck for ideas? Here are some suggestions that might be developed into new kits:

Crypt Ranger. Cemeteries, battlefields, or other locales associated with death are his primary terrain. His followers are non-evil undead.

Dragon Killer. Similar to the Giant Killer, he has special abilities that increase his effectiveness when fighting dragons.

Extra-Planar Ranger. His primary terrain is another plane of existence. His followers include extra-planar creatures.

Militant Ecologist. He's a conservation expert who retaliates violently against despoilers, polluters, and poachers.

Lycanthropic Ranger. He can change into an animal and counts werecreatures among his followers. Werebears and weretigers are suggested.

Ranger-Knight. He's a private landowner primarily interested in protecting and expanding his own holdings.

Survivalist. He can thrive in any terrain, under any conditions. He can improvise deadly weapons from the simplest materials.

Demi-Rangers

According to the *Player's Handbook*, only humans, elves, and half-elves can be rangers. But using the rules in this book, it's possible to include characters of other races with ranger-like abilities in a campaign. However, lacking the necessary qualities to become rangers in the true sense, these other races are subject to specific limitations. They are known as demi-rangers.

Demi-rangers are restricted in the following ways:

- Demi-rangers *must* take character kits. Only a few kits are available to each race, as indicated in Table 53. Further, they must meet all the initial ability score requirements for both the ranger class and the kit.
- Demi-rangers use only the basic Tracking proficiency; they do not track as rangers, nor can they specialize in a primary terrain if that optional rule is being used.
- Demi-rangers do not get the two-weapon attack ability of standard rangers.
- Demi-rangers *do* add their racial modifier (if any) to their move silently and hide in shadow abilities.
- Demi-rangers are limited as to the maximum level they may achieve. Table 53 lists the maximum level for each kit.
- Demi-rangers attract 2d3 followers instead of the 2d6 normally allowed rangers. (Dwarf demi-rangers will rarely have elf or half-elf followers; gnomes will have an exceptionally high number of burrowing mammals.)
- Demi-rangers are restricted as to their terrain types. These include:
- *Dwarf:* Arctic, Hill, Mountain, Desert.
- *Gnome:* Arctic, Forest, Hill, Underdark.
- *Halfling:* Aquatic, Forest, Plains, Jungle (exception, Explorer).
- Halfling demi-rangers are unable to learn the priest spells normally available to rangers. Dwarf and gnome demi-rangers may learn priest spells (from appropriate spheres) but not until they reach 10th level. As indicated in Table 53, they learn fewer spells than other rangers and cast them at lower levels.

Table 53: Demi-Rangers

Race Kit	Maximum Level
Dwarf	
Guardian	15
Mountain Man	15
Warden	15
Gnome	
Forest Runner	11
Pathfinder	11
Stalker	11
Halfling	
Explorer	9
Feralan	9
Sea Ranger	9

Table 54: Demi-Ranger Spell Progression and Dexterity Modifiers

Demi-ranger Level	Casting Level	Priest Spell Level	
		1	2
1-9	-	-	-
10	1	1	-
11	2	2	1
12	3	2	2

Race	Hide in Shadows	Move Silently
Dwarf	–	–
Gnome	+5%	+5%
Halfling	+10%	+15%

New Kits for Demi-Rangers

Just as you're free to create new ranger kits, it's also possible to design kits specifically for demi-rangers. Follow the suggestions outlined in the Creating New Kits section above. The DM has the right to disallow *any* kit he feels is inappropriate for his campaign.

Some suggestions for demi-ranger kits:

Dwarven Spelunker. This is a subterranean ranger whose primary terrain encompasses caves and underground passages.

Gnomish Terraformer. He pursues techniques for physically reshaping the lay of the land.

Halfling Agronomist. He's a master of agriculture and animal husbandry.

Dual-Classed Rangers

Dual-classed characters must be human. A dual class ranger may be of any character kit, presuming the DM allows it in his campaign.

To change from a ranger to another class, the ranger must have a minimum score of 15 in Strength, Dexterity, and Wisdom. He must have a score of 17 or better in the prime requisites of the new class.

If a character from another class wants to switch to a ranger, he must have a minimum score of 15 in his prime requisites and a score of 17 or better in Strength, Dexterity, and Wisdom.

Multi-Class Rangers

The main multi-class option open for a ranger is the half-elf cleric/ranger. The half-elf advances in both classes simultaneously, up to 16th level ranger and 14th level cleric. All the usual rules for multi-class characters as given in the *Player's Handbook* should be followed.

> ### Optional Rule: The Ranger-Druid
> Generally, a ranger/druid combination is not possible, due to the conflicting alignments of the classes. However, campaign conditions may allow their creation, should the players and DM decide that they wish to experiment with them.
>
> First, there must be a nature deity of good alignment whose specialty priests are druidic. Second, the priesthood must have an allied group of rangers. Given these conditions, a half-elf ranger/druid character may be possible.
>
> Such a character is still bound by racial level limits, in this case 16th level ranger and 9th level druid. Even if the optional level advancement for exceptional ability scores is used, such a character is unlikely to become a 12th level druid (a level for which the character must fight). At the very least, the character will have formidable enemies among conservative members of the priestly hierarchy, and is likely to become the target of subtle plots. Also, such a character would be under constant pressure from divided loyalties, as his chosen professions will tend to pull him in different directions.

It's strongly suggested that you incorporate the optional proficiency rules into your campaign, especially if you're using the character kits from Chapter 4. This chapter presents all of the non-weapon proficiencies relevant to the ranger from the *Player's Handbook*, along with descriptions of a few new ones and clarifications of some old ones.

Compiled Proficiencies

Table 55 lists all of the nonweapon proficiencies normally available to the ranger, which includes all of the proficiencies associated with the warrior, wizard, and general groups. Rangers may also acquire proficiencies from the priest and rogue groups described in Chapter 5 of the *Player's Handbook*, but at a cost of one additional proficiency slot above the listed number.

Bold-faced entries are new proficiencies described in this chapter.

Italicized entries require the player to select a specific area of specialization. For instance, a ranger proficient in artistic ability must specialize in one particular art form, such as painting, sculpture, or origami. Spending another slot on this proficiency allows him to improve an already chosen art form, or to pick another one.

Entries marked with an asterisk (*) are proficiencies with special applications for rangers, explained in the Clarifications and Modifications section.

Clarifications and Modifications

The following modifications are used in addition to the information in the proficiency descriptions given in Chapter 5 of the *Player's Handbook*. The modifications apply to rangers only. Except where specified otherwise, rangers must spend the slot points indicated in Table 55 to acquire any proficiency.

Whenever a proficiency bonus is indicated, the bonus is added to the normal check modifier. For example, if a terrain-specialized ranger with a Wisdom of 14 uses direction sense (Wis +1) in his primary terrain (+2), the check is made at Wis +3. A roll of 17 or less on 1d20 is a success.

Animal Handling

A ranger's animal empathy ability (see Chapter 2) can produce essentially the same calming effect on an animal as the animal handling proficiency. If a ranger also has the animal handling proficiency, he may attempt to soothe an animal *either* by making a proficiency check or by using his animal empathy ability—but not both.

If an animal is among a ranger's followers, neither *animal empathy* nor the animal handling proficiency is necessary to control the follower. Use the guidelines in Chapter 3 instead.

The animal handling proficiency has no effect on a ranger's species enemy.

Animal Training

Rangers are more efficient than other characters at training animals. In the Standard method (see Chapter 3) a ranger needs two months to train an animal to perform a general task. Training for a specific trick requires 2d4 weeks. At the end of the training period, he makes a proficiency check. If the check is successful, the animal has learned the task or trick. If the check fails, the ranger may make a second attempt at teaching it the same task (requiring another two months) or trick (requiring another 2d4 weeks), followed by a second proficiency check. If this second proficiency check fails, the animal is too dumb or too stubborn to learn that particular trick or task. The ranger may repeat the training process with a different trick or task. An animal can learn a maximum of 2d4 tasks or tricks, in any combination of the two.

The animal training proficiency isn't necessary to train followers. Use the guidelines in Chapter 3 instead.

A species enemy can't be trained by the ranger, neither with the follower guidelines nor the animal training proficiency.

Riding, Airborne and Land-based

A ranger cannot use his species enemy as an airborne or land-based mount. If the mount is a follower, use the guidelines in Chapter 3 instead of the proficiency rules.

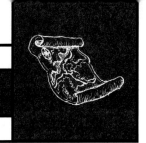

Survival

All rangers have basic survival skills in their primary terrain. Additional proficiency slots may be spent to add more terrain types. Thus, if a ranger spends slots to acquire this proficiency, he must choose a terrain type other than his primary terrain, giving him the survival proficiency in two types of terrain.

Tracking

Most rangers will have this proficiency in outdoor land terrain without spending any slots, as discussed in Chapter 2. Generally, success chances in urban, man-made, or aquatic terrains are halved, unless a specific kit description says otherwise. Some kits give tracking in alternative terrains instead of the usual outdoor land environment.

Table 55: Nonweapon Proficiencies

Proficiency	# of Slots Req'd.	Relevant Ability	Check Modifier
Agriculture	1	Int	0
Alertness	1	Wis	+1
Ancient History	1	Int	−1
Animal Handling*	1	Wis	−1
Animal Lore	1	Int	0
Animal Training	1	Wis	0
Armorer	2	Int	−2
Artistic Ability	1	Wis	0
Astrology	2	Int	0
Blacksmithing	1	Str	0
Blind-fighting	2	NA	NA
Boating	1	Wis	+1
Bowyer/Fletcher	1	Dex	−1
Brewing	1	Int	0
Camouflage	1	Wis	0
Cartography	1	Int	−2
Carpentry	1	Str	0
Charioteering	1	Dex	+2
Cobbling	1	Dex	0
Cooking	1	Int	0
Dancing	1	Dex	0
Direction Sense	1	Wis	+1
Distance Sense	1	Wis	0
Endurance	2	Con	0
Engineering	2	Int	−3
Etiquette	1	Cha	0
Falconry	1	Wis	−1
Fire-building	1	Wis	−1
Fishing	1	Wis	−1
Foraging	1	Int	−2
Gaming	1	Cha	0
Gem Cutting	2	Dex	−2
Heraldry	1	Int	0
Herbalism	2	Int	−2
Hunting	1	Wis	−1

Proficiency	# of Slots Req'd.	Relevant Ability	Check Modifier
Languages, Ancient	1	Int	0
Languages, Modern	1	Int	0
Leatherworking	1	Int	0
Mining	2	Wis	−3
Mountaineering	1	NA	NA
Navigation	1	Int	−2
Persuasion	1	Cha	0
Pottery	1	Dex	−2
Reading/Writing	1	Int	+1
Religion	1	Wis	0
Riding, Airborne	2	Wis	−2
Riding, Land-based	1	Wis	+3
Riding, Sea-based	2	Dex	−2
Rope Use	1	Dex	0
Running	1	Con	−6
Seamanship	1	Dex	+1
Seamstress/Tailor	1	Dex	−1
Set Snares	1	Dex	−1
Signaling	1	Int	−2
Singing	1	Cha	0
Spellcraft	1	Int	−2
Spelunking	1	Int	−2
Stonemasonry	1	Str	−2
Survival	2	Int	0
Swimming	1	Str	0
Tracking*	–	Wis	Special
Trail Marking	1	Wis	0
Trail Signs	1	Int	−1
Veterinary Healing	1	Wis	−3
Weaponsmithing	3	Int	−3
Weaponsmithing, Crude	1	Wis	−3
Weather Sense	1	Wis	−1
Weaving	1	Int	−1

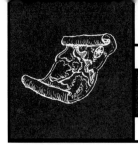

New Proficiencies

Rangers of any character kit can acquire these proficiencies by spending the points listed in Table 55. The "Crossover Groups" mentioned at the end of the description are eligible to buy the proficiency at the normal cost. Groups not mentioned may buy the proficiency by paying one additional point beyond the listed cost.

Alertness

A character with this proficiency is exceptionally attuned to his surroundings, able to detect disturbances and notice discrepancies. A successful proficiency check reduces his chance of being surprised by 1. (This replaces the description of this proficiency in *The Complete Thief's Handbook*.)

Crossover Groups: General.

Boating

This proficiency allows the character to pilot any small boat, such as a kayak or canoe, operating it at maximum speed. It also allows make minor repairs and improvements in these boats, such as waterproofing them and patching holes. A successful proficiency check enables the character to handle the craft in treacherous situations; for instance, maneuvering the boat though choppy water without capsizing it, or avoiding collisions when guiding it through a narrow channel choked with rocks or ice. Note that while the navigation and seamanship proficiencies deal with ships in oceans, seas, and other large bodies of water, the boating proficiency is confined to small craft on rivers, lakes, on oceans close to shore, and over similar terrain, usually on relatively calm waters.

Crossover Groups: General.

Camouflage

By using this proficiency, the character can attempt to conceal himself, his companions, and inanimate objects by using natural or man-made materials. Successful use assumes the availability of all necessary materials. In forests and jungles, the character can use shrubbery, mud, and other readily available resources. Arctic or similarly barren terrain usually requires special clothing, paints, or other artificial materials (although "digging in" is an old trick which may be applicable in such terrain, depending on local conditions). It takes a character a half-hour to camouflage himself or another person, two or three hours to conceal a cart or inanimate object of comparable size, and a half-day to hide a small building.

Neither human, demihuman, monster, nor animal passersby will be able to see a camouflaged character, presuming the character makes a successful proficiency check. Camouflaged companions will also go unnoticed; only one proficiency check is required for the entire group.

Objects may also be camouflaged. Objects the size of a person require no penalty to the check; cart-sized objects require a –1 penalty, while building-sized objects require a –3 penalty. The DM may adjust penalties based on these guidelines.

Camouflaging has no effect on predators that locate prey by scent or other keen senses; a hungry wolf can still sniff out a camouflaged human. A camouflaged person has no protection against a passerby who accidently brushes against or bumps into him. Likewise, a camouflaged person may reveal himself if he sneezes, cries out from the sting of a bee, or makes any other sound.

Note that camouflaging is only necessary for persons or objects that would otherwise be partially or entirely exposed. A person hiding behind a stone wall wouldn't need to be camouflaged to avoid detection, nor would a buried object.

Crossover Groups: Fighter, Rogue.

Cartography

This proficiency grants skill at map making. A character can draw maps to scale, complete with complex land formations, coastal outlines, and other geographic features. The character must be reasonably familiar with the area being mapped.

The DM makes a proficiency check in secret to determine the accuracy of the map. A successful proficiency check means that the map is correct in all significant details. If the roll fails, the map contains a few errors, possibly a significant one. A roll of exactly 20 means the map contains a serious errors, making it useless.

Crossover Groups: General.

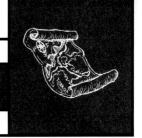

Distance Sense

This proficiency enables a character to estimate the total distance he's traveled in any given day, part of a day, or a number of consecutive days equal to his level. For instance, a 7th level character can estimate the distance he's traveled in the previous week. The estimate will be 90% accurate.

Crossover Groups: General.

Falconry

This is most properly the Animal Training (Falcon) proficiency. A character with this proficiency is an expert in training and handling falcons, enabling him to teach them tricks and tasks (This proficiency also allows the training of hawks at a –1 penalty. Owls are a separate proficiency and can be trained at –2).

A character can teach a falcon 2d4 (2-8) tricks or tasks in any combination. It takes 2d6 weeks to teach the falcon a trick, three months for a task. At the end of a training period, the character makes a proficiency check. If the check succeeds, the falcon has learned the trick or task. If the check fails, the falcon is incapable of learning more.

If not using falconry training equipment (see Chapter 7), the success roll required for training is penalized by –2.

Crossover Groups: General.

Note: The foregoing is the standard proficiency. Optionally, the training rules for rangers given in Chapter 3 can be used. Training times and number of tricks/tasks may vary.

Sample general tasks:

Hunting: The falcon is trained to hunt its natural prey: small mammals and game birds; and to return with them to the falconer. Nearly all trained falcons receive this training first.

Ferocity: The falcon receives a +1 bonus to all attack and damage rolls, and a +2 morale bonus.

Guard: The falcon shrieks at the approach of strangers. If approached closer than 20' or 30', the falcon will attack unless ordered not to. The bird can recognize designated friends.

Homing: The falcon recognizes one place as its roost and returns there upon command.

Loyalty: The falcon is exceptionally loyal to an individual selected by the trainer. It has a +4 saving throw bonus against charm, control, empathy, or friendship attempts by others. Further, it comes when the individual summons it, guards its master from attack and may perform unusual acts of loyalty as decided by the DM.

Species Enemy: The falcon is trained to recognize an entire species as a natural enemy. Its basic reaction will be hostile, it will reject empathy, and have a +4 saving throw bonus against the enemy's charm or control attempts. It will attack the species enemy in preference to others.

Track: The falcon will track a designated creature and return. It can retrace its path to lead the falconer to the creature.

Sample specific tricks:

Attack: The falcon will attack on command a creature designated by the falconer until called off. The falcon's base morale is at least 11. The falcon receives a save vs. rods against another ranger's animal empathy ability.

Capture Prey: A hunt-trained falcon will return with the prey alive and unharmed.

Catch Object: Upon command, the falcon will catch a small object thrown into the air or a small falling object and return to the falconer.

Distract: The falcon is trained to feint at an opponent. The opponent must make a saving throw vs. paralysis or lose its next action.

Eye Attack: The falcon is trained to strike at an opponent's eyes. A beak hit has a 25% chance of striking an eye. An opponent struck in the eye is blinded for 1d4 rounds and has a 10% chance of permanently losing sight in the eye.

Hand Signals: The falcon can be commanded by hand signals as well as by voice.

Hide Object: The falcon takes an object from the falconer, flies away with it, and conceals it. The falcon will retrieve the object on command.

Pit Fighting: The falcon is trained as a fighting bird. It has a +2 attack bonus against any fighting bird that is not so trained.

Recall: The falcon will immediately return to the falconer upon receiving the command.

Nemesis: The falcon is trained to attack a specific individual. The falcon never checks morale when attacking the individual.

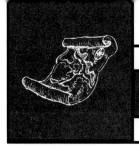

Foraging

By using this proficiency, a character can search a wilderness area to locate a small amount of a desired material, such as a branch suitable for carving into a bow, enough kindling to start a fire, a medicinal herb, or a component required for a spell. The character must spend 2-8 (2d4) hours searching, and the material must theoretically be available in the area being searched (for instance an icicle isn't available in the desert, nor dry kindling on the ocean floor). The DM doesn't confirm if the material sought is actually available until after the character has searched for the designated period. If the DM decides the material isn't in the area, no proficiency check is necessary; he merely reveals that the search was in vain.

If the DM decides the material is indeed available, a successful proficiency check means the character has found what he's been looking for. As a rule of thumb, the character locates no more than a handful of the desired material, though the DM may make exceptions (if searching for a few leaves of a particular herb, the character may instead find an entire field).

If the check fails, the material isn't found. The character may search a different area, requiring another 2-8 hours and a new proficiency check.

Crossover Groups: Warrior, Rogue.

Persuasion

This proficiency enables the character to make a compelling argument to convince a subject NPC character to see things his way, respond more favorably, or comply with a request. The character engages the NPC in conversation for at least 10 rounds (meaning that the subject must be willing to talk with the character in the first place); subjects whose attitudes are threatening or hostile aren't affected by this proficiency.

A successful proficiency check means that the subject's reaction is modified by +2 in favor of the character (see Table 59 in Chapter 11 of the *DUNGEON MASTER Guide*). This bonus is *not* cumulative with any other reaction modifiers, such as those derived from Charisma; other reaction modifiers don't apply. For every additional slot a character spends on this proficiency, he boosts the reaction modifier by +1 (for example, spending two slots on this proficiency gives a +3 reaction bonus).

Crossover Groups: General.

Riding, Sea-based

This proficiency allows the character to handle a particular species of sea-based mount The type of mount must be specified when the proficiency is acquired. The character may spend additional slots to enable him to handle other species.

In addition to riding the mount, the proficiency enables the character to do the following:

- When the mount is on the surface of the water, the character can leap onto its back and spur it to move in the same round. No proficiency check is required.
- The character can urge the mount to leap over obstacles in the water that are less than 3' high and 5' across (in the direction of the jump). No proficiency check is required. Greater jumps require a proficiency check, with bonuses or penalties assigned by the DM according to the height and breadth of the obstacle and the type and size of mount. Failure means the mount balks; an immediate second check determines if the character stays on the mount or falls off.
- The character can spur the mount to great speeds. If an initial proficiency check fails, the mount resists moving faster than normal. Otherwise, the mount begins to move up to 2d6 feet per round beyond its normal rate. Proficiency checks must be made every five rounds. So long as the checks succeed, the mount continues to move at the faster rate for up to two turns. After the mount moves at this accelerated rate for two turns, its rate then drops to ⅔ of its normal rate. It can move no faster than ⅔ of its normal rate until allowed to rest for a full hour.

If the second or any subsequent check fails, the mount's movement drops to half its normal rate. It continues to move at this half-speed rate until allowed to rest for a hour.

- If a sea-based mount on the surface of the water is attacked, it will normally submerge unless it makes a successful morale roll. If the morale roll fails, the rider can command the mount to re-surface by making a successful

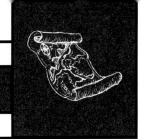

proficiency check. If the check fails, the rider can attempt another check each round thereafter, so long as he is physically able. While submerged with the mount and attempting to force it to surface, the rider risks drowning (see Chapter 14 of the *Player's Handbook*). Because he's exerting himself, the number of rounds the rider can hold his breath is equal to half his Constitution score.

Crossover Groups: General.

Signaling

This proficiency gives the character the ability to send messages over long distances. The character must designate his preferred method for signaling. Typical methods include smoke signals, whistling, waving flags, drums, or reflecting mirrors. For each additional slot spent, the character may choose an additional method.

Because signaling is essentially a language, messages of reasonable complexity can be communicated. A practiced signaller can transmit as many as 10 words per combat round.

To interpret the signal, the recipient must be able to see or hear it. He must also have the signaling proficiency and know the same signaling method as the sender. To send a message and have it understood, both the signaler and the recipient must make successful proficiency checks. If one fails his roll, the message is distorted; the message can be sent again in the following round, and proficiency checks may be attempted again. If both checks fail, or if either character rolls a natural 20, an incorrect message was sent and received; the message has the opposite of the intended meaning. Characters without the signaling proficiency, as well as characters who have the proficiency but use a different signalling method, can't understand the signals.

Crossover Groups: General.

Spelunking

A character with this proficiency has a thorough understanding of caves and underground passages, including their geology, formation, and hazards. The character generally knows what natural hazards are possible and what general equip-

ment a spelunking party should outfit itself with. A successful proficiency check can reveal the following information:

- Determine, by studying cracks in the walls and pebbles on the floor, sniffing the air, etc., the likelihood of a cave-in, flash flood, or other natural hazard. This only works with respect to natural formations, and is negated if the natural formations have been shored up, bricked in, or otherwise tampered with.
- Estimate the time required to excavate a passage blocked with rubble.
- While exploring extensive underground caverns, a successful check reduces the chance of getting hopelessly lost when confronted by multiple unmarked passages, sinkholes, etc. to a maximum of 30%, assuming good lighting (see *DMG* Table 81-82).

Crossover Groups: Warrior.

Trail Marking

By notching trees, scattering pebbles, piling stones, and clipping weeds, the character can mark a trail through any wilderness area. Providing he moves at ⅔ his normal movement rate, he can mark a continuous trail as long as he likes; however, the longer the trail, the less likely he'll be able to follow it back.

A successful proficiency check enables a backtracking character to follow his own trail for a distance equal to his level in miles. If he fails a check, he loses the trail. For instance, assume a 3rd level character marked a 12-mile trail. His first successful proficiency check enables him to follow this trail back three miles. A second successful proficiency check means he can follow the trail another three miles. The third check fails, and he loses the trail; he's only been able to follow his trail for a total of six miles.

The tracking proficiency isn't necessary to use the trail marking proficiency. However, when a ranger loses his own marked trail, he may still attempt to follow it using his tracking proficiency. Any other characters with the tracking proficiency may also attempt to follow a ranger's marked trail, using the rules applicable to the tracking proficiency.

A marked trail lasts unless it is obscured by precipitation, a forest fire, or the passage of time (an

undisturbed trail marked in a forest should last for weeks, while an arctic trail may last less than a day during periods of heavy precipitation; the DM decides). A ranger or other character with the tracking proficiency may still attempt to follow an obscured trail using the tracking rules.

Crossover Groups: Warrior.

Trail Signs

A character with this proficiency can read symbolic messages indicated by an arrangement of stones or other physical objects. The character must designate the method of leaving messages preferred by his family, tribe, or culture. Typical methods include piling rocks, stacking branches, or building snow sculptures. When the character encounters such a message, he understands the meaning if he makes a successful proficiency check. ("A dragon dwells in these woods." "Eat the green berries for restored health.") The message is meaningless to characters without the trail signs proficiency. A character with the trail signs proficiency who uses methods other than the one encountered can try to read it at half the normal chance for success. This proficiency can also be used to identify the cultural group or tribe that has left a specific trail sign.

Crossover Groups: Warrior, Rogue.

Veterinary Healing

The character can attempt to heal all types of normal animals, following the same procedures described in the description of the healing proficiency (returns 1-3 hit points if done within one round of wounding, once per creature per day; continued care can restore 1 hit point per day during non-strenuous traveling for up to 6 creatures; gives a +2 to save vs. poison if treated for 5 rounds within a round after poisoning; diagnose disease, magical origins identified, natural diseases take mildest form and shortest duration). Supernatural creatures (such as skeletons or ghouls) or creatures from another plane (such as aerial servants or xorn) cannot be treated with this proficiency.

This proficiency is not cumulative with the healing proficiency—the first used will take precedence. The veterinary proficiency can be used on humans, demihumans, and humanoids at half the normal chance for success.

Crossover Groups: Priest.

Weaponsmithing, Crude

This proficiency allows the making simple weapons out of natural materials. This skill is most often found in those from a primitive, tribal, or savage background.

The crude weapons are limited to natural materials: stone, wood, bone, sinew, reed, and the like. Crude weapons take a certain amount of time to make. The DM may add additional primitive weapons to the basic list.

The chance for success is based on the character's Wisdom, with a –3 penalty. Any warrior or a character with the hunting proficiency has a +3 bonus. The fashioner must be proficient in the use of the weapon.

If successful, the weapon can be used normally. If failed, the weapon is so badly flawed as to be useless. On a roll of 20, the weapon seems sound, but will break upon first use. On a roll of 1, the weapon has no chance of breaking except against a harder material.

Optional: Crude weapons check for breaking upon inflicting damage; roll 1d6. Bone weapons break on a roll of 1 or 2, stone weapons break on a roll of 1.

Crossover groups: Warrior.

Weapon	Construction Time
Arrows	7/day
Axe, Battle	4 days
Axe, Hand	1 day
Axe, Throwing	6 days
Bow, Long*	15 days
Bow, Short	12 days
Dagger	2 days
Dart	3 day
Javelin	1 day
Knife	2 days
Quarterstaff	1 day
Spear	2 days
Staff Sling	3 days
Warhammer	5 days

* Seasoning the wood takes 1 year.

A ranger who reaches 8th level can learn and use certain spells. Unlike a wizard, he doesn't need a spell book, nor does he need to roll to learn spells. Instead, he obtains spells like a priest, acquiring the spells he wants to memorize through meditation and prayer. Chapter 8 examines the relationship between rangers, priests, and faiths in more detail.

Unlike priests, rangers have access to spells only from the animal and plant spheres. As shown on Table 5 in Chapter 1, a ranger can cast spells at an increasingly higher level as he himself advances in level; a 9th-level ranger casts spells as a 2nd-level caster, while a 12th-level ranger casts spells as a 5th-level caster. Also note that a ranger choose to memorize *any* plant or animal sphere spell of the level shown on Table 5; for instance, a 13th-level ranger can have any three 1st-level spells from the plant and animal spheres and any two 2nd-level spells from the plant and animal spheres memorized at one time.

This chapter presents several new spells that the ranger should find especially useful, along with a few new magical items. For quick reference, Table 56 lists all spells available to the ranger. **Bold-face** spells are described in this chapter; the rest are detailed in the *Player's Handbook*.

New Spells

First-Level Spells

Allergy Field (Alteration)

Sphere: Plant
Range: 10 yards/level
Components: V, S, M
Duration: 3 rounds + 1 round/level
Casting Time: 4
Area of Effect: 5-foot/level cube
Saving Throw: Neg.

This spell causes characters entering the affected area to suffer extreme allergic reactions. It may be cast on any field, meadow, forest, or other outdoor area with an abundance of plant life, causing the plants to produce pollen, antigens, or similar allergens. Characters coming in contact with the affected area who fail their saving throws vs. spell, experience swelling of the eyes, fits of sneezing, and dull headaches for the next 2-5 (1d4+1) turns. During that time, they make all attack rolls and ability checks at a –1 penalty.

The spell affects a cubic volume whose sides are 5 feet long per level of the caster; thus, a 9th-level caster could affect a 45'×45'×45' cube. The spell lasts until the end of the indicated duration, or until the first frost, whichever comes first.

The material component for this spell is a pinch of ragweed.

Recover Trail (Divination)

Sphere: Plant
Range: Special
Components: V, S
Duration: Special
Casting Time: 4 + Special
Area of Effect: Special
Saving Throw: None

A caster who has lost a quarry's trail while using the tracking proficiency can use this spell to proceed. The spell only works in terrain containing some type of vegetation (such as trees, grass, or seaweed). The quarry must have left some potential trail on which the spell can act (the spell cannot track a creature that has *teleported* or *plane shifted*, for example).

If successful, within an hour after casting the spell, the vegetation in a particular area will begin to flutter, as if being blown by a gentle breeze. If the wind is already blowing, the vegetation moves up and down, or moves in another unusual way to attract the caster's attention. When examining this area, the caster will notice a footprint, broken twig, or other sign previously overlooked, indicating to correct trail. The spell has a success chance of 60% + 2% per level of the caster.

This spell will immediately negate a *pass without trace* spell if cast directly for that purpose, otherwise it will still function normally to allow tracking along the disguised trail.

Any spellcaster with access to both the plant sphere and the tracking proficiency can use this spell.

Revitalize Animal (Necromancy)

Sphere: Animal
Range: Touch
Components: V, S
Duration: Permanent
Casting Time: 4
Area of Effect: One animal
Saving Throw: None

This spell allows the caster to heal an animal by transferring life force (hit points) from himself to the animal. If the animal is touched with one hand, it regains 1d4 hit points, just as if it had received a *cure light wounds* spell. Touching the animal with both hands restores 2d4 hit points. In either case, the caster temporarily loses the number of hit points that the animal regains. The caster will recover his lost hit points 1-4 hours later (if he transferred 3 hit points, he recovers 3 hit points in 1-4 hours). The caster's recovery of these hit points has no effect on the restored animal.

During the 1-4 hours before the caster recovers his transferred hit points, he feels weak and dizzy, making all attack rolls at a –1 penalty during that time. Should the ranger die during that 1-4 hour period, the recovery process stops immediately and *no* hit points are recovered.

The animal cannot recover hit points beyond the normal allotment. For instance, an animal that normally has 10 hit points, but has been reduced to 6 due an injury, can't receive more than 4 hit points from this spell. Also, the caster will have at least 1 hit point remaining after using this spell; if the caster has 6 hit points, he won't transfer more than 5 to a damaged animal.

Revitalize animal works on animals only; it has no effect on humans, demihumans, humanoids, magical creatures, etc. The spell is not reversible; that is, an injured caster can't receive hit points from an animal.

Second-Level Spells

Animal Eyes (Necromancy)

Sphere: Animal
Range: 0
Components: V, S, M
Duration: 3 rounds + 1 rnd/level
Casting Time: 5
Area of Effect: One creature
Saving Throw: None

By using this spell, the caster can temporarily see through the eyes of any animal. The caster points at any single animal within 100 yards, then closes his eyes and remains stationary. In his mind's eye, he sees whatever the animal is seeing. If the subject animal is a squirrel studying the party from a tree branch, the caster sees himself and the party from the perspective of the squirrel. If the subject animal is a bird soaring overhead, the caster gets a bird's eye view of the area below.

The spell has no effect on the subject animal, nor can the caster control the animal's actions in any way. The animal is unaware of the spell and acts as it normally would. The spell persists until the end of its duration, or the caster moves or takes another action. The caster may voluntarily negate the spell by opening his eyes. The spell also ends if the animal is killed, or moves more than 100 yards away from the caster.

The subject animal must be one normally found in nature. It may not be supernatural, human, demihuman, nor of extraplanar origin.

The spell requires a glass lens no larger than one inch in diameter as a focus, which is not consumed in the casting.

Locate Animal Follower (Divination)
Reversible

Sphere: Animal
Range: 60 yards + 10 yards/level
Components: V, S, M
Duration: 8 hours
Casting Time: 5
Area of Effect: 1 animal follower
Saving Throw: None

Occasionally, a ranger's animal follower may wander away in search of food or a mate. An animal follower may also be abducted or trapped. The *locate animal follower* spell helps the ranger find such lost creatures.

The spell takes affect once the ranger fixes in his mind the follower being sought. The spell locates only that specific follower.

Once the spell is cast, the ranger slowly turns in a circle. If the follower is within range, the ranger senses when he is facing in the direction of the sought follower. If the follower isn't within range, the spell doesn't work. If the follower moves out of the area of effect, the spell is immediately negated. As soon as the ranger sees the lost follower, the spell ends. The spell is blocked by lead.

The spell works only on a natural animal follower (including giant animals); not a supernatural creature, human, demihuman, humanoid, or other. If the follower is dead, the spell still seeks it out, providing other conditions of casting are met.

The material component is a hair, feather, scale or other physical remnant of the lost follower.

The reverse of this spell, *obscure follower,* hides an animal follower from detection by spells, crystal balls, and similar means for eight hours.

Third-Level Spells

Call Follower (Conjuration/Summoning)

Sphere: Animal
Range: 0
Components: V, S
Duration: Special
Casting Time: 6
Area of Effect: 10 mile radius/level
Saving Throw: None

A ranger who has not yet received his full allotment of followers can use this spell in an attempt to summon one. After the spell is cast, the DM secretly consults the list of followers he's chosen for the ranger, or rolls an appropriate table. If the DM decides that a potential follower exists within the area of effect, the follower appears within the next 24 hours. If the DM decides that a follower isn't available within the area of effect, nothing happens (no follower appears). Note that the ranger can't request a specific type of follower; as always, the type of follower is up to the DM. The spell can be attempted no more than once per month.

DM Note: Notes on staging the arrival of the follower are also given in Chapter 3.

Chatterbark (Divination)

Sphere: Plant
Range: Touch
Components: V, S
Duration: Special
Casting Time: 1 turn
Area of Effect: One tree
Saving Throw: None

A variation of the 4th-level priest spell, *speak with plants,* this spell enables a ranger to ask a simple question to a tree and receive a spoken response. The tree can be any species, so long as its trunk is at least 1 foot in diameter. Before casting the spell, the ranger must spend at least an hour carving a humanoid face in the trunk; if the ranger has a proficiency in wood carving (a variation of artistic ability), he can carve a suitable face in one turn.

After carving the face, the ranger spends 1 turn casting the spell, at which time the face becomes animated, twitching and grimacing as if just awakening from a long sleep. The tree face then looks at the caster expectantly, waiting for a question. The caster may ask the tree any single question that can be answered in a single word or short phrase. Typical questions might include: "Has a dragon passed this way within the last few days?" "Has it rained here recently?" "Are there any fruit trees nearby?" The tree answers the question honestly. If the question is beyond the scope of its knowledge, the tree says, "I don't know." After answering, the face disappears.

The DM should keep in mind that a typical tree doesn't know very much, as it has little experience, never travels, and rarely interacts with other living things in meaningful ways. As a rule of thumb, a tree's knowledge is limited to things it has observed (passersby, weather conditions) and general information about the immediate area (animal populations, location of landmarks). A tree can't give dependable advice or make judgements. If the DM is in doubt about what a particular tree knows, the tree answers, "I don't know."

Animal Trick (Enchantment)

Sphere: Animal
Range: 30 yards
Components: V, S
Duration: 1 round/level
Casting Time: 6
Area of Effect: One animal
Saving Throw: Special

This spell temporarily enables any animal to perform a trick it normally doesn't know or lacks the intelligence to execute. The animal must be within 30 yards of the caster and must be able to hear his spoken commands. If these conditions are met, the animal will do exactly what the ranger tells it. A lion will batter down the door of a cell, a cat will fetch a key and carry it in its mouth, a parrot will draw a circle in the sand with its claw. A creature with less than 5 hit dice and no prior allegiances receives no saving throw. Any willing creature predisposed to aid the caster (such as an animal follower) will not resist this spell at all.

The animal can't execute a trick or task that exceeds its physical limitations. A snake can't pick a lock, and a horse can't play a trumpet. Note also that the caster must give specific instructions, not general commands. If the caster commands a lion to "Get something to help me put out this fire," the puzzled lion won't know what do to. However, if the caster says, "Take this bucket in your mouth, dip it in the stream, and carry the water back to me," the lion will do as it's told.

The caster can take other actions while the animal is completing the trick. Once the animal completes its trick, the caster may give it additional tricks to complete until the spell expires. If the spell expires while the animal is in the middle of a trick, or if the spell is broken by some means, the animal immediately stops what it's doing.

Polymorph Plant (Alteration)

Sphere: Plant
Range: Touch
Components: V, S, M
Duration: Permanent
Casting Time: 6
Area of Effect: One plant
Saving Throw: None

This spell enables a ranger to transform any single plant, including a fungus or mold, into any other type of plant of the ranger's choice. The change is permanent. The changed plant has the physical appearance of its new form, but not all of the associated properties. If edible, the new form tastes as bland as cotton. If normally used as a spell component, the new form has only a 50% chance of actually functioning as a component. If normally used for medical purposes (such as for a

healing salve or poison antidote), the new form has only a 50% chance of having any beneficial properties.

Only living plants can be polymorphed; the spell won't work on a fallen leaf, a nut, or a picked fruit. The size of the plant is not relevant; a blade of grass may be polymorphed into a towering oak tree and vice versa. The new form doesn't have to be indigenous to the environment; an evergreen tree on a frigid mountain may be polymorphed into a cactus (although it may not thrive for long).

Neither the original vegetation nor its polymorphed form can be an intelligent plant or a plant-like creature. Nor are unnatural plant forms allowed; a mushroom may be transformed into a normal-sized cornstalk, but not a 50-foot-tall cornstalk or a stalk that produces apples instead of corn.

The material component for this spell is any seed.

Table 56: Ranger Spells

Level	Name	Sphere	Level	Name	Sphere
1	Allergy Field	Plant	3	Call Animal Follower	Animal
1	Animal Friendship	Animal	3	Chatterbark	Plant
1	Entangle	Plant	3	Hold Animal	Animal
1	Invisibility to Animals	Animal	3	Plant Growth	Plant
1	Locate Animals or Plants	Both	3	Polymorph Plant	Plant
1	Log of Everburning*	Plant	3	Slow Rot*	Plant
1	Pass Without Trace	Plant	3	Snare	Plant
1	Recover Trail	Plant	3	Spike Growth	Plant
1	Revitalize Animal	Animal	3	Summon Insects	Animal
1	Shillelagh	Plant	3	Tree	Plant
2	Animal Eyes	Animal	4**	Animal Summoning I	Animal
2	Barkskin	Plant	4**	Call Woodland Beings	Animal
2	Charm Person or Mammal	Animal	4**	Giant Insects	Animal
2	Goodberry	Plant	4**	Hallucinatory Forest	Plant
2	Locate Follower	Animal	4**	Hold Plant	Plant
2	Messenger	Animal	4**	Plant Door	Plant
2	Snake Charm	Animal	4**	Repel Insects	Animal
2	Speak With Animals	Animal	4**	Speak With Plants	Plant
2	Trip	Plant	4**	Sticks to Snakes	Plant
2	Warp Wood	Plant		*Tome of Magic	
3	Animal Trick	Animal		** Seeker Kit	

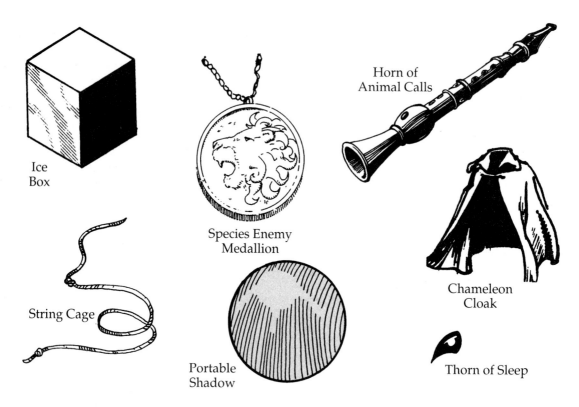

Ice Box

Species Enemy Medallion

Horn of Animal Calls

Chameleon Cloak

String Cage

Portable Shadow

Thorn of Sleep

New Magical Items

The following magical items are intended for rangers, but if the DM so chooses, he may allow fighters, wizards, and other character classes to use them, too. All of these items are relatively rare and should turn up no more often than a typical item listed in the Miscellaneous Magic Tables in Appendix 2 of the *DUNGEON MASTER Guide*; if you like, you may use any of these items as an option when a DM's Choice is rolled.

Chameleon Cloak. This lightweight cloak, which covers the wearer from neck to foot and also includes a hood, may be worn comfortably over studded leather or lighter armor. The color of the cloak automatically changes to blend in with the surrounding terrain. If the wearer enters a jungle, the cloak becomes mottled with patches of green and brown. If the wearer enters a plain of snow, the cloak turns white. At night, the cloak becomes black. The color changes are instantaneous.

A *chameleon cloak* allows a character to be personally camouflaged, as if using the camouflage proficiency, in any terrain. The *chameleon cloak* can only conceal one person at a time. The cloak conceals with an effective Wisdom equal to its rating.

d20 roll	Wisdom Rating	XP
1-6	15	750
7-15	16	800
16-19	17	850
20	18	900

Horn of Animal Calls (1200XP). This wooden instrument, painted bright red with tiny silhouettes of various animals along the sides, resembles a recorder about six inches long. The instrument can duplicate the cries and calls of any animal. The user closes his eyes, pictures the animal in his mind, then blows into the instrument. The sound is indistinguishable from the cry of the actual animal. The instrument can be used to call particular animals or frighten them away. The DM deter-

mines the effect of any particular use of the horn; for example, summoning 2d4 animals might be 80% likely in an animal's home terrain, with an arrival time of 1-4 rounds.

Ice Box (800 XP). This is an airtight box one foot square, made of black metal with a single hinged panel. Opening the panel reveals the hollow interior. Centered on the outside of the panel is a white metal pointer resembling a small arrow. This pointer can be rotated in any direction to regulate the temperature inside the box. If pointed straight up (toward the hinges), the temperature remains at 70°F. For every complete clockwise rotation of the arrow, the temperature inside the box drops 1 degree. Therefore, if the arrow is rotated 30 times, the temperature drops to 40°F. Rotating the arrow counter-clockwise raises the temperature 1 degree per rotation. The temperature can't be lowered below zero degrees or elevated beyond 70 degrees. The box is useful for making ice and preventing food spoilage.

Portable Shadow (1,000 XP). Similar in appearance to a *portable hole,* a *portable shadow* resembles a gauzy black circle about 10 feet in diameter that can be folded up into a packet about 6 inches square. When unfolded and laid on any horizontal surface, the *portable shadow* looks like any normal area of shade, as dark as a shadow cast by a tree or other solid object under a midday sun. This magical item is useful for concealment and makes as good a hiding place as any naturally shaded area; rangers, thieves, and others have their normal chance of hiding in shadows when standing in a *portable shadow.* The shadow can be picked up by lifting the edge and folding it like a tablecloth.

Dungeon Masters should use common sense adjudicating the use of a *portable shadow.* If a character attempts to use it to hide in shadow while crossing a featureless plain, the presence of a "black hole" attached to nothing will be more likely to attract attention than to divert it. However, it can provide a shady place to cool off away from the desert sun.

Species Enemy Medallion (750 XP). A character wears this copper disk on a chain around his neck and under his clothing so that the metal touches his chest. When the character comes within 100 yards of his species enemy, the medallion becomes warm, alerting him to the enemy's presence. The intensity of the warmth varies according to the number and proximity of the enemy. The medallion doesn't get hot enough to cause damage, nor does it reveal the exact location or number of enemies in the vicinity.

String Cage (500 XP). This looks like a piece of white thread 20 feet long, flecked with gold. When arranged in a circle so that the ends touch, the *string cage* creates an invisible barrier that prevents any creature contained inside from leaving. The invisible barrier has the strength of a *wall of force* and has the shape of a closed cylinder about 6' tall. The *string cage* only functions if placed on the ground or other solid surface; if moved, the barrier dissipates. Because of its light weight, the string can't be thrown like a lasso; if rocks or other weights are attached, its magic is negated. Therefore, the device is mainly useful to contain creatures that are sleeping, trapped, restrained, or cooperative.

A *string cage* can contain any single creature, so long as the creature fits inside the circle. Physical attacks and most spells have no effect on a *string cage.* The creature trapped inside can't move it. A *disintegrate* spell destroys the device, as will a *rod of cancellation* or a *sphere of annihilation.* A creature contained in a *string cage* can escape by using *dimension door, teleport,* or a similar spell.

Only the person who originally formed the circle can separate the ends and free the creature inside. Otherwise, a *string cage* lasts for 3-12 (3d4) hours, at which time the ends separate automatically. A *string cage* can be used only once per day.

Thorn of Sleep (100 XP each). The *thorn of sleep* looks like the thorn of a plant, about three inches long. It is dry and smooth to the touch. If pricked by the thorn, a creature must make a saving throw vs. paralyzation. Failure means the creature falls into a deep slumber. The creature will not waken until attacked or strongly roused. Noises, even those of battle, will not awaken the sleeping creature. Each thorn can be used but once. Only 1-8 thorns will be found at any one time. A *thorn of sleep* can be projected by a blowgun.

To help him thrive in a variety of environments, the ranger has developed a wide range of specialized equipment. This chapter describes some of the more useful items, along with some of the more unusual.

Table 57 lists costs and weights of clothing, transport, and miscellaneous equipment. Table 58 provides similar information for weapons; see Chapter 6 of the *Player's Handbook* for the meaning of weapon size, speed factors, and type.

Clothing

Aba. This desert robe is made of lightweight fabric and covers the entire body. Typical colors include brown, gold, black, and white. Elaborate embroidery, made of brightly colored cloth strips or gold thread, often decorates the hem. A silken or cotton sash ties the aba at the waist.

In deserts and other dry climates, such garments help prevent evaporation, allowing the wearer to retain more moisture and function more comfortably. Assuming adequate water, a character wearing a desert robe is no more likely to suffer heat exhaustion on days of extreme heat than a normal person would on days of moderate temperatures. Note that desert robes don't help in areas of high humidity; in humid environments, as much skin should be exposed as possible to encourage cooling from the evaporation of perspiration.

Arctic Coat. Designed for protection against extreme cold, the arctic coat is a knee-length single-piece garment with a billowing hood. The long sleeves allow the wearer to warm his hands by drawing them inside and holding them against his chest. Arctic coats are usually made of thick bear fur, lined with seal skin for comfort. An arctic coat keeps the wearer comfortable in temperatures well below zero degrees F.

Rain Poncho. A one-piece garment resembling a large cloak with a head-sized hole in the center, a poncho helps keep the wearer dry during rain storms. Ponchos are made of canvas or similar material, often treated with a waterproofing oil. A poncho can double as ground cover and can also be used as an emergency tent. Crude ponchos are sometimes woven from grass or reeds.

Snowshoes. Each about three feet long, these oval-shaped wooden frames are laced with leather webbing to allow the wearer to walk across snow without sinking. A character newly introduced to wearing snowshoes moves at half his normal rate until he gets used to them. After a day or so of practice, he moves at his normal rate. A character wearing snowshoes receives no bonuses for charging.

Terrain Suit. Made of lightweight material, usually fine linen or silk, the terrain suit consists of a long-sleeved shirt or blouse and long trousers, dyed in various colors to help the wearer blend in with his surroundings. Styles include arctic (colored solid white), sand (mottled patches of various shades of brown, for desert and similarly sandy terrain), woodland (patterns of green and brown, for forests and jungles), and urban (black). A terrain suit must be precisely made and fitted to the person to wear it. It is worn most commonly by Stalkers, though some individual tribes and groups of warriors, woodsmen, or thieves use them, too. (As a rule of thumb, terrain suits should be slightly more common than elven chain mail.)

A terrain suit gives the same advantages as the camouflage proficiency when worn in the appropriate terrain, using a base Wisdom rating of 14. A character wearing a terrain suit with the camouflage proficiency uses his Wisdom (or 14, whichever is higher) with an additional +1 bonus.

Waterproof Boots. These thick boots are made of tough, water-resilient hide (such as alligator or caribou) treated with a waterproofing oil (typically derived from seals or minks). The wearer tucks his trousers inside the boots, then ties them near the knees with a leather drawstring. The boots keep the feet dry, even when wading in water.

Wilderness Harness. This device resembles a thick leather belt with straps that cross over the wearer's back. Both the belt and the straps contain a series of small pouches, useful for storing supplies, ammunition for missile weapons, and other materials. A secret compartment in the back section of the belt conceals a 6-inch-long flat knife (the knife comes with the harness; see Table 58 for statistics).

Transport

Dog Sled. One of the best ways to travel in snowy or icy terrain, a dog sled consists of a wooden frame for carrying supplies, wooden runners extending the length of the sled, a platform on which the passenger stands, and a lattice on the front to which the dog team is harnessed. About 6-11 dogs (or equivalent) can pull a sled 10 feet long and 3 feet wide, carrying up to 880 pounds (including the weight of the sled). Fewer animals are required for smaller sleds. A typical 8-dog sled travels at a movement rate of 15 with a load of about 680 lbs., including the sled.

When adjudicating movement via dog sled, DMs should take into account that animals not bred or trained to pull a sled can create a considerable amount of trouble for the driver—tangling traces, fighting with nearby animals, and so on—and movement could be slower than expected.

Kayak. This is a single-person boat, fast-moving and easy to maneuver. Its lashed wooden frame is about ten feet long and two feet wide, covered with canvas, sealskins, or hides of similar water-dwelling animals. The skins are attached to the frame, allowed to tighten by drying, then coated with oil to make the craft water resistant. The passenger squeezes into the hole in the top of the craft and sits so his legs extend into the bow. To seal out water, the opening of the kayak has an "apron" (often made of whale intestines) which the kayaker laces around his waist. He propels the kayak with a single long oar with a paddle on either end. A kayak can move 200'/round (its movement rate can be rounded down to 6) and it can carry 250 pounds.

Water Sled. This resembles a dog sled with inflated skins in place of runners, enabling the craft to float on the surface of the water. Long leather reins, treated with waterproofing oil, connect with the animals pulling it, usually a team of eight seals or six dolphins. A water sled carries no more than two passengers (about 480 pounds, including the sled), unless the animals pulling it are exceptionally fast and strong. Made to ride as much above the water as in it, the sled can achieve a top movement rate of 15 if pulled by strong steeds, but 9-12 is a more sustainable speed.

Miscellaneous Equipment

Breathing Tube. This simple device helps a character function underwater. A breathing tube made of a hollow reed, about a foot long, strengthened with wax and treated with waterproofing oil. The user places the tube in his mouth, then submerges himself with the end of the tube protruding from the water. The tube enables the submerged user to breathe indefinitely.

Camouflage Paint Kit. This compact leather case contains several cakes of greasepaint (in various shades of brown, green, yellow, and black), applicator brushes, a jar of paint removal cream, and a small mirror. Characters apply the paint to areas of exposed flesh to help them blend in with their surroundings. A kit contains 12 uses.

By itself, camouflage paint doesn't give a character any particular advantage. However, when used with a terrain suit (described above), it boosts the character's success chances by +1. The camouflage proficiency is required to apply the camouflage paint well; those without this proficiency have *half* the usual chance of success. A character using camouflage paint and a terrain suit gains a +2 bonus to his camouflage check.

Chain Leash. Made of chain links with a leather muzzle, this leash can be adjusted to fit any animal ranging in size from a small dog to a wolf. The length of the leash varies from 6-12 feet long. When using a properly-fitted chain leash on an animal, a character receives a +1 bonus to his animal training proficiency checks. Chain leashes are available in other sizes and lengths to fit larger and smaller animals.

Falconry Gauntlet. Also called a *perch glove*, this is a heavy arm-length glove of thick leather upon which a falcon or hawk can perch.

Falcon Training Equipment. This equipment makes falcon training more efficient. A character using the falconry proficiency without this equipment suffers a –2 penalty to training proficiency checks. One set is required for each falcon.

Each set consists of *jesses* (leather bands with rings, attached to the falcon's legs), *talon guards* (metal coverings for the bird's claws to prevent it

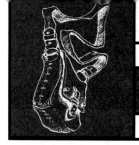

from harming the owner during training), a *creance* (a slender leather leash attached to the jesses, held by the user or secured to the perch glove), and a *hood* (a leather covering fitting over the falcon's head that restricts vision; the hood forces the falcon to rely on its senses of hearing, touch, and taste). Customized or richly appointed equipment, such as an embroidered hood or golden jesses, is also available, usually at double or triple the normal price.

Fishing Tackle. This meticulously crafted set of polished wooden lures, colorful flies made of feathers and catgut cord, bone hooks, and cork bobbers can be quite useful in the hands of a skilled fisherman. If used by a character with the fishing proficiency, the proficiency checks are modified by +1.

Healing Kit. This is a waterproofed leather or canvas backpack or handbag containing cloth bandages, splints, needles and thread (for stitching wounds), ointments, and a selection of herbs for soothing pain (these don't heal damage). It also has room for special medicines, such as poison antidotes or healing potions, but these are not included in the standard kit. The kit is useful in treating injuries of all types; a character with the healing or veterinary healing proficiency without this kit or equivalent may not be able to use the proficiency, depending on the situation.

Insect Repellent. Applying this rare, minty cream over a character's face, arms, and other areas of exposed flesh repels bees, ants, and all other types of insects less than 1 Hit Die in size. One application wears off after 8 hours. A jar of insect repellent contains 12 applications.

Scent Lure. A scent lure is a pungent liquid used to attract animals in the wild. Each scent lure attracts a specific type of animal, usually woodland game such as deer, wolf, or fox; individual animals of the species find the odor irresistible.

Each bottle of scent lure contains five applications. One application near a tree, rock, or snare has a 15% chance of attracting an animal of the given species within 24 hours, presuming the animal passes within 100 yards of the application (the DM determines if an animal comes close enough). Extra applications do not increase the chance of attraction. The scent evaporates in 24 hours.

Sleeping Bag. More comfortable, but bulkier than blankets, the sleeping bag is made of two layers of canvas or wool, stuffed with down for warmth. The user slips inside the sleeping bag and secures the open side by fastening several buckles or tying a series of leather straps.

Sun Goggles. Arctic or mountaineering sun goggles are made from solid wood. The wearer peers through two narrow slits. These reduce or eliminate the effects of dazzling lights, such as fatigue from traveling under very bright sun (for example, across deserts, or flat plains on cloudless days). Sun goggles also prevent snowblindness, where the eyes become swollen from exposure to bright sun reflecting off ice and snow. (Attack penalties for snowblindess vary from –1 to –4.)

Sun goggles will not prevent blindness caused when a *light* spell is cast directly against the wearer's eyes. Sun goggles also reduce the field of vision; the wearer can't see above or below without moving his head. This may increase chances of being surprised or attacked from a blind side, at the DM's option.

Sunburn Ointment. Characters risk damage from sunburn in any terrain during seasons of bright sunlight, not only in deserts, but also in the arctic, where the sun reflects off the ice and snow. If characters don't protect exposed flesh with scarves, mask, or other covering, they risk suffering 1 point of damage from sunburn per day. An application of sunburn ointment, gives protection against sunburn for a full day. A jar of sunburn ointment contains 14 applications.

Sunburn ointment gives no protection from magical or non-magical fire; it is ineffective against any source of damage other than the sun.

Sunburn ointment is rare, found only in the best-stocked shops in large cities.

Survival Kit. A character may strap this small leather pouch, about four inches on each side and an inch thick, around his thigh, upper arm, or anywhere else where it can remain concealed. The kit contains a number of small items useful in emergencies: a scrap of parchment and piece of graphite (for writing messages), a fish hook, a 25-foot length of fishing line on a spool, one gold piece (good for bribing guards), a small razor (for

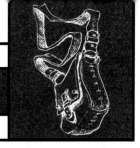

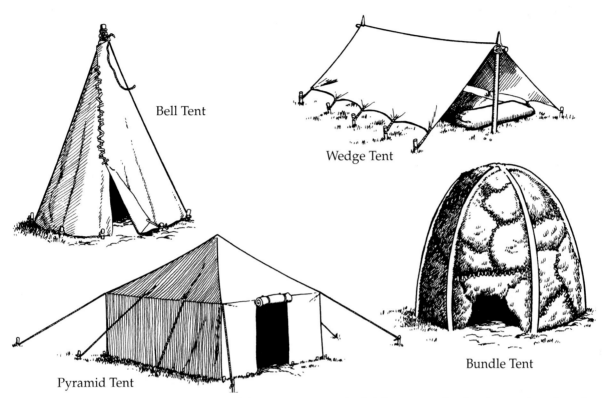

Bell Tent

Wedge Tent

Pyramid Tent

Bundle Tent

severing rope or inflicting 1 hit point of damage against captors), a wooden whistle (for signaling), a cloth pad (for making an emergency bandage), and a few pieces of sugar candy and dried fruit (for quick energy, or luring animals). Similar items may be substituted to customize individual kits.

Tents. These portable shelters, usually made of canvas or tanned animal skin, provide shelter from the elements for weary travelers. They're easy to erect and light to carry. Here a few of the most popular small tents, suitable for one or two occupants:

• *Bell Tent.* This is one of the simplest tents, consisting of a single sheet of fabric arranged around a pole to form a cone. Ropes attached to stakes surrounding the bottom of the tent are pulled to stretch the fabric tight. Though quick to construct and easy to transport, bell tents don't provide much protection against strong winds.

• *Wedge Tent.* Also known as an A-frame tent or a wall tent, the wedge tent is built on a frame consisting of two vertical poles with a horizontal pole secured between them. The fabric

is laid across the horizontal pole, then stretched with ropes attached to stakes. The wedge tent is somewhat sturdier than the bell tent, although like that tent, it provides only modest protection against severe weather.

• *Pyramid Tent.* Combining elements of both the bell and wedge tents, the pyramid tent frame is made of four vertical poles arranged in a square, with horizontal poles attached between them. A longer pole rises from the center of the square. The fabric extends from the center pole to form four slanting walls, secured with stakes. The sturdy pyramid tent resists light to moderate winds.

• *Bundle Tent.* Particularly useful in cold climates, the bundle tent consists of from six to eight ribs about five feet long, connected to each other by the tent covering. The covering consists of two layers of skin from a furry animal, such as a bear or caribou. The layers are arranged fur-side out, creating a pocket of air for extra insulation. The tent opens like an umbrella to form a domed shape or folds into a bundle.

Traps. These finely-crafted metal traps can be set up in a matter of minutes. Two general types are available; both come in *small* (rabbit), *medium* (wolf), and *large* (bear) varieties. A character using either type of trap adds a +1 bonus to his set snares proficiency checks.

- *Enclosing Trap:* This type of trap resembles a box. It catches animals alive. Lured by edible bait or a shiny object, the animal enters the box and steps on a trigger which causes the front of the box to snap shut.
- *Killing Trap:* A killing traps has two metal jaws lined with sharp points. A small platform, which holds a lure, rests in between the jaws. The slightest pressure on the platform causes the jaws to snap shut, killing the animal.

Tinderbox, Waterproof. This waterproof box contains flint and steel, along with a small supply of wood shavings for kindling. The box keeps the contents dry during a rainstorm or when submerged underwater. Once per round, a character can attempt to start a fire using these materials. A roll of 1 or 2 on a 1d8 is necessary to start a fire in normal, dry conditions. A 1 on a 1d8 is necessary if the area is damp; the DM may require more difficult rolls (for instance, a 1 on 1d12) in wet terrain, or may rule that a fire can't be started at all.

Weaponblack. When rangers or thieves apply this oily paste to their weapons or armor, it makes the metallic surfaces non-reflective and nearly invisible. Modify their base chance to hide in shadows by +5%. A coat of weaponblack lasts until the character engages in melee combat, at which time enough of the substance flakes away to negate any camouflaging advantage. The substance is flammable; if lighted, a sword coated with the paste will become the equivalent of a *flametongue* for 2-5 rounds, and will also inflict 1d4 points of heat damage upon the wielder unless he is magically protected. A vial of weaponblack contains 1 application. This substance is uncommon and only available through shady under-the-counter dealing.

Weapons

Flail, Grain. This consists of a leather strap two or three feet long that connects a wooden handle to a block of wood about a foot long. Farmers use the grain flail to thresh wheat, barley, and other grassy crops. It also makes a good bludgeoning weapon.

Hatchet. This one-handed woodsman's axe has a broad blade, a smooth wooden handle for a good grip, and its own leather scabbard for the head, which can be strapped to the wearer's belt. The hatchet is useful for chopping wood and serves as an excellent melee weapon.

Ice Pick. This special type of metal awl is used to break holes in frozen lakes for ice fishing and to chip away ice chunks when building snow houses. (Note, however, that the snow blade, or *iuak*, described below, is the primary tool for such a job.) Consisting of a bone or wood handle and a sharp metal point about six inches long, an ice pick also can be used as an impaling weapon.

Snow Blade. Also called an *iuak*, the snow blade resembles a machete made of bone, about two feet long and six inches wide. The end is flat rather than pointed. Mainly used by arctic rangers to slice blocks of snow to make shelters, the snow blade also doubles as a weapon.

Machete. Farmers in tropical regions use this 3-foot-long flat blade to chop cane and clear undergrowth. Wielded like a sword, it can inflict serious damage. The price of a machete includes a canvas sheath.

Ritiik. This 6-foot-long weapon consists of a wooden shaft with a point and a hook on the same end. Primarily used by primitive tribes of arctic and tundra regions for hunting bear and other large game, the ritiik is thrust, not thrown. When the point pierces the animal, the user jerks and twists the shaft to embed the hook.

Scythe. A curved blade attached to a 5-foot wooden pole, this farm tool is used to cut grain at harvest and also doubles as a weapon. A user wields the scythe by holding the short wooden bars on the end opposite the blade. The scythe is always used as a two-handed weapon.

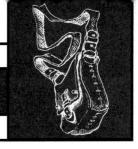

Table 57: Clothing, Transport, and Misc. Equipment

Item	Cost	Weight (lb.)
Aba**		
Common	9 sp	3
Embroidered	20 gp	3
Arctic coat**	10 gp	5
Boots, Waterproofed	4 gp	2
Breathing Tube	2 sp	*
Camouflage Paint Kit	50 gp	1
Chain Leash	6 gp	1
Dog Sled	30 gp	40
Falconry Gauntlet	5 sp	1
Falconry Training Equipment	10 gp	1
Fishing Tackle	2 sp	1
Healer's Kit	25 gp	1
Insect Repellant	5 sp	*
Kayak (& paddle)	35 gp	50
Poncho, Rain	6 gp	2
Scent Lure	3 gp	*
Sleeping Bag	3 gp	8
Snowshoes	2 gp	1
Sun Goggles	1 gp	*
Sunburn Ointment	2 gp	*
Survival Kit	10 gp	*
Tents		
Bell	4 gp	10
Bundle	20 gp	12
Pyramid	15 gp	15
Wedge	5 gp	10
Tinderbox, Waterproof	8 sp	*
Trap		
Enclosing***	3/7/12 gp	3/8/15
Killing***	2/5/10 gp	5/10/20
Water Sled	35 gp	30
Weaponblack****	2 gp	*
Wilderness Harness	2 gp	1

* Weight is inconsequential (a few ounces).

** Price is double to triple this amount unless bought in a desert setting.

*** Prices and weights are for small, medium, and large sizes, respectively.

**** Rare. Only available under-the-counter.

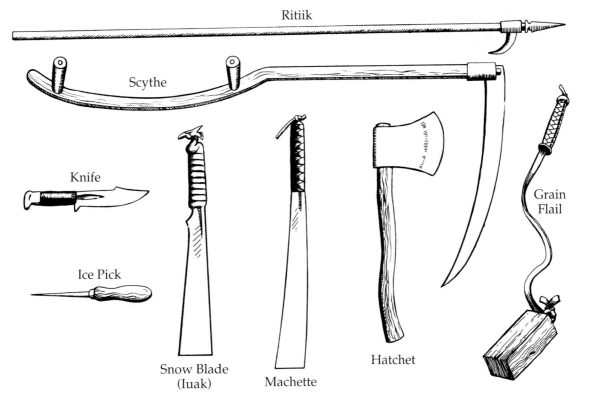

Ritiik

Scythe

Knife

Ice Pick

Snow Blade (Iuak)

Machette

Hatchet

Grain Flail

Table 58: Weapons

Item	Cost (gp)	Wt. (lb.)	Size	Type	Speed Factor	Damage S-M	L
Flail, Grain	3	3	M	B	6	1d4+1	1d4
Hatchet	2	3	S	S	4	1d4+1	1d4+1
Ice Pick	1	1/2	S	P	2	1d4	1d3
Knife, Harness*	-	-	S	P/S	2	1-2	1
Machete	30	4	M	S	8	1d8	1d8
Ritiik	10	6	L	P	8	1d6+1	1d8+1
Scythe	5	8	M	P/S	8	1d6+1	1d8
Snow Blade (iuak)	10	3	M	S	4	1d4	1d6

Optional Weapons from *The Complete Fighter*

Item	Cost (gp)	Wt. (lb.)	Size	Type	Speed Factor	Damage S-M	L
Belaying Pin	2 cp	2	S	B	4	1d3	1d3
Gaff/Hook							
Attached	2 gp	2	S	P	4	1d4	1d3
Held	5 cp	2	S	P	4	1d4	1d3
Main-Gauche	3 gp	2	S	P/S	2	1d4	1d3
Stiletto	5 sp	1/2	S	P	2	1d3	1d2
Sword							
Cutlass	12 gp	4	M	S	5	1d6	1d8
Rapier	15 gp	4	M	P	4	1d6+1	1d8+1
Sabre	15 gp	5	M	P	4	1d6+1	1d8+1

*The harness knife's cost is included as part of the cost of the wilderness harness (Table 57). The knife itself weighs only a few ounces.

Optional Weapon Notes

Belaying Pin: A short wooden rod used on ships (rigging lines are tied to them). This can be used as an improvised club. If using related proficiencies, the belaying pin is related to club and mace.

Gaff/Hook: This is a metal hook with a metal or wooden crossbar at the base. "Attached" means the hook has been used to replace a hand.

Main-Gauche: A large-bladed dagger with a basket hilt, used as a secondary weapon in a two-weapon fighting style. Gives +1 to disarm attempts. Hilt gives +1 to parry and the effect of an iron gauntlet when punching.

Stiletto: A narrow-bladed knife, with a sharpened point only. Has a non-magical +2 bonus against ring mail, chain mail, and plate mail. Knife proficiency covers the stiletto.

Cutlass: Short heavy slashing sword, sharp along one edge, with a basket hilt (+1 to parry, punch as iron gauntlet). If using related proficiencies, related to dagger, knife, and short sword.

Rapier: Long-bladed sword, with point only, requires its own proficiency. A basket hilt can be added for 2 gp (+1 to parry, +1 lb., punch as iron gauntlet). If using related proficiencies, this is related to sabre.

Sabre: A light slashing sword. Can be fitted with a basket hilt for 2 gp (+1 parry, +1 lb., punch as iron gauntlet). If using related proficiencies, this is related to rapier.

Each ranger is a unique individual with his own feelings, motivations, and personal history. Because there are an endless number of possibilities for ranger personalities, step-by-step guidelines for generating them are not practical, nor are they particularly desirable. Strong characters have constantly evolving personalities, reflecting their experiences as well as their players' inclinations. Just about anything goes, so long as the DM approves and the resulting character is fun to play.

Look over the topics in this chapter and consider how they relate to your character. Ask yourself how he become a ranger in the first place. Where does he come from? What drives him? What makes him feel angry, happy, fulfilled? How does he spend his free time? As you answer these and other questions, your mental image of the character should begin to sharpen. Before you know it, he'll be as familiar as an old friend.

Demographics

The total number of rangers is difficult to determine. Because of their independent nature and tendency to avoid civilized society, rangers aren't likely to cooperate with a formal census. Additionally, many rangers reside in the most remote regions of the world, making a population count impractical if not impossible.

Still, it's safe to say that rangers are among the less numerous of the character classes, if for no other reason than the demanding ability score requirements limit their number. It's a good bet that there are fewer rangers than bards. They're perhaps more common than paladins. Beyond these generalities, it's anybody's guess.

Terrain preferences are a little easier to ascertain. Most rangers prefer forests, hills, and plains, thanks to the flourishing animal life and comfortable climates. Rugged mountains, and jungles attract the more adventurous rangers, while only the hardiest rangers make their home in the harsh lands of the desert and arctic. As a rough guideline, assume that about 40% of all rangers have Forest as their primary terrain, about 15% have Hill, another 10% or so each have Jungle, Mountain, or Plain, and the rest are more or less equally divided among Swamp, Desert, Arctic, and Aquatic.

Race

Unless the demi-rangers described in Chapter 4 are allowed in your campaign, rangers must be human, elf, or half-elf. Roughly 70% of all rangers are human, 10% are elves, and 20% are half-elves. Even in demi-ranger campaigns, less than 1% of the ranger population are dwarves, gnomes, or halflings.

Gender

Gender plays no part in determining one's aptitude for becoming a ranger. About half the ranger population is male, and the other half, female, reflecting the percentages in the general population.

Social Background

No particular social background predominates in the ranger population. Lower, middle, and upper class rangers are more or less equally represented, with a slight bias toward the lower classes at low levels because these are closest to the land.

Certain kits also tend to favor certain social classes. Feralans and Greenwood Rangers tend to come from lower economic backgrounds, while Falconers, Sea Rangers, and Wardens often come from wealthier families. Social class, however, is only one element that influences a ranger's personality. A Guardian with a lower class background who has worked his way up might behave little differently than one with middle class origins.

Family

More relevant to the ranger's choice of career is the size of his family and his role within it. Because his duties place him into a life of relative isolation, the best candidates for rangers are those with few family ties. Orphans and late children are disproportionately represented in the ranger population, as are those who have been disowned or cast out by their families.

Age

There are no rigid age requirements for rangers. However, few adolescents are capable of commanding the respect due a ranger, while many older individuals have trouble managing the rigors of the wild. Consequently, the majority of rangers fall between the ages of 18-60.

Alignment

All rangers are of good alignment, and the number of lawful good, neutral good, and chaotic good rangers are approximately equal. The more independent and isolated a ranger, the less likely he'll be lawful good. Lawful good rangers are often drawn to the Guardian, Justifier, and Warden kits. The Pathfinder and Explorer kits tend to have more than their share of neutral good rangers. Chaotic good rangers are generally associated with the Feralan and Mountain Man kits.

Becoming a Ranger

Unlike many other character classes, rangers have no clear career paths. Wizards may be taught in magic academies and clerics may be recruited by a church, but no structured training centers exist for rangers. There are guilds for thieves and worldwide hierarchies for druids, but rangers stubbornly resist organizations of any kind. Since the ranger class stresses self-reliance and independence, it's not surprising that the circumstances under which they acquire their skills are as varied as the rangers themselves. Here are some of the most common ways to become a ranger, along with a few kits typically associated with them. Of course, the standard ranger might have any of these.

Apprenticeship

An elderly ranger may wish to make sure that his territory will be in good hands after his death. Rather than award conservatorship of the territory to another ranger or a local government, he may instead decide to recruit an apprentice. The elder not only teaches the ways of the wilderness to the young man or woman, but also passes along his values, ensuring that his philosophy will live on. Friends or family members of the elder make ideal candidates for apprentices, as do orphans and human followers.

Suggested Kits: Falconer, Forest Runner, Greenwood Ranger, Guardian, Pathfinder, Sea Ranger, Seeker.

Self-Determination

Individuals attracted to this character class may take it upon themselves to master the necessary skills without a formal apprenticeship. Such an individual may be motivated by curiosity (he's fascinated by nature and longs to learn what books can't teach), a compelling event (an army of orcs makes a surprise attack against his village from an unpatrolled forest; he vows to guard the forest to prevent a recurrence), or a restless urge to explore the world (he feels smothered by the secure but boring life his parents have planned for him).

A self-determined ranger often takes a circuitous route to learning his craft. He may begin by petitioning his lord or king to allow him to accompany military personnel on wilderness excursions, learning from observation how soldiers survive in the field and track their enemies. He may offer to keep house or work for a sage or hedge wizard in exchange for private lessons in botany and other natural sciences. A few years as a neophyte in a nature-oriented church may give him access to priestly magic. And a surreptitious partnership or adoption by a notorious thief may teach him the knack of hiding in shadows and moving silently.

Suggested Kits: Explorer, Forest Runner, Guardian, Justifier, Pathfinder, Sea Ranger, Seeker, Stalker.

Conscription

Occasionally, a king or other official requires a ranger to explore, settle, or administer a recently annexed territory. A replacement may be needed for a ranger who has retired or died. If a suitable candidate isn't available, the most suitable young man or woman may be drafted. Generous authorities may reward the draftee's family with a

monthly stipend in exchange for the cooperation of their son or daughter. More often, however, the authorities offer no remuneration, expecting some type of service from all citizens; recruitment as a ranger is generally preferable to the risky life of a soldier or dull routine of a bureaucrat.

Conscripted rangers often receive first-class training, perhaps at the hands of elder or retired rangers. Some countries have special units of border runners or scouts, which can provide a training ground for the potential ranger. Terms of services range from several years in most cases to a few decades in extremely militaristic societies. Though many choose to re-enlist when their service terms expire, most conscripted rangers eventually part company with the established rulers and continue their careers as free agents.

Suggested Kits: Justifier, Giant Killer, Pathfinder, Sea Ranger, Warden, Stalker.

Happenstance

A common way for a young character to become a ranger is though circumstances beyond his control. The following are typical. A youth who makes his way to an uninhabited island after his ship sinks has to master the skills of a ranger in order to survive. The lone survivor of a pioneer family slaughtered by grizzly bears wanders for years in the wilderness, becoming a ranger in the process. A youth captured by slavers escapes into the wilderness and eventually learns ranger skills. He returns much later as an accomplished ranger with a mission to destroy or drive out the band of slavers who imprisoned him.

Suggested Kits: Beastmaster, Explorer, Feralan, Guardian, Mountain Man, Pathfinder.

Divine Intervention

For purposes of their own, the gods may choose a mortal to receive the skills of a ranger. If the gods see a need for a protector of a favored tract of land, or desire an advocate for threatened animals, they may seek out a youth with the prerequisite physical skills, mental agility, and moral attitude. If the youth is open to their offer—generally, the gods won't bother with an unreceptive candidate—he will be guided through a lengthy series of quests and training exercises to develop the skills necessary to become a ranger. In some cases, the gods may grant him the skills directly.

Suggested Kits: Beastmaster, Greenwood Ranger, Guardian, Justifier, Mountain Man, Sea Ranger, Seeker.

Social Misfit

Society has no use for some of its citizens, shunning them because of their appearance, race, social standing, or nonconformist philosophies. Outcast youths often find solace in the wilderness. Animals, they discover, are far less judgmental than humans. In time, those with strong wills and a knack for survival may become rangers through sheer tenacity.

Suggested Kits: Feralan, Greenwood Ranger, Guardian, Mountain Man, Stalker.

Common Traits: the Classic Ranger

Perhaps the most important aspect of creating a three-dimensional character is determining his core traits, the values and principles upon which he bases his philosophy. A character with specific values tends to be more consistent in his reactions. And while few real-world people are wholly consistent, the more consistently a character behaves, the more lifelike he'll appear in the context of a game.

While no two rangers are exactly alike in their outlook, all share a set of common traits which form the foundation of their personality. These traits are described in general terms below, and are not intended to straitjacket a good role-player. A player doesn't necessarily have to incorporate all of these traits into his character, but he should think carefully before setting them aside. In a sense, these traits are as crucial to defining the ranger character class as his ability scores.

Strong Ethics

Rangers have firm values that impel them to promote goodness and justice. Regardless of whether he's lawful good, neutral good, or chaotic good, a ranger has definite ideas about the difference between right and wrong. He behaves hon-

estly, and most rangers believe in altruism and service. Selfishness and greed are antithetical to the ranger. He champions the powerless and fights for the weak. In many cases, a ranger's respect for life extends to animals as well as humans. Though in essence rangers are warriors, most have no fondness for war. Even when fighting for a cause in which he believes, the ranger looks forward to the end of the conflict and the natural healing process promised by peace.

Love of Nature

A ranger is as much a creature of the wilderness as a lion or wild horse. Many rangers find urban life suffocating and would no more make their homes in a city than volunteer for a prison sentence. A typical ranger prefers songbirds to orchestras, flowers to jewelry, and forests to grand castles. Most rangers are sophisticated enough to handle themselves well in urban settings, but they generally can't wait to finish their business and leave.

Solitary

By virtue of his duties and disposition, the ranger spends a lot of time alone. Most rangers come to enjoy the solitary life, and have no particular need for the company of other people. In most cases, animals satisfy a ranger's desire for companionship.

On the positive side, the ranger's penchant for solitude encourages him to be self-reliant and independent. On the negative side, rangers may come across as remote and detached, even antisocial. While a ranger may be perfectly capable of social etiquette, his companions may believe that he's not especially interested in fostering lasting friendships.

Taciturn

By observing wild animals, many rangers have learned the importance of keeping their emotions in check. A juvenile wolf who charges impulsively is certain to scare away his prey. A young lioness who makes unprovoked, pointless attacks against the pride leader may find herself ostracized and alone. Consequently, rangers often conceal their feelings from friends and strangers alike, revealing little about themselves in actions or words. For all but the ranger's closest companions, it's often difficult to tell if he's happy or sad, angry or forgiving, troubled or content.

Though rangers certainly experience emotions as deeply as anyone else, many suffer in silence when wounded, and grieve in private at the loss of a beloved animal or comrade. A ranger's companions invariably find him to be a dependable, competent, and trustworthy professional. But as a person, he often remains an impenetrable enigma.

Devout

Many rangers are deeply and privately spiritual, perceiving their access to spells and their appreciation of nature as gifts from a greater power. Whether a ranger worships nature itself as a unifying force or follows an established religion, he combines his love of nature with his faith to form the foundation of his moral code. Such rangers regularly reaffirm their commitment through moments of quiet reflection. (See Chapter 9 for more about rangers and religion.)

Daily Life

When a ranger is not adventuring, he still has plenty to do to keep busy. Some of the more common ranger activities are described below.

Most of a ranger's daily routine occurs off stage; that is, neither the player nor the DM need keep a detailed record of what a ranger does between adventures. However, a creative DM may use elements of a ranger's routine as the basis for an adventure—while patrolling his territory, a ranger intercepts a goblin who turns out to be a scout for an advancing army; or as a springboard for a ranger to acquire a new follower—a bear rescued from poachers takes a liking to the ranger. A ranger's routine might also generate encounters to introduce him to important NPCs—the ranger provides first aid to a hunter who turns out to be a powerful official in a prosperous kingdom; or gain him experience—the ranger earns experience points by fighting a small forest fire.

Of course, not every ranger regularly engages

in all of these activities. A ranger occupying an arctic territory doesn't have to worry much about forest fires, while a Warden probably spends more of his time enforcing laws than a Greenwood Ranger or Feralan. Still, the activities described here should give you a good idea of how a typical ranger fills his day.

Patrolling

The ranger spends much of his free time patrolling his territory. He may follow the same route every day, or he may wander wherever his fancy takes him. He keeps an eye out for signs of trouble, such as eroded fields or withered plants, and makes contact with other sentient residents, listening to their problems or engaging in small talk. Some rangers ride mounts, particularly if they have a lot of ground to cover, but most prefer to patrol on foot, which enables them to traverse obstacles more easily, as well as minimizing the chance of drawing attention to themselves.

Though patrolling is necessary to keep abreast of the condition of their territories, rangers also patrol for the sheer pleasure of basking in the open air and savoring nature's splendor.

Monitoring Strangers

A ranger is ever-watchful for strangers in his territory. Followers or other contacts may alert him to the presence of strangers, or he may become aware of them himself by noticing disturbances in the terrain or observing them directly.

In most cases, a ranger monitors strangers discretely, watching them from the cover of trees or shadows, or requesting his followers to make regular reports of their activities. Usually, a ranger can ascertain the intention of strangers without ever making direct contact with them. Most turn out to be harmless travelers or hunters who pose no threat to the ranger or his territory, and the ranger leaves them alone.

If a stranger's motives are more ambiguous—

for instance, if he's chopping down trees or hunting animals beyond his needs—the ranger will confront him, politely but firmly inquiring about his intentions. Generally, the abrupt appearance of an intimidating ranger, particularly if he's accompanied by a bear or two, elicits immediate cooperation. If the stranger explains himself satisfactorily, the ranger departs, perhaps implying that he'll be back if the stranger doesn't keep his nose clean. Should the stranger resist the ranger's authority, the ranger may take whatever actions he deems necessary to ensure compliance, using violence as a last resort.

However, physical confrontations are rare. More commonly, strangers require directions, medical care, or advice. A ranger is usually willing to help, especially if his assistance facilitates their leaving his territory more quickly. If the strangers are lost, the ranger will point out the best route leading to their desired destination. In some cases, he'll volunteer to guide them. Most rangers have a rudimentary knowledge of first aid, and can bind sprained ankles, splint bones, and attempt to resuscitate for drowning victims. A ranger can explain which plants are edible and which are poisonous. He can direct strangers to sources of fresh water, orchards of ripe fruit, and safe campsites.

In return, the ranger may well insist that strangers clean up after themselves, avoid disturbing local habitats, and preserve the natural beauty of the environment. Those who violate the ranger's trust can expect a brisk escort out of his territory.

Trailblazing

A ranger who occupies an undeveloped wilderness must spend a fair amount of time making and maintaining trails. Some of these trails may be permanent roads or paths, usable by anyone traversing the ranger's territory. Other trails may be known only to the ranger, concealed by dense woods or similar terrain. The ranger and his followers use these concealed trails to get from place to place while monitoring the movement of strangers. Although animals in their native habitats are efficient trailmakers, the ranger may improve their trails by making the footing safer, or

linking feeding grounds, watering holes, grazing pastures, and lairs.

An effective trail system requires a thorough understanding of the land, including the precise location of streams, hills, and other significant terrain features. A ranger occupying a small territory may be able to hold this information in his head. For larger regions, the ranger may need to keep maps. In this case, a conscientious ranger will regularly review and update his maps, adding new features and looking for discrepancies.

Constructing a new trail begins with clearing debris and smoothing the ground. This may involve cutting trees, pulling stumps, and filling in holes. If a road passes though a valley or ravine, the ranger may have to dig ditches to direct rainwater away from the trail. He may then need to plant grasses along the roadside to prevent soil from washing into the ditches.

Trail maintenance is an ongoing chore, requiring weeding in the spring and ice removal in the winter. In exceptionally harsh climates, the ranger may have to build snow fences, which are constructions of wood or stone that run parallel to a trail. During blizzards, blowing snow piles up along the fence instead of covering the trail.

Wildlife Management

A dutiful ranger looks after the interests of the wildlife in his territory. He tracks down poachers and unprincipled hunters, relocates creatures that have been displaced by natural disasters, and cares for young animals whose parents have been killed. He notes fluctuations in animal populations and tries to determine if an excess of predators (or prey) is only a temporary adjustment to current conditions, or if it foreshadows a more serious problem. A sudden drop in the number of songbirds or frogs, for instance, may indicate that the insects they eat have been poisoned by some outside source.

Conservation

A ranger is dedicated to the preservation of his environment. He uses timber, water, and other natural resources judiciously and encourages others to do the same. If he cuts a tree, he replaces it

with a new seedling. If he raises herd animals, he keeps them moving so as not to overgraze a pasture. If he farms, he rotates his crops so as not to exhaust the soil, replacing the nutrients with natural fertilizers.

Unfortunately, the ranger must continually struggle against the carelessness and greed of those who don't share his concerns. They strip the land of timber and minerals, and level entire forests to build new cities. For commerce or sport, they hunt scarce species to extinction. They relentlessly farm the same acreage until the soil can no longer support crops, and dump raw sewage and other waste products into lakes and rivers until the water is no longer fit to drink.

The ranger employs several methods to counter this selfishness and indifference. He educates travelers passing through his territory, demonstrating the importance of proper waste disposal and the danger of smoldering camp fires. He negotiates with local villages to regulate mining and farming, and to set aside virgin forests and jungles as protected sanctuaries. In extreme situations, a ranger may resort to guerilla tactics, such as sabotaging oppressive and ruinous activities.

A ranger must also be constantly vigilant for natural disasters. As prevention is the key to effective disaster management, a ranger remains alert for the earliest signs of trouble, taking immediate steps to intervene before the problem becomes a full-blown catastrophe.

Here are some the most common natural disasters a ranger might have to face:

Insects/Disease. Infestations of beetles, locusts, aphids, and other insects can strip forests and pastures in a matter of days or weeks. Molds and rusts can ravage woodlands if unchecked. Old trees, which aren't as resistant to disease as younger ones, are particularly vulnerable. To prevent the spread of destructive insects and fungi, rangers remove and dispose of infested plants as quickly as possible.

Flood. An excess of precipitation, sudden snowmelt, or high winds producing strong coastal waves may result in flooding. Floods can wash away valuable topsoil, destroy trees and buildings, and drown the unprepared. Rangers reduce the severity of river flooding by planting and maintaining the trees and grasses in ele-

vated lands. This vegetation controls runoff and absorbs melted snow, preventing it from running off into rivers and causing the water to rise over the embankments. Ambitious rangers with leadership skills will sometimes coordinate the local population to assist him building levees to contain rivers prone to flooding. This must be handled with care, as such rivers can silt up, causing worse problems later.

Seacoast floods, on the other hand, are almost impossible to prevent. A ranger's best strategy for dealing with them is to become familiar with the weather patterns that precede them. With sufficient warning, a ranger can warn others to seek protection in the highlands until the storm subsides.

Earthquake. Violent shifting of the earth's inner layers may produce earthquakes, which can occur anywhere in the world. Earthquakes can indirectly cause flooding and fires, but the biggest danger comes from avalanches, falling rocks, trees, mudslides, and collapsing buildings.

As with seacoast floods, there's not much a ranger can do to prevent earthquakes, but he can learn to recognize the signs that precede them. Unusual animal behavior (such as the agitated prancing of small mammals), spontaneous geyser eruptions, and clusters of small tremors often indicate an impending major earthquake. While the warnings may not come long in advance, a forewarned ranger can spread the word to head for plains or open fields, which may be safer havens in the event of a major earthquake.

Drought. Higher than average temperatures and a lack of rainfall may result in a drought. When water is scarce, rivers dry up, vegetation withers, and animals suffer from dehydration.

Rangers can't accurately predict when droughts will occur. However, in regions of irregular rainfall, he can check tree rings, which give an excellent indicator of rain received in previous seasons. Thick rings occur in wet years, thin rings in dry years. Since wet periods tend to alternate with dry periods, studying the rings can help the ranger anticipate the next drought. A ranger can't offset the overall effects of a drought, but he can reduce the local impact of the drought on marginal habitats by storing water, and encouraging others to do the same.

Fire. Fires are perhaps the most devastating of all natural disasters. A fire not only wipes out trees and vegetation, it also kills animals and pollutes lakes and rivers with ash. Travelers who carelessly burn trash or toss unwanted torches into the brush are a common source of fires. While lightning strikes are a primary cause of forest fires, some fires are intentionally set by enemies.

Rangers occupying forests or other territories susceptible to fire constantly watch for smoke. Tall mountains make the best vantage point, but where mountains are unavailable or where scaling them frequently is impractical, rangers may construct lookout towers—simple platforms supported by long poles and nearby trees. A rope or wood ladder gives the ranger access to the tower.

Fighting fires isn't easy, nor is it something one ranger can effectively do alone. Because fires spread so rapidly, particularly in dry seasons, a ranger's chance of stopping a fire decreases with every moment it's allowed to burn. Water or dirt can be used to smother small fires. If a ranger has prepared for help beforehand, he can coordinate the building of a fireline—an area cleared of all vegetation and other combustible material. This helps contain larger fires, but an adequate fireline usually requires the efforts of many individuals working as a team. Once a fire is extinguished, a close watch must still be kept for many days, lest a smoldering limb start the fire blazing once again.

Law Enforcement

Certain rangers, such as Wardens and Sea Rangers, may be charged with enforcing the laws of the local ruler. They arrest and punish poachers, patrol the lands they guard, and sometimes negotiate land use agreements with farmers, loggers, and others. If a royal decree protects a particular animal species, the ranger may be charged with enforcing it. Some rangers have the authority to act as judge and jury, allowing them to try cases on the spot and pass sentences as they see fit. Fines may be levied for minor infractions, such as trespassing, while more severe crimes, such as killing an animal from the king's private stock or picking fruit from the king's tree, may be punishable by death. In such cases, the ranger will have a charter or royal writ from the ruler.

The Ranger's Personality

After considering the ranger's background, core traits, and routine duties, let's focus on his personality. The purpose of this section is to help players and DMs determine how ranger characters may behave in a campaign—for instance, how he responds to NPCs, interacts with other PCs, and reacts in combat situations. There are several courses to consider.

To begin with, you can consult the previous volumes in the *Complete Handbook* series. The first four books *The Complete Warrior, Priest, Wizard,* and *Thief* provide lists of archetypes drawn from literature, film, and other fictional and mythological sources. In these books, players are encouraged to adopt the Folk Hero, the Vigilante, or other archetypes as models for their characters' personalities. Many of these archetypes can also be adapted to ranger characters; the archetypes in *The Complete Fighter's Handbook* are especially applicable.

The Complete Bard's Handbook features a series of tables containing traits associated with intellect, interests, and other personality components. The key traits listed on these tables can be picked or determined randomly. The tables can be used for rangers as well as bards (or for that matter, any other character).

You can also refer to the kit descriptions in Chapter 4 of this book, many of which suggest traits associated with a particular ranger type. Players can use the descriptions as springboards for working out the details of their rangers' personalties.

Another way to shape a character's personality is to come up with a single word that summarizes his identity. This word—which we'll call the *defining characteristic*—describes the essential nature of the character and how he comes across to others. While a character's personality is comprised of many elements, the defining characteristic is the most dominant, the trait from which all other personality components arise.

If basing a personality on a single word seems restrictive or artificial, think about how you describe people in your own life. A particular teacher may be *crabby,* a close friend may be *funny,* a favorite game designer may be *eccentric.* Defining characteristics may also spring to mind for fic-

tional characters; consider the *noble* Sir Galahad, the *brilliant* Sherlock Holmes, the *stingy* Ebenezer Scrooge. The defining characteristic forms an overall impression. The details come afterwards.

There's no best method for choosing a defining characteristic. Whatever word seems appropriate to you is good enough, so long as it brings the character into focus and feels right. To get you started, a sample list of defining characteristics appropriate for rangers is given below. The descriptions are intentionally vague, since personal interpretations are more important than rigid definitions. After all, it's *your* character!

You'll know if you've chosen a good defining characteristic if you can immediately begin to visualize how the ranger will respond in various situations. For instance, an *arrogant* ranger may enter a deserted castle without hesitation, certain that he can contend with whatever dangers wait inside. In combat, he may fight aggressively and enthusiastically, each blow accompanied by a declaration of his own magnificence. If defeated, the arrogant ranger may sulk for days, his ego taking longer to heal than his fleshly wounds. Of course, it's not necessary to think through every situation before it occurs—having your character react spontaneously is a big part of what makes role-playing fun—but deciding on a primary characteristic can be a lot of help in getting him off the ground.

If you like, you can choose secondary traits that complement the defining characteristic. These secondary traits, called *corollary characteristics*, add dimension to the character; in combination with the defining characteristic they help define a unique individual. The entries below list several corollary characteristic suggestions for each defining characteristic. Choose one or two that appeal to you, or make up your own. Any corollary characteristics are fine, so long as they don't contradict the defining characteristic; an *arrogant* ranger might also be *proud* and but it's unlikely he'd be *shy,* too.

Some kits work with certain defining characteristics better than others, and each entry below lists a few recommendations. However, don't feel restricted by them. You can use any defining characteristic with any kit that feels right to you. Likewise, you can mix and match the various corollary

characteristics, or ignore them altogether. You may also use the defining characteristics in conjunction with the archetypes from the first four *Complete Handbooks* or to supplement the trait tables from the *Complete Bard.* Regardless of your approach, the goal remains the same—to create ranger personalties that are believable and interesting.

List of Defining Characteristics

Altruistic

A selfless humanitarian who puts the welfare of others before his own, the Altruistic ranger tirelessly fights for the common good. Unhampered by jealousy or self-interest, he commands respect from friends and foes alike. He shows mercy to his opponents, compassion to the dispossessed, and unwavering loyalty to his friends.

Corollary Characteristics: Kind, honest, reserved, introverted, reverent, courteous.

Suggested Kits: Beastmaster, Greenwood Ranger, Guardian, Seeker, Warden.

Analytical

An agile mind and eclectic interests mark the Analytical ranger. He loves knowledge and relishes every opportunity to ponder the mysteries of nature. New cultures, unusual creatures, and scholarly strangers fascinate him. He respects intellectual prowess more than physical skills, and may seek to negotiate with a potential opponent rather than engage in combat.

Corollary Characteristics: Ponderous, meticulous, dignified, thoughtful, cautious, dispassionate.

Suggested Kits: Explorer, Seeker, Stalker.

Arrogant

An arrogant ranger believes he can do no wrong. He views indecision as weakness and compromise as cowardice. He glories in the memory of his accomplishments, which typically have been both numerous and impressive. If there are stronger, smarter, or more skilled rangers than himself, he is unaware of them—or at least, he chooses not to acknowledge them.

Corollary Characteristics: Haughty, confident, patronizing, energetic, extroverted, optimistic.

Suggested Kits: Falconer, Forest Runner, Giant Killer, Mountain Man, Warden.

Boisterous

A boisterous ranger has little patience with social etiquette. He says what he thinks and behaves as he pleases, and may be oblivious to how his actions might offend others. A man of action, he likes to get to the point, avoiding what he considers to be time-wasting conversation and endless planning. Beneath it all, there often beats a heart of purest gold.

Corollary Characteristics: Brash, impulsive, lusty, spontaneous, intimidating, vulgar.

Suggested Kits: Feralan, Forest Runner, Giant Killer, Mountain Man, Pathfinder.

Distrustful

Usually as a result of limited contact with other people, the distrustful ranger remains emotionally distant from strangers and comrades alike. He may be cordial and cooperative, but he rarely gets close to anyone other than his animal followers. He is awkward in social situations, uncomfortable in large groups, and suspicious of friendly overtures. The reason is usually hidden in his past.

Corollary Characteristics: Suspicious, paranoid, cold, reflective, lonely, moody.

Suggested Kits: Beastmaster, Falconer, Feralan, Forest Runner, Mountain Man.

Inspiring

The inspiring ranger radiates authority and confidence, making him a natural leader. He instinctively takes charge in times of crisis, displaying bold initiative when others hesitate to act. His companions depend on his decisiveness and common sense, and he rarely lets them down. Always, he is the first to the battlefield and the last to leave.

Corollary Characteristics: Flamboyant, fearless, cheerful, driven, virtuous, honorable.

Suggested Kits: Explorer, Forest Runner, Justifier, Sea Ranger, Warden.

Laconic

The laconic ranger is a soft-spoken, thorough professional. He says little, sees much, and lets others go their own way as he goes his. He takes quiet pleasure in a job well done, and avoids needless confrontation with lazy, the foolish, and the incompetent (though he might remark with shrewd humor upon their foibles). He nearly always lends his neighbor a helping hand.

Corollary Characteristics: Steady, thoughtful, pithy, keen, practical, skilled, canny.

Suggested Kits: Falconer, Guardian, Justifier, Pathfinder.

Melancholy

The melancholy ranger shoulders the weight of the world. Plagued with self-doubt and tormented by the injustice of a seemingly indifferent universe, he is preoccupied with his own misery and prone to deep depression. Ironically, though he may perceive himself as a failure, he may actually be quite accomplished. Whatever success he experiences, however, doesn't seem to bring him much pleasure.

Corollary Characteristics: Brooding, quiet, cynical, tentative, impulsive, neurotic.

Suggested Kits: Guardian, Greenwood Ranger, Justifier, Warden, Seeker.

Merry

The merry ranger is full of the joy of life. He spreads springtime and sunlight wherever he goes, regardless of how bleak the situation may be. Always ready with a tale, a story, or a practical joke to break the tension, he puts the counsel of the eternal doom-sayer to shame. Though he may, in fact, have serious problems of his own, these never discourage him for long, nor does he inflict them on his companions.

Corollary Characteristics: Bright, flippant, vibrant, honest, buoyant, optimistic.

Suggested Kits: Forest Runner, Mountain Man, Pathfinder, Sea Ranger.

Mysterious

The mysterious ranger envelops himself in an aura of secrecy, keeping even the most pedestrian details of his background hidden from his companions. He seldom speaks, and when he does, his words may be ambiguous or laden with cryptic overtones. Though he dutifully fulfills his role within a party, he minimizes his contact with his comrades. For no apparent reason, he may disappear for days at a time, then reappear as unexpectedly as he departed. He may whisper poetry to his followers, make bizarre notations on the trunks of trees, or brew sweet-smelling soup which he

dumps on the ground rather than drink, all without explanation. His strange behavior may be due to religious reasons, cultural requirements, or merely a desire to keep his companions at arm's length.

Corollary Characteristics: Eccentric, threatening, somber, distant, taciturn, studious.

Suggested Kits: Feralan, Pathfinder, Seeker, Stalker.

Nurturing

The nurturing ranger serves as a caretaker and counselor, supporting his companions and followers in times of stress. He comforts the troubled, reassures the doubtful, and soothes the anxious. He has a kind word for all and strives to bring out the best in his friends by bolstering their self-esteem. He may leave leadership roles to others, preferring to work in the background, or a loss of leadership or sudden crisis may bring him to the fore.

Corollary Characteristics: Diplomatic, inquisitive, philosophic, humble, passive, empathetic.

Suggested Kits: Falconer, Guardian, Greenwood Ranger, Seeker.

Obsessed

A single, all-consuming goal motivates the obsessed ranger to the exclusion of all else. Typical obsessions include destroying a species enemy, revenge on an overlord who illegally annexed his territory, or locating a animal believed to be extinct. Though an obsessed ranger may function effectively within his party, the party's objectives are always secondary to his own. Often, such a character will mature out of the obsession as the campaign continues.

Corollary Characteristics: Irritable, grim, passionate, anxious, determined, tireless.

Suggested Kits: Explorer, Giant Killer, Justifier, Sea Ranger.

Experience

As explained in Chapter 2 of the *DUNGEON MASTER Guide*, rangers gain experience much like other warriors. Table 59 summarizes their standard experience awards.

Table 59: Ranger Experience

Action	XP
Per hit die of creatures defeated	10/level
Monster experience	Typ*
Other group experience	Typ*

* **Typ** = Typical share of experience, as described in the *DMG*.

Table 59 is fine as far as it goes, but for those using the guidelines in this book, it may not go far enough. If the DM decides that a little more detail is needed when determining experience awards for rangers, he may decide to use Table 60 to award experience points instead DM.

Table 60: Optional Individual Experience Awards

Action	XP
Per spell level cast to overcome foes or problems, or further ethos*	100
Per successful use of special ability (class or kit)	100
Per Hit Die of creatures defeated	10/level
Per Hit Die of species enemy defeated	20/level**
Follower, per trick or task trained	100
Monster experience	Typ***
Other group experience	Typ***

* Like priests, rangers gain experience for using spells to promote their philosophies and principles. A ranger who's accepted the responsibility of protecting a forest would not gain experience for using *charm person or mammal* to coerce an woodcutter into finding some tasty fruit, but he would gain experience for using the spell to ensure the woodcutter helps him put out an uncontrolled fire in the forest.

** The ranger receives double the normal amount of experience points when defeating a species enemy (20/level). In addition he receives a 1,000 experience point bonus for defeating the long-range plans of a species enemy.

*** **Typ** = Typical share of experience, as described in the *DMG*.

FREDFIELDS ©88

Rangers and Religion

Most rangers are privately religious, convinced that there are powers at work in the world much greater than themselves. Though different rangers may worship in different ways, all regard the embodiment of their devotion with awe and respect, and try to abide by the ideals it represents.

Aspects of Faith

Rangers manifest their faith in a number of ways:

Inner Peace

A ranger's devotion gives him a sense of purpose, a feeling that his life has a purpose. Even though his role may seem at times to be minor, he feels that he has a definite place in the scheme of things.

Code of Behavior

A ranger's beliefs give structure to his life by providing a set of principles for him to follow. Being of good alignment, rangers tend to adopt beliefs that encourage honesty, compassion, and selflessness.

Access to Spells

In practical terms, the access to spells enjoyed by the high level ranger is one of the most immediate and visible results of a life of service. Much like a druid, the ranger receives his spells as a consequence of his beliefs. Though prayer or meditation, the ranger asks for the spells he wishes to memorize, and in most cases, his requests are granted.

Unlike the druid and other priests, the ranger's access to spells is limited. A priest, after all, devotes much energy to the service of his faith, while a ranger's other activities and duties place great demands on his time. For this reason, the ranger is able to acquire spells only when he reaches 8th level, and then has only minor access to the plant and animal spheres. The ranger can fill his spell slots with any spells of the appropriate level listed for those spheres. Some kits may have expanded or restricted spell use.

Types of Faith

Many rangers venerate nature itself. Others develop private faiths, more follow recognized religions that are based on established traditions and doctrines. Rangers aren't necessarily affiliated with churches or monasteries; in fact, rangers generally avoid formal religious organizations, preferring to worship alone or with a small group of trusted followers. Certainly the travels of most rangers often take them far from the centers of organized religion. As a result, a ranger's worship may differ from that of a priest, even if they technically share the same faith.

Regardless of how a ranger practices his faith, there will be some power that is the beneficiary of his devotion. Most rangers worship the divine in nature; monotheistic rangers worship one particular god, while polytheistic rangers may worship several. A few base their faith on an individual philosophy. All of these approaches provide support to their disciples, as well as access to the spells available to the a ranger. In game terms, they all function identically.

Nature

Many rangers choose nature itself as the focus of their devotion. Nature worshipers revere nature as a process and a source of life; whether it was designed by a greater intelligence or arose from the interaction of primal forces is largely irrelevant. Ethics and morals are derived from observing the natural order, and the perception of the majesty of the natural world and its relationship to the ranger is a closely personal one. The natural life force of the world can be felt by the ranger who becomes attuned to it. Any ranger may be drawn to the worship of nature. For some rangers, particularly those with few ties to the civilized world (such as Beastmasters, Feralan, Greenwood Rangers, and Mountain Men), the pull is especially strong.

Gods

Gods are supernatural beings considered by their worshipers to be the supreme sources of might and authority. Often, a god embodies a particular principal that is manifested or promoted in

the material world.

The total number of gods is impossible to know, as are the number and identities of the rangers who worship them. These factors will vary from campaign world to campaign world. DM's who design customized pantheons for their own campaigns should consider including gods specifically intended for rangers. Gods concerned with agriculture, animals, plants, birth, fertility, geology, weather, and hunting are appropriate, providing they're of good alignment. One place to go for ideas is *The Complete Priest's Handbook,* which contains many suggestions for adding religions to a campaign, and dozens of sample priesthoods.

Rangers with gods worship them in a variety of ways. Some may erect simple shrines to their deities that complement the natural features of their primary terrain. For instance, a ranger whose primary terrain is Forest might plant a private grove. An Arctic ranger might build a towering ice pillar.

Religious practices for the same deity may also vary from ranger to ranger, depending on their primary terrain. Prior to an important hunt, a Desert ranger might immerse his hands in the sand, a Forest ranger might conduct a spirited dance under a tall tree, and a Plains ranger might snap an arrow in two to attract the god's attention (a smooth break may be interpreted as an omen of a favorable hunt, while jagged edges may indicate that the god discourages hunting at that particular time).

Philosophy

A belief system derived from intellectual concepts rather than supernatural forces or the natural world may also be the basis for a ranger's religion. The sheer intensity of the believers' devotion is sufficient to attract the magical energy necessary to cast spells.

Worshipers of philosophic faiths tend to concentrate in small sects in isolated areas of the world. For example, the Iulutiun rangers of the Great Glacier, for example, follow an animistic philosophy called *qukoku,* which holds that all creatures share a life essence called *eaas.* The teachings of *qukoku* maintain that all creatures are morally equivalent, and that animals and men share the same emotions and intellect, which their *eaas* compels them to express in different ways. (For more about the Iulu-

tiuns and *qukoku,* see the FORGOTTEN REALMS® FR14 *Great Glacier* sourcebook.)

Expressions of Faith

Regardless of whether a ranger worships nature, gods, or a philosophy, he is assumed to engage in various practices to affirm his faith. Some of these practices may be formally established; for instance, a particular group of disciples may be required to kneel before the setting sun every day. Other practices may be self-imposed; a ranger may decide for himself that the best way to express his devotion is to refrain from violence during nights with a full moon. Once a player establishes a practice as routine for the ranger, the player and DM can assume the character continues it "off stage" unless campaign events dictate otherwise.

It's up to the DM, in conjunction with the player, to decide what, if any practices a ranger should follow in order to remain true to his faith. Typical practices might include any of the following:

Meditation. Having private moments of quiet reflection and communion is a common practice. These may take the form of the soft verbal recitation of sacred verse, spoken at the same time every day, to periods of silent meditation, performed whenever the ranger gets a chance. Observing particular phenomena, such as a shooting star, or experiencing certain events, such as acquiring a new follower, may inspire special periods of this type.

Offerings. The ranger make regular offerings of food or treasure. Offerings may be given to the underprivileged, cast into the sea, or buried in the ground. Small offerings, such as a scrap of meat or a few copper pieces, usually suffice.

Symbol Display. The ranger may declare his devotion to the world by displaying the symbol of his faith. The symbol may be a distinctive article of clothing, a brooch or pendant, a tattoo, or a tiny mark made on a tree or stone wherever the ranger spends the night. The ranger might mark his animal followers with the deity's symbol. The symbol may be engraved in a collar or bracelet, shaved into the animal's fur, or notched in the animal's horn.

Pilgrimage. The ranger may make a periodic journey to a sacred location, such as a temple, mountain peak, or holy village. The pilgrimage may take place on a particular date (say, the first

day of spring) or whenever he gets the chance within a particular timeframe (he must make the pilgrimage once a year).

Taboos. Some faiths may impose strict prohibitions on the ranger's behavior. For example, the ranger may not be allowed to eat meat, wear head coverings, or start more than one fire in the same day.

Players and DMs may also make up their own religious requirements. Remember that a ranger might follow practices unlike other disciples of the same faith; just because most worshipers of a nature deity make shrines out of polished stone doesn't mean that a ranger can't build a shrine out of deer bones. Care should be taken to ensure that the practices don't conflict with the requirements of the ranger's character kit (it's unreasonable to expect a Sea Ranger to make an annual pilgrimage to the middle of a desert).

Most importantly, any routine practices should be simple enough that they don't distract from the campaign or tie up an undue amount of the ranger's time and effort. A ranger who has to come up with a weekly offering of 500 gp or must spend four hours per day in solitude won't be welcome in very many parties.

Once the practices are established, the ranger is expected to follow them. Should a ranger fail to uphold the requirements of the religion, or intentionally violate them, he may lose the use of his spells for a brief period, he may become ill, or one or more of his followers may desert him. The DM determines the penalty based on the severity of the ranger's negligence. In most cases, a warning should be enough (which the ranger may experience as a dream or vision), but continued abuse may call for a more severe response.

Rangers and Druids

Rangers have much in common with druids. For instance, both classes are predominantly oriented toward nature. Both receive spells in similar ways; in fact, both of the ranger's spheres are shared with druids. Both strive to live up to the tenets of a higher power. They are natural allies against raiders, evil humanoids, and others who would despoil and ruin the land.

Some rangers won't form anything other than casual relationships with druids. They may work with them on projects of mutual interest and occasionally call on them for guidance or advice, but otherwise the rangers go their own way, oblivious to how druids exercise their faith and not particularly concerned with what goes on in their places of worship. In special circumstances, however, rangers and druids may establish more formal alliances, especially when a druid becomes a ranger's follower.

Any ranger may acquire a low-level druid as a follower, and may do so for a variety of reasons. If the ranger is skilled in areas in which the druid is deficient, the druid may seek him out as a teacher. The druid's superior may instruct him to serve a ranger as part of a penance, or to serve as a go-between for a network of wilderness protectors that exchanges information and favors. Or like other human followers, the druid may be drawn by the ranger's reputation, hoping for a working relationship that will allow the projects of both to prosper.

Secretive and mysterious, a druid may never let on as to why he's chosen to follow a ranger. He may simply show up, tag along, obey orders, then abruptly disappear a few weeks later. His initial appearance may be equally cryptic; a ranger who believes he's acquired a lizard or raccoon follower may be shocked to discover that the animal is, in fact, a shapechanged druid.

Likewise, a low-level ranger may become a follower of a druid. Though many druids are reluctant to take on such strong-willed characters, open-minded druids are often receptive to rangers with a thirst for nature lore and a commitment to conservation.

Most of the time, however, rangers and druids operate independently. On occasion, they may find themselves competing for dominance of the same territory. A novice ranger who wishes to move into a region occupied by a druid may be wise to petition for permission, even though such permission is rarely required by law. Failure to do so may result in lasting resentment at best, open hostility at worst. Should the ranger act courteously and respectfully, permission is usually granted.

Conversely, an initiate assigned to a ranger's territory would do well to request an audience with the ranger before settling in. Most rangers will appreciate the gesture, which minimizes the likelihood of misunderstandings or conflicts. A ranger probably won't attempt to drive away a

druid who doesn't bother to make contact—assuming that the druid otherwise behaves himself—but relations between them may remain strained indefinitely.

Because their outlooks are so similar, rangers and druids can usually share the same territory without any trouble, though their paths may seldom cross. Druids tend to keep to themselves even more than rangers. They are less likely than rangers to involve themselves in the affairs of men. Since they're of neutral alignment, druids aren't particularly interested in promoting the ranger's conception of justice. Rangers tend to work more openly, druids more deviously.

Rangers and druids may informally agree to divide the responsibilities of their territory. The ranger may agree to deal with human and demi-human travelers, while the druid handles the problems of the native animals. They may join forces to contend with a natural disaster, only to part company when the danger has passed.

Rangers and Clerics

Low-level clerics may become followers of rangers for many of the same reasons as druids. Not all clerics make suitable followers. The cleric must be of good alignment and should be several experience levels lower than the ranger. Since most rangers are human or half-elven, clerics of these races are the most likely to sign on, though a ranger will rarely reject a follower solely on account of race. Gender considerations usually aren't important, but a cleric with a strict upbringing may hesitate to follow a ranger of the opposite sex.

The faith of a clerical follower should be compatible with that of the ranger. This doesn't mean that the faiths must be identical—an inquisitive cleric might want to follow a ranger solely to study the nuances of an unusual religion—but the goals of the faiths can't be diametrically opposed. For instance, if the cleric believes that anyone who prays to inanimate objects is a heathen, he won't follow a ranger who worships mountains.

A cleric serves the ranger in the same way as other followers—assisting him in combat, performing routine chores, and offering advice. In turn, the ranger benefits from the cleric's priestly skills and loyalty. The cleric may be able to assist

with some of the ranger's religious requirements; for example, the cleric might handle the blessing of new followers, or come up with the daily offering of food or treasure. If they share the same faith, the cleric may teach the ranger new ways to worship, as well as engaging him in enlightening conversations concerning all things spiritual.

As with all followers, a cleric will remain in the company of a ranger as long as the relationship is mutually beneficial. When the cleric reaches the end of his penance or learns what he wants to know, he may express his desire to leave. A gracious ranger will grant this request, either dismissing or releasing the cleric at the earliest opportunity. Should the cleric prove to be a nuisance—or worse, if the ranger finds the cleric's religious practices to be unacceptable—the latter may be dismissed without explanation.

Conversely, a ranger may find it advantageous to serve as a temporary follower of a cleric. He may seek out a cleric because an obligation requires him to spend a period of time working for a church, or because he wishes to learn more about that religion in a structured setting. Alternately, a ranger may volunteer to protect a clerical stronghold, or his deity may have commanded him to become a follower to show his dedication. Regardless of his motivation, a ranger usually serves as a follower for a limited period of time, seldom exceeding a few months. He typically begins his term of service early in his career, usually before reaching 3rd level. When his term ends, however, he may continue an informal relationship with that particular church for a much longer period.

Clerics of 8th level or higher who establish large places of worship may accept ranger followers. Some clerics may have gender, racial, or kit preferences for their followers, but usually they'll accept any ranger whose faith is compatible with their own and who demonstrates a sincere commitment to serve. Once accepted, the ranger is expected to obey his clerical superiors and adhere to their traditions. The ranger may be required, for instance, to pay a weekly offering for the upkeep of the fortification, take a vow of chastity, or wear a distinctive cloak or other garment. He may also be expected to perform any number of special duties. Typical duties might include:

- Performing routine maintenance on the stronghold. This may include repairing damage,

sweeping floors, polishing metalwork, cleaning latrines, and so on.

- Constructing a wilderness shrine or temple. Usually, this is performed under the supervision of a superior. The ranger handles most of the manual labor.
- Recopying faded sacred texts on fresh parchments. Often the language will be unfamiliar to the ranger, as some clerics believe that copying foreign script enhances the disciplinary benefits of the practice.
- Supervising the fortification's herd animals. This includes feeding, watering, administering to sick animals, and cleaning barns and stables.
- Tending the church's gardens and harvesting the crops.
- Protecting the stronghold against monsters and enemy armies.

A ranger can expect to be disciplined if he refuses to obey his superiors or becomes derelict in his duties. For minor infractions, he may be confined to his quarters or given additional chores. Major infractions may result in beatings or even a banishment from the fortification. In extreme cases, the ranger's superiors may be able to exert their influence to permanently separate the ranger from their religion, causing him to lose all associated privileges and benefits.

In the context of a game, a ranger's term as a clerical follower may take place between adventures, or it may be incorporated into a campaign, possibly as a springboard for an expedition involving the entire party (the ranger must complete a quest for his cleric, and recruits other companions to help him).

A ranger's term as a clerical follower may have a variety of consequences, for weal or woe. On the good side, he may make some powerful new contacts and learn some new skills. He may even acquire a new follower or two of his own (a low-level cleric or fighter decides to accompany the ranger when he leaves). On the other hand, the ranger may become burdened with new duties to perform (in exchange for his training, his clerical superiors now expect him to offer extra donations every month in their honor). At any time, he may be unexpectedly summoned to the clerical stronghold to help train novices or defend against attackers.

Though they generally avoid organizations and communal events, many rangers participate in informal get-togethers called *forgatherings* or *moots*. At forgatherings, rangers can exchange ideas, barter for supplies, and participate in contests of skill, as well as catch up on gossip and blow off steam. Attendance at forgatherings is by no means mandatory, but most rangers look forward to the opportunity to spend a few days socializing with others who share the same general philosophy and professional challenges.

These are often times of much merriment and celebration. Old friends are greeted warmly and new rangers are initiated, sometimes with raucous practical joking. There are food and fun for all, and tests of skill and prowess to pass the time and take each other's measure.

Attending a Forgathering

A ranger can go through his entire life without ever hearing about a forgathering, let alone attending one. But chances are that sooner or later, he'll hear a rumor about an upcoming forgathering, or receive an invitation from another ranger. He may also notice strange symbols etched on trees or stones, intended as guideposts to lead attendees to the forgathering site (depending on how secret is the location of the meeting, a ranger might need the trail sign proficiency to translate the symbols).

In most cases, forgathering attendance requires no prior arrangements. These gatherings are by their nature informal, and they are rarely interrupted by serious business except under the most unusual circumstances. Any ranger who shows up is usually welcome; rangers who bring extra meat, fruit, or wine to share are welcomed with open arms. Attendees are expected to supply their own bedding, tents, and food. First-timers may be required to perform extra chores, such as guard duty or trash disposal.

A ranger may bring non-ranger companions with him as guests, providing the guests keep to themselves and stay out of the way. The ranger is responsible for his guests' behavior; should they cause trouble or make nuisances of themselves, both the ranger and his guests will be summarily ejected. It's unlikely that ranger will be welcome at any future forgatherings unless things are smoothed over.

Types, Sites, and Dates

There are as many types of forgatherings as there are rangers. Some are held in well-traveled forests, others in remote deserts. Some attract only specific kit types, such as Mountain Men or Sea Rangers, while others are primarily intended for specific races, such as elves. In general, however, most forgatherings are open to any ranger who cares to come.

Though some established forgatherings occasionally change locations and dates, most are held in the same place and at the same time every year for the convenience of the attendees. Any open wilderness area, reasonably isolated, can serve as a forgathering site. Forests, mountains, and plains are preferred, as they give the easiest access to the greatest number of rangers. Because travel can be difficult in the winter, and summer can bring uncomfortably hot temperatures, forgatherings are usually held in late spring or early fall. Most forgatherings last from two to three days, but some drag on for several weeks or until the last few diehards call it quits and head for home.

Specifics about individual forgatherings are hard to come by, since rangers tend to keep the details to themselves. Brief descriptions follow, the pieced-together bits and pieces of information that have trickled out over the years regarding a few of the best-attended and longest-lived meetings: feel free to add to them and adapt them to your campaign world.

Equinox Festival

One of the most important annual meetings is the gathering at this festival, held during the six days following the first full moon after the autumn equinox. Rangers of every type and specialty can be found here, though standard rangers outnumber all the others. The site shifts every other year, alternating between a heavily forested area and a plains region, far from any civilized settlement. The organizers announce next year's site at the end of the current festival. As this is primarily a trade fair, rangers bring a wide variety of goods to sell, and haggle with each other long into the night. Prices tend to be high, but so does the quality.

Glass Eye Concourse

This is one of the wildest and least structured forgatherings, attracting Mountain Men by the dozens, along with a few rowdy Giant Killers, Pathfinders, and Forest Runners. The name derives from the person who organized the first of these forgatherings, a rowdy Mountain Man who lost an eye in a drunken sharpshooting contest. Held near the base of a tall mountain in mid-spring, the Glass Eye Concourse features a weekend of physical contests, lewd jokes, and lots and lots of cheap ale.

High Tide Assembly

In contrast to most forgatherings, the High Tide Assembly is downright sedate, emphasizing philosophic discussion and formal lectures. This forgathering takes place during the first high tide of spring on a quiet seashore. The Assembly lasts for three days. Seekers, Sea Rangers, and Explorers are the primary attendees. By tradition, the forgathering climaxes with a wild boar hunt. Following a traditional feast, the bones of the wild boars are tossed into the sea, to the accompaniment of triumphant cheers and whistles.

Solstice Jamboree

Most often held in a central plains location, the Solstice Jamboree attracts all types of rangers, as well as a number of bards and druids. The event lasts for six days, beginning on the first day of the summer solstice. Lavish banquets, featuring exotic meats and rich candies are held three times daily, and general good fellowship is encouraged. This is an important event, for much serious business is discussed on the side. Comrades who died the previous year are honored on the last day of the forgathering with poetry recitations and silent meditations.

Physical Layout

Most forgathering sites have few permanent features or structures. Upon their arrival, attendees construct any necessary buildings or fixtures, and take them down when the forgathering ends. Forgathering fixtures are simple but functional, with building materials consisting usually of wood, stones, and mud. Here are a few features common to most sites:

Sleeping Area. The driest and clearest patch of ground makes the best sleeping area. Attendees pitch their tents or lay out their sleeping bags in lines, spaced well apart. In colder climates, the sleeping area is located where the sun (whatever there is of it) can warm the earth before nightfall. In warmer climates, shady locations are preferred.

Dining Area. A typical dining area consists of a few benches or logs for sitting on, some stone barbecue pits, and a simple lean-to for storage. The optimum location for the dining area is several hundred feet from the sleeping area, positioned so that breezes don't carry the cookfire smoke in the direction of resting rangers. A stream nearby for washing up is also desirable, if available.

Fire Pit. A pit for burning waste is constructed near the dining area, preferably away from trees or brush to minimize the chance of a fire getting out of control. It's located where the prevailing breezes don't carry the smell of burning garbage toward the sleeping or dining areas.

Barn. A barn, stable, or pen is constructed to house the rangers' animal followers for the duration of the forgathering. Large forgatherings may require several pens and stables to accommodate a variety of species. Rangers are responsible for the feeding and grooming of their animals, and are also held accountable for their animals' behavior; it's considered a grievous breech of etiquette for a lion follower of one ranger to eat the goat follower of another ranger.

Chapel. The forgathering chapel may be as simple as a stone platform, or as elaborate as a full-sized cabin with a podium and wooden pews. Religious symbols are not exhibited here, so that the chapel may accommodate worshipers of diverse beliefs. Most often, the chapel is isolated from the main forgathering site, erected in a nearby woodland or other quiet location.

Campfire. The communal campfire, typically constructed in a central location, serves as the focal point of the forgathering. The campfire burns all night and day, continually tended and fed deadfall logs. At any hour, rangers can be found crowding around the camp fire, roasting meat and exchanging stories.

Activities and Events

As forgatherings are primarily intended as social events, rarely are there fixed agendas or schedules. Activities tend to develop spontaneously, continue as long as the rangers show an interest, and end when the participants have had enough. Following are a few of the activities and events most likely to occur:

Trading.

Trading goes on virtually non-stop at most forgatherings, ranging from private transactions between individuals to dozens of rangers peddling their wares in what amounts to an open air market. Merchandise includes both the common (rope, saddles, boots) and the unusual (chainlink leashes, camouflage paint, homemade wine). Weapons and maps are especially in demand, particularly bows and quarterstaves with hand-carved designs, and maps of exotic territories that detail the newest trails. Rangers pay for their purchases in fur, food, and trinkets as well as gold pieces.

Magical items are occasionally available, but many rangers are more inclined to loan them to needy comrades rather than sell them outright. Rangers who borrow magical items are expected to return them at the next forgathering. Being men and women of integrity, the borrowers rarely fail to honor their agreements.

News and Gossip.

Information flows freely at forgatherings, and most rangers are eager to learn about the trials and tribulations their comrades have experienced in the previous year. They hear of marriages, births, and deaths, as well as followers acquired and abandoned. They learn which expeditions resulted in new discoveries and which ended in disaster. Rumors abound of lost civilizations, hidden treasures, and gruesome monsters. An attentive ranger may hear about employment opportunities or new hunting grounds. If he's lucky, an unattached ranger may make contact with a potential mate.

Training.

The typical forgathering attracts rangers with a wide range of skills. Often, they're willing to give instruction to novices for a small fee or as a gesture of friendship. If he locates a willing teacher, a ranger may be able to pick up hunting or tracking tips, acquire cooking secrets from a master chef, or learn how to construct emergency shelters from an elder woodsman. (The optional training rules in Chapter 8 of the *DUNGEON MASTER*™ *Guide* can be used to allow rangers to acquire new skills as a result of their forgathering experiences.)

Contests.

No forgathering would be complete without games and contests for rangers to demonstrate their skills and compete for prizes. Conservative forgatherings feature debates, target shooting, and knotting matches (where contestants see who can untangle complex knots in the shortest time). The Glass Eye Concourse and similarly rowdy forgatherings feature contests of a more physical nature, such as head-slamming (contestants butt heads as hard as they can until one passes out), dagger juggling (often done blindfolded), and bear wrestling.

Mountain Men in particular have a tradition of rather intense competition. For example, Mountain Men enjoy a bizarre drinking contest where bitter roots, fish scales, rotten vegetables, and other distasteful substances are mixed with water; whoever consumes the most of this vile brew is declared the winner.

Other contests common to forgatherings include horse races, rabbit hunts, and mock battles using swords and spears bound with thick layers of cloth. Winners are awarded silver pendants, hiking boots, or other prizes donated by the more affluent attendees. If donations aren't available, each participant puts a few coins in a pot before a contest begins; whoever wins claims the pot. Wagering is rampant for all types of contests, with rangers betting everything from animal pelts and dried meat, to arrowheads and leather gloves.

Class Description

Rangers are a sub-class of fighter who are adept at woodcraft, tracking, scouting, infiltration, and spying. All rangers must be of good alignment, although they can be lawful good, chaotic good, or neutral good. A ranger must have a Strength score of at least 13, Intelligence of at least 13, Wisdom of at least 14, and Constitution of at least 14. If the ranger has ability scores of greater than 15 in Strength, Intelligence, *and* Wisdom, he gains the benefit of adding 10% to experience points awarded by the referee.

Unlike other members of the fighter group, rangers have eight-sided Hit Dice (d8) but at first level they get 2, rather then 1, Hit Dice. It should also be noted that rangers get 11 Hit Dice rather than the 9 of other fighter-types. Table 61 shows the experience points needed for each level, along with the associated titles. Table 62 lists the number of attacks per round a ranger can make at various levels.

Table 61: Experience Levels (1st Edition)

Level	XP Needed	Hit Dice (d8)	Level Title
1	0	2	Runner
2	2,251	3	Strider
3	4,501	4	Scout
4	10,001	5	Courser
5	20,001	6	Tracker
6	40,001	7	Guide
7	90,001	8	Pathfinder
8	150,001	9	Ranger
9	225,001	10	Ranger Knight
10*	325,001	11	Ranger Lord
11	650,001	11+2	Ranger Lord (11th level)
12**	975,001	11+4	Range Lord (12th level)

* Rangers gain 2 hit points per level after the 10th.

** 325,000 experience points per level for each additional level above the 12th.

Table 62: Attacks Per Round (1st Edition)

Level	Attacks/Round*
1-7	1/1 round
8-14	3/2 rounds
15+	2/1 round

* This applies to any thrusting or striking weapon.

Special Abilities

In addition to considerable prowess as fighters, rangers have druidic and magical spell capabilities when they attain high levels. Thus, they are very formidable opponents, for they have other abilities and benefits as well.

When fighting humanoid-type creatures of the "giant class," listed hereafter, rangers add 1 hit point for each level of experience they have attained to the points of damage scored when they hit in melee combat. Giant class creatures are listed on Table 66. **Example:** a 5th level ranger hits a bugbear in melee combat, and the damage done to the opponent will be according to the ranger's weapon type, modified by his Strength, and +5 (for his or her experience level) because the opponent is a bugbear (a "giant class" humanoid).

Rangers surprise opponents when rolling 1-3 on 1d6 and are themselves surprised only when rolling 1 on 1d6.

Tracking is possible both outdoors and underground (in dungeons and similar settings). Underground, the ranger must have observed the creature to be tracked within 3 turns (30 minutes) of the commencement of tracking, and the ranger must begin tracking at a place where the creature was observed. Table 63 lists the ranger's chance to track creatures underground in various situations.

Table 63: Underground Tracking Chances

Creature's Action	Chance to Track
Going along a normal passage or room	65%
Passes through normal door or uses stairs	55%
Goes through a trap door	45%
Goes up or down a chimney or through a concealed door	35%
Passes through a secret door	25%

Outdoors, a ranger has a base 10%, plus 10% per level, chance of following a creature (1st: 20%, 2nd: 30%, etc). Table 64 shows the modifications to the base chance.

Table 64: Outdoor Tracking Modifiers

Situation	Modifier
For each creature above 1 in the party being tracked	+2%
For every 24 hours that have elapsed	–10%
For each hour of preparation	–25%

At 8th level, rangers gain limited druidic spell ability. Additional spells are added through 17th level. At 9th level, rangers gain limited magic-user spell ability, as with druidic spell ability (see Table 65). Rangers can't read druid, cleric, or magic-user spells from magical scrolls in any event.

Table 65: Spell Progression (1st Edition)

	Spell Level				
Ranger	Druidic			Magic-User**	
Level	1	2	3	1	2
8	1	-	-	-	-
9	1	-	-	1	-
10	2	-	-	1	-
11	2	-	-	2	-
12	2	1	-	2	-
13	2	1	-	2	1
14	2	2	-	2	1
15	2	2	-	2	1
16	2	2	1	2	2
17*	2	2	2	2	2

*Maximum spell ability
**The ranger must check which spells he can learn, just as if he was a magic-user.

At 10th level (Ranger Lord), rangers are able to employ all non-written magical items which pertain to *clairaudience, clairvoyance, ESP,* and *telepathy.*

Also at 10th level, each ranger attracts 2-24 (2d12) followers. Note that these henchmen once lost can never be replaced, although mercenaries can be hired, of course. These followers are determined by the DM who then informs the ranger.

Special Restrictions

Any change to non-good alignment immediately strips the ranger of all benefits, and the character becomes a fighter, with eight-sided Hit Dice ever after. He can never again regain ranger status.

Rangers may not hire men-at-arms, servants, aides, or henchmen until they attain 8th level or higher.

No more than three rangers may ever operate together at any time.

Rangers may own only those goods and treasures which they can carry on their person and/or place upon their mount. All excess must be donated to a worthy communal or institutional cause (but never to another player character).

Rangers do not attract a body of mercenaries to serve them, but when (and if) rangers construct strongholds, they conform to the fighter class in other respects.

The following is a list of "giant class" creatures for which the ranger receives his special combat bonus.

Table 66: Giant Class Creatures

bugbear	kobold
cyclops	meazel
cyclopskin	norker
dune stalker	ogre/merrow
ettin	ogre mage
giant (all)	ogrillion
giant-kin (all)	orc/orog
gibberling	quaggoth
gnoll/flind	spriggan
goblin	tasloi
grimlock	troll/scrag (all)
hobgoblin/kaolinth	xvart

Optional Rule (from *Unearthed Arcana*) The Ranger's Weapons

By the time a ranger gains a fourth weapon proficiency at 4th level, the character's weapons must include:

• a bow (of any sort) or light crossbow*
• a dagger or knife
• a spear or an axe
• a sword (any type)

* This choice must be made at 1st level.

Ranger Kit Record Sheet

Player _____ _____**Character**

Kit [_____] **DM** _____ **Campaign** _____

Requirements

Ability Scores _____   Races _____

Alignments _____   Primary Terrain _____

Species Enemy _____   Followers _____

_____   _____

Description** _____
_____
_____
_____

Role** _____
_____
_____
_____

Secondary Skills	**Weapon Proficiencies**	**Nonweapon Proficiencies**
		B = Bonus R = Required S = Suggested
_____	_____ _____	
_____	_____ _____	_____ _____
_____	_____ _____	_____ _____
_____	_____ _____	_____ _____
_____	_____ _____	_____ _____

Armor/Equipment _____
_____
_____

_____   _____
_____   _____
_____   _____
_____   _____

Special Benefits* _____ _____
Other

#1 _____ _____

#2 _____ _____

#3 _____ _____

#4 _____ _____

Special Hindrances* _____

Notes _____
_____
_____

** = These categories should be fully detailed on another sheet of paper.

This form may be photocopied for personal use in playing AD&D® games.

©1993 TSR, Inc. All Rights Reserved.

Ranger Character Record Sheet

Player _____ Character _____

Date Created _____ Kit Name _____

Race _____ Alignment _____

Ability Scores

STR	Max Press _____ lbs. ___	Open Doors _____ ( ) in 20	Bend Bars/ Lift Gates _____ %
DEX	Surprise: 1-3 in 10 _____		
CON	System Stock _____ %		
INT	(Missing entries go in other areas of this record sheet.)		
WIS	Max/ Henchmen _____	Loyalty Base _____	Reaction Adjustment _____
CHA			

Saving Throws

Paralyzation/Poison/Death Magic	
Rod/Staff/Wand	
Petrification/Polymorph	
Breath Weapon	
Spell	

+/–	Condition	+/–	Condition

Experience

+10% Bonus if 16 Str, Dex, and Wis

Level [ ]

Limit [ ]

Individual XP	#	Worth
Thief Skills		100 –
Spell Levels		100 –
Special Ability		100 –
Train Follower		100 –
Hit Die Defeated		10/lev 10/lev
Species Enemy		20/lev –
Other		PHBR or DMG

TOTAL

Next Level

Hit Points

Current

Total

1st–9th level = 1d10+ _____
10th on = +3 only _____ (Con.)
■ Regenerate _____ / _____
Death: Max # [ ] Initial (Con. + 1)
To date _____ Resurrection Survival _____

Armor Class

AC

Worn _____
_____

△ BASE

+/–	Condition	+/–	Condition

Level Changes

THACO	All
HP	All
Saves	Odd levels
Proficiencies	3, 6, 9, 12, 15, 18
Thief Skills	1-15
Spells	8-16
Followers	10th

Target's AC	10	9	8	7	6	5	4	3	2	1	0	–1	–2	–3	–4	–5	–6	–7	–8	–9	–10
Attack Number																					
Weapon Slots	= 4 + (1 at 3, 6, 9, 12, etc.)				THACO = 20 (–1 every level past 1st)															

Combat

Weapons	Attack Adj. Usual	0	–2	–5	#AT ROF	Damage S/M	L	Sp	Ty	Sz

Shots Fired

Type	#	Used

Attack +/–	Condition	Both +/–	Condition	Damage +/–	Condition

Notes

125

Ranger Character Record Sheet

Nonweapon Proficiencies
Slots ☐ + _____ + 3 + (1 at 3, 6, 9, 12, etc.)

Proficiency	Req.	Ability Score	+/– Mod.	+ Add'l Slots	Total

Notes

■ Secondary Skill: _____

Thief Skills	Base	Race	Dex.	Armor	Kit	Total
Hide in Shadows						
Move Silently						

Racial Abilities

Spells
Casting Level _____
1st_____
2nd_____
3rd_____

Primary Terrain _____
Species Enemy _____
Animal Empathy Modifier _____
(begin at –1; level 4, –3 at
level 7, –4 at level 10, etc.)

Survival Check _____
(= Int.)
Tracking Score _____
(= Wis.)

Special Benefits
#1_____   _____
#2_____   _____
#3_____   _____
#4_____   _____

Kit Notes

Ranger Character Record Sheet

Age

_____ + _____ = [ ]   ___/___/___
Natural   Unatural   Year   Date Born

Middle [ ]   −1 Str & Con; +1 Int & Wis
Old [ ]   −2 Str & Dex; −Con; +1 Wis
Venerable [ ] −1 Str & Dex & Con; + Int & Wis

Maximum Age [ ]

Vital Statistics

Sex   ☐ M ☐ F

Height _____ ft. _____ in.

Weight _____ lbs.

Hair _____

Eyes _____

Skin _____

Personality Traits

_____
_____
_____
_____
_____
_____
_____
_____

Followers

Name/Species	Notes
_____	_____
_____	_____
_____	_____
_____	_____
_____	_____
_____	_____
_____	_____
_____	_____
_____	_____
_____	_____

Notes

Equipment Carried

Used	Item/Location	Unit cost/wt.	Used	Item/Location	Unit cost/wt.	Used	Item/Location	Unit cost/wt.

cp	1/100*
sp	1/10*
ep	1/2*
gp	1*
pp	5*

*10 of these = 1 lb.

Debts/Will _____

Vision ■ Infravision _____ ft.

Light Source	Radius	Duration	Used

Movement Rate

Base ■ 12 ■ 6

Encumbrance	lbs. Carried	MV	✓	Attack	Penalty AC
Unenc.	−			−	−
Light (2/3 MV)	−			−	−
Mod. (1/2 MV)	−			−1	−
Heavy (1/3 MV)	−			−2	+1
Severe (1)	1			−4	+3

127

JOIN THE ADVENTURE!
ENTER NEW WORLDS OF EXCITEMENT AND FUN IN EVERY ISSUE!

Dragon MAGAZINE

Dungeon ADVENTURES FOR TSR ROLE-PLAYING GAMES

The leader of the role-playing world offers gaming advice, new ideas, reviews, monsters, cartoons, and treasures not found anywhere else!

The module magazine for AD&D® and D&D® game players leads you to the limits of the known gaming universe!

FILL OUT AND MAIL THE SUBSCRIPTION FORM BELOW
to receive the world's greatest gaming magazines.